Children of the Moon

Book 1 in the

'Remember the Future'

Time Travel Adventures

by

Evadeen Brickwood

Can you imagine, suddenly living in the past? Not last year or in the Roman Empire, but a really, really long time ago?

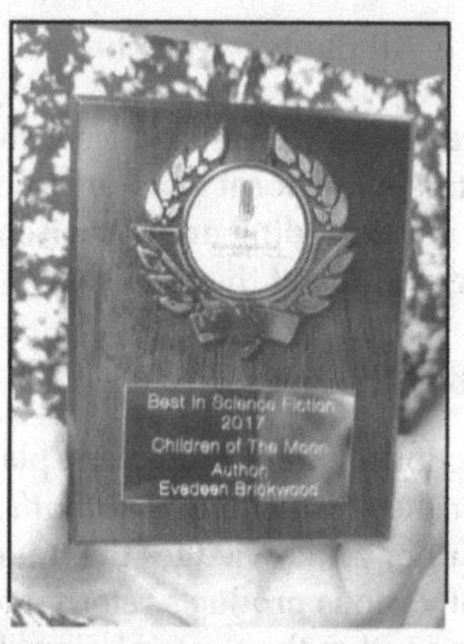

"Children of the Moon" won the

2017 Book Talk Radio Club Award

in the Science Fiction Category

For Peter, Franciska and Svenja

who time-travelled with me

Acknowledgements

A big thank you to my family for putting up with the long hours I spent writing behind closed doors. I love you guys. I'm also grateful to all my editors and test readers for their honest comments (in no particular order): Christopher Hojem, Kevin Richie, Michaela du Plessis, Andrew Nkadimeng, Nokuthula Vilakazi, Lyndall Kenyon, Susan Cooper, Michelle Edridge, Beverly Birchleigh, Barbara Powalka, Zai Whitaker, Melesia Tully and Phyllis Hyde; and especially Peter Böttner and Phyllis Hyde for their enthusiasm, constructive proof-reading and unwavering support. The time travel idea was fueled by videos on interviews with Prof. Thomas Bearden and Prof. Dr. Rupert Sheldrake and the novel 'Timeline' by the late Michael Crichton. I studied too many sources on prehistory to mention them all, but I would like to highlight non-fiction works like 'Fingerprints of the Gods' by Graham Hancock, the Oera Linda book, 'Chariots of the Gods' by Erich von Däniken 'and Forbidden Archeology' by Michael Cremo. A special thanks to Andreas Eschbach for his advice and Graham Hancock for placing my profile on his website.

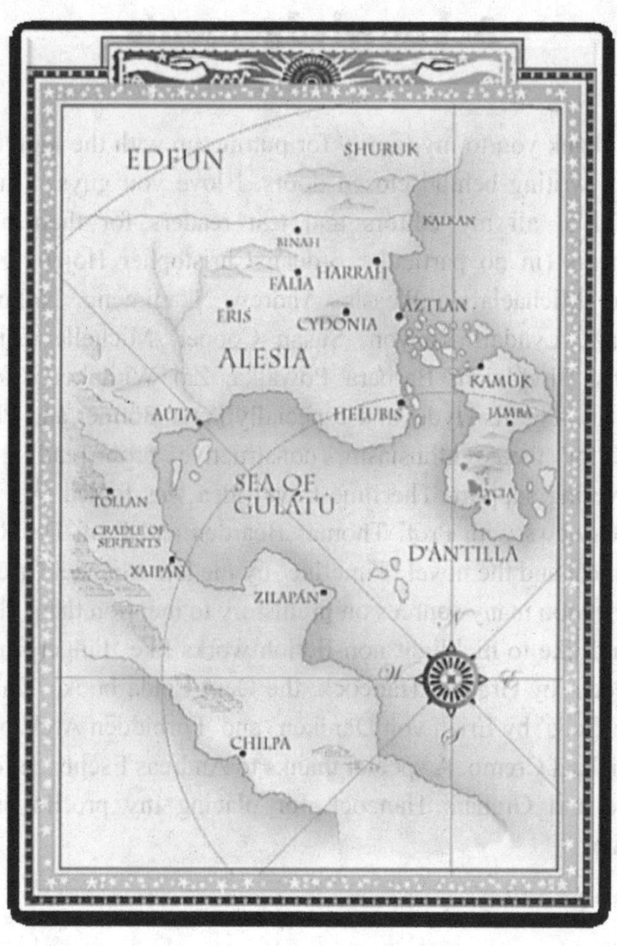

EDFUN
SHURUK
KALKAN
BINAH
HARRAH
FALIA
AZTLAN
ERIS
CYDONIA
ALESIA
KAMUK
AUTA
HELUBIS
JAMBA
SEA OF
GULATÚ
LYCIA
TOLIAN
CRADLE OF
SERPENTS
D'ANTILLA
XAIPÁN
ZILAPÁN
CHILPA

A pale half-moon watched over the commotion in the parking lot at Carter Valley Inn. It was cool this morning, but the weather could change rapidly in spring.

The place was packed with impatient school children. Many of them only half-listened to Dr. Broadbent's speech and some even yawned. Why didn't they go already?

"Ladies and gentlemen, I hope we understand each other. Please keep in mind that under *no* circumstances is *anyone* to go near the escarpment. I fully expect to see everyone safe and sound on top of the hill by lunchtime."

The principal of the 'Pemberton Academy for Advanced Learning', a well-known school for gifted kids, made sure that his instructions were carried out properly.

"Stay on the footpath - yes, you too over there!" The culprit quickly stepped back onto the rocky footpath. "Remember poor Tom Fraser—"

General murmur arose. They all knew that Tom Fraser had tripped and fallen off the cliff three years ago. Luckily, he had been okay. Sort of.

"There we go," Dr. Broadbent said with satisfaction. "The junior grades follow Dr. Naidoo and Mr. Van Straten. The senior grades line up to my left, right here. You will walk with Mrs. Meyer and Dr. Wilkins."

Dr. Naidoo was so short that she almost disappeared between the students in the ensuing chaos. She tried to make herself heard in a shrill voice, "Victor and Brandon, come back here this minute!"

Dr. Broadbent pushed sparse strands of hair back from his

shiny forehead and began to assign the students to groups. Soon orderly columns started to move uphill. Only three of the seven-graders hung back right from the start.

Chryséis Cromwell seemed to have hurt her ankle and sat down on a wooden bench. Her best friends Katherine and Trevor sat down next to her and they watched the others file past.

"Hey, lazy buggers. What are you still doing here?" they teased the three friends.

Chryséis pulled a face in faked pain as she rubbed her ankle and moaned, "Oh that really hurts."

Chryséis Cromwell was eleven, had lots of freckles on her cute nose and blonde hair that was tied up in a ponytail. Her usually bold blue eyes took on a suffering expression as soon as somebody looked her way.

Katherine MacDougal was twelve and rather pretty with her long, auburn hair. She came from England and was as shy as a dormouse, according to the self-confident, younger Chryséis, who had an opinion on absolutely everything.

The third conspirator was the quiet Trevor Huxley from Chicago. He was twelve like Katherine and attended Pemberton on a scholarship.

It wasn't easy to get into an exclusive school like that and it helped that Trevor was very smart. His parents had never really understood their gifted son, but a scholarship meant that they didn't have to pay for their son's education.

Because of the divorce, it was just better for everyone, if he went to boarding school.

Trevor loved to daydream. In his thoughts, he could do as he pleased: fly on sun rays beyond the grey clouds in Chicago to the African jungle, or work on an alternative to washing machines, or cruise the blue Mediterranean Sea. And when he felt like it, he could even travel back in time to ancient Rome.

The three of them had never done anything like this

before, but today they had good reason. So they sat on the wooden bench and waited.

It didn't take long for one of the teachers to approach them with a stern face to see what was going on. Of course, they were prepared. Katherine grew nervous all the same and started to fidget so badly that Trevor had to shove her a couple of times.

Would Dr. Wilkins buy the sore ankle or would he notice that they were up to something?

"And what's that?" the educator asked. "Chry-sé-is Cromwell, shouldn't you be with your group?"

"My foot rolled off that stone over there," Chryséis complained. "It hurts."

She pointed to a random stone on the ground. The teacher's expression softened. He stared at the spot, but there was nothing unusual on the ground.

"I see," Dr. Wilkins said and scratched his long nose.

Thankfully, he liked Chryséis. Excellent student, and her mother, Professor Cromwell, wrote such interesting articles in the scientific magazine, he enjoyed as a bit of light reading at bedtime.

He decided to give Chryséis the benefit of the doubt and gave her an encouraging look. Chryséis was to stay at the little inn and wait for the other students to come back in the afternoon.

"The two of you—" he waved Katherine and Trevor over, "you come with me."

Oh no, they had to stay together! According to plan, they also had to avoid cars, buildings and especially people. Electromagnetic interference was just about the last thing they needed for their experiment. The sooner the teacher left, the better.

"Ahem, Dr. Wilkins," Chryséis said bravely. "I'd really like to go to our picnic on the hill. Maybe we should just take it slowly. I'm sure my friends will help me. It doesn't hurt so bad anymore, see."

She stood up on wobbly legs and smiled. It worked.

Dr. Wilkins agreed. "Alright, then," he said and told Trevor and Katherine to look after Chryséis. Then he caught up with his group and helped a flustered Mrs. Meyer herd some of the students back onto the path.

Dr. Wilkins turned around briefly and saw Chryséis limping, as was to be expected, and leaning onto Trevor's arm. Then he went to the front of his group and soon disappeared behind a rock face.

"Phew, at last," Katherine said relieved.

Chryséis bent down and rubbed her ankle, then she recovered in record time. "I'm going to get lame for real, if I keep this up much longer... okay, so what now?"

Trevor stopped and scanned the hill. He pointed with his chin to some larger rocks. "See, how the path kind of forks to the right over there?"

"Yes - and?!"

Trevor had already mapped out the best site, just right for their purposes. Also rather close to the escarpment, but that couldn't be helped.

"We aren't supposed to go so near to the edge!" Katherine said immediately. Her stomach ached with nervousness. "What if we get caught? And what about Tom Fraser?"

"What about him? He'd fall over his own feet when he had half a chance," Chryséis said.

"Yes, but..."

"Give us a break, Katie. If we don't do it today, we can forget about the whole thing."

"We'll be careful." Trevor started walking. "The others won't see us for a while. At least not until they get to the top of the hill. By then, we're back on the path."

"I knew that." Katherine caught up with them. "And what if we can't find a portal up there?" She was still skeptical, despite weeks of careful preparations.

"Oh stop it already." Trevor was eager to get going. *Today!* "There has to be a time warp around here somewhere."

"I guess," Katherine mumbled and trudged after them.

"I found a time warp in the school garden last week, remember?"

Sure, she remembered. Trevor had told them all about it, over and over. It had been his job to test the time-portal-finder... and what a test it had turned out to be!

First a shimmering, holographic spot had appeared that was growing larger all the time. That was the closest description Trevor could think of for the warp in the space-time continuum.

Then behind that 'curtain' a vortex had opened up. Churning like a washing machine during the spinning cycle - and Trevor had jumped in. Just like that!

On the other side, he'd seen a large 'thing' with shiny scales and steaming breath, stretched out right there before him. Creepy! The 'thing' had moved in waves and given Trevor the grandmother of all shocks.

He'd lost no time and pressed the 'Return' button and had found himself back in the school garden at exactly the same point in time when he had left.

The possible monster couldn't scare them off. It had been a real trip through time, no matter how short. Back at the lab, they'd thought up better safety features and now it was time for the first experiment together. THE experiment.

They climbed over sticks and stones, until they stood in front of a stone platform, shielded by rocks on three sides and virtually invisible from the footpath. The fourth side was open toward the valley. Just what they needed.

"Okay, here we are," Trevor announced.

"Then let's get going!" Chryséis took a deep breath and jumped effortlessly onto the rock terrace.

Trevor and Katherine did the same. Trevor plunked his daypack on the ground and took out a plain object that looked a bit like a flat metal-pear and fitted snug in the palm of his hand. The time-portal-finder. Chryséis had dubbed the time-portal-finder TPF, and the name had stuck.

The three friends were proud of their handiwork. It had taken loads of time and effort to get the TPF looking like that. It had all started with Katherine's physics project - quantum physics project to be precise. The vacuum battery - an endless source of energy.

At first, it hadn't even crossed her mind to use this energy source for time travel. Trevor had come up with the idea and now they had to test the whole thing.

Time travel was perfect proof that the endless energy source actually worked and wasn't just some sort of legend. Of course the project was unusual, but they had come this far, right? This year's physics project would be a rip-roaring success!

The TPF was fitted with a row of black buttons on the right side. They were there, to dial the target epoch.

With three bigger red buttons on the left, they would save reference points in time. First of all, they would save the time of departure. This was one of the new safety features, the first model did not have. The other red buttons would be programmed with other reference point in time, they liked. A kind of shortcut.

Then there was a big white button right in the middle. When it was pressed, the TPF located a time warp. When it was pressed again, it activated a portal. A small display above the buttons indicated the number of years travelled. At the moment, it was set to '0'.

Tiny stickers under the black buttons had numbers on them were still blank. The sticker under the red button at the top showed the date of departure. 21 February 2015.

"Here are the other TPFs with their own integrated vacuum battery. One for each of us. Here and... here." Trevor handed the girls identical-looking devices, in see-through plastic wraps.

"I put them into sandwich bags, so they won't get wet."

"Ah, I was wondering..." Katherine said. "So that's what you've been up to all day yesterday."

"Good thinking, Trev. In case we land in the ocean or so," Chryséis quipped and let the TPF slide into her jacket pocket.

"Right, if we lose one or this one here gets damaged, we still have the others as a reserve," Katherine said.

Trevor carried on talking with a serious expression. "The top red button is for today's time reference. We discussed that. We have to all press it at the same time - when we are ready to travel."

"Sure thing. Now, the VICs - one virtual invisibility cape for each of us." Chryséis opened the front pocket of her daypack and pulled out thin, black plastic hair bands. They had a tiny box on top and a deep-set button on the side. The VIC was probably the best thing.

Katherine and Chryséis had come up with the idea after Trevor's strange time travel experience. One never knew what lay in wait. In principle, it had something to do with the bending of light waves. In case of an emergency, one pressed the button - and simply disappeared.

Trevor wanted to put his aliceband on this morning, but that would have been just weird. Imagine, a boy wearing an aliceband to the school outing! They had also decided to keep the VICs switched off inside the time portal. One never knew what might interfere with the frequency. The risk was too great.

"Oh flip." The u-shaped plastic bands were entangled and Chryséis struggled to get them out of the pocket. Katherine looked worried. "Hurry up, Chris! This is taking forever."

"Okay, okay."

In the end, Katherine helped her untangle the alicebands. "All right then," Chryséis said with triumph in her voice. They put on their VICs, careful not to touch the flat button on the side.

"Can we go now?" Chryséis asked all excited. She

didn't notice, how pale Katherine had become. 'Time travel' - the words echoed in Katherine's mind. Her mouth felt so dry. She swallowed hard, but the fear didn't want to go away. Now of all times she had to panic! Then, a completely useless question shot through her mind: 'Can you breathe prehistoric air just like that or is it dangerous?'

This whole experiment was insane. Dangerous even! Katherine swallowed again and fought the urge to run.

There was still time to cop out… no, it was too late. She couldn't let her friends down now!

Trevor had already activated the big white button on the TPF and tried to find a good spot, pointing the TPF here and there. And sure enough, something began to shimmer by one of the grey rocks. Another curtain-thing. A portal to the space-time continuum!

"I knew it!" Trevor cried.

Chryséis stared mesmerised at the shimmering spot. A time warp, this had to be a time warp! For the first time in her life, she didn't know what to say.

"All together. Now!" On Trevor's signal, they pressed the red button through the plastic cover, locking in today's time reference. Done. Step one completed.

"I'm going to activate now. Get ready."

The girls grabbed each other's hand and Trevor pushed the big white button a second time.

It had all begun like any other school year after the winter holidays and the experiment in Carter Valley was still a pie in the sky.

As so often, Walt, the janitor, had fetched Katherine and other students from the Etheridgeville airport.

Time travel was pretty much the last thing on Katherine's mind as she sat comfortably in the back of the old-fashioned, black Volvo. She gazed dreamily at the passing landscape while trying not to pay attention to Privesh and Hendrik, who were having a boring discussion about sport.

Looks almost like England, she thought. If one ignored the long bearded moss swaying from the branches of Eucalyptus tree. She had never seen that in England. And the sky was never such a bright blue.

A tiny cloud between the trees shifted to the left as the road swerved through the broad school gate. Ah, there was another cloud not far from the first. That's more like it.

Katherine sighed and settled back into the snug leather seat. As always, the holidays had been way too short. She missed her gentle French mother and Dad and their comfortable home in Oxfordshire. And Aunt Trudie, Mom's sister. She was always so nice and funny.

She didn't really miss her two younger brothers, Graham and Frederick. They were really naughty and bothered her endlessly.

Dad was often away on business. The lingering smell of leather and cigars always reminded Katherine of him.

When her Dad was home, she loved to sit on his lap and listen to his deep, sonorous voice. He'd tell her fascinating stories, like the one about a wedding in Pakistan he had been invited to.

'The bride wore a red and gold sari dress and the groom's eyes were hidden behind a veil of golden lametta,' he had reported. 'Women were dancing around balancing metal water jugs on their heads.'

They made Dad ride on a painted elephant! Katherine could see the scene right in front of her as she smelled the leather of the car seat. This time, Dad had been home for only three brief days before flying back to Hong Kong.

Would things be better, if her parents weren't wealthy? Sometimes, all Katherine wanted was the luxury of growing up without being shipped off to boarding school. It seemed so unfair. Why couldn't she just grow up like everybody else? Well, *almost* everybody else. There were many kids with rich parents at Pemberton.

The rambling school building painted in rust and white, with its impossible spires and towers, appeared behind the sweeping green lawns at the end of the driveway. Katherine asked herself for the umpteenth time, who had thought that up.

Loads of shrubs and trees dotted the Pemberton school grounds. All that exuberant vegetation kept two gardeners quite busy throughout the year. Murmuring water features sparkled between masses of flowers as the car purred past a nine-hole golf course.

The sports facilities at Pemberton weren't to be scoffed at, either. Too bad that Katherine wasn't interested in sports.

They left the tennis courts behind as the car began to wind its way up the alley between high bluegum trees.

Walt steered the black Volvo deftly up the broad driveway.

A familiar bump in the road jolted Katherine from her dreamy mood. A red squirrel with feathery tail darted up and down the trunk of a large tree as they reached the gravelled parking lot. Directly in front of the entrance with its sweeping stairs.

Children walked around everywhere between the parked cars, while adults in smart clothes stood chatting next to piles of luggage. A familiar sight.

The school magazine proudly declared that Pemberton-students came from all over the States, Europe and from far-flung countries like Korea, South Africa and New Zealand. The academy enjoyed an excellent reputation all over the world.

A sobbing boy of perhaps eight years was obviously new to the school and clung to his increasingly impatient mother. "Mom, I don't want to stay here. Mom, please..."

She scolded him under her breath and pulled his clawing hands from her expensive pink designer suit.

"Lester..., stop it this minute. No, don't do that... please... stop it!"

At the same time, she tried to make a good impression on Woody Kranich's mother, who was a fashion editor from California. Defeated, Lester sat down on his designer suitcase with a sad expression.

For Katherine, there had been a few tears in the privacy of her first class seat on the Boeing that had carried her from London to New York. By the time her connecting flight had reached Etheridgeville, Katherine's tears had dried up. After all, her parents tried to give her the best education they could afford. Nothing one could do about it, anyway.

The Volvo came to a solid halt. On top of the broad steps, the great doors were flung invitingly open.

'Pemberton Academy for Advanced Learning', announced a polished brass sign next to the dark wooden entrance.

"Right, here we are," Walt said. His voice was raspy like a vegetable grater. "Out with you guys. I'll get your things from the trunk in a jiffy and take them up to the entrance hall."

Walt was an amicable fellow with grey, wiry hair. He had been the janitor, chauffeur and supervisor of staff forever – even longer than the fat cook Mrs. Hadley - and proud to be an employee of importance.

He admired Dr. Broadbent and was fond of the students. Well, most of them. He appreciated it, if they didn't trample on his flowers or played fountain with the water hoses. Water was expensive these days.

Too clever for their own good some of those kids are, Walt thought to himself and opened the trunk of the car. *Just too clever.*

Katherine and the two boys jumped onto the crunching gravel. She felt hot in her woollen skirt and twin set. They were more suitable for the cool British weather than the much warmer Georgia. Then it didn't matter anymore. Katherine had detected Chryséis and Trevor.

Trevor stood in a group of boys, close by. They were telling stories about their holidays. Chryséis held the hand of her colourfully dressed Mom.

Most of the kids wouldn't be seen dead, holding their Mom's hand, but Chryséis couldn't be bothered with other people's opinions. Prof. Cromwell was a bit eccentric, but other than that, really nice. Not like many of the other rather square parents.

The three friends shared an interest in quantum physics and global warming and were in the top ten of their grade. This year, they would be in the seventh grade. Seventh grade sounded so grown-up!

*

Trevor was glad to be back at school after a never-ending holiday. He had spent the first two weeks cooped up in his Dad's small flat in Chicago, 'The Windy City', with his new computer. His Dad never spoke much and it had been too cold to go outside. The few friends he still had at home, had been on vacation.

Trevor knew that his Dad meant well, but they were just light years apart. His parents had been divorced by the time Trevor was three, and he began to spend much time with his beloved grandmother.

Granny had nursed him when he had broken his arm as a little boy, they went for walks in the park and she had made up the most amazing stories.

But then Granny had died two years ago of pneumonia in the cold of winter and Trevor felt so lonely as if he had lost his entire family right then.

Dad's new girlfriend Peggy-Sue had also been there in Chicago. She always wore this puzzled look on her heavily made-up face. She was a waitress at the diner around the corner. Dad had obviously not looked very far to find a girlfriend. Trevor couldn't talk at all to the giggling Peggy-Sue and avoided her most of the time.

By the end of his stay in Chicago, Trevor was sick of greasy burgers and peach cobbler. He was sure that his Dad and Peggy-Sue were just as relieved to see him leave on the bus bound for Iowa.

Trevor listened to music on his headphones for most of the trip and braced himself for his stay in Iowa. His mother was now Mrs. Hadwen and seemed happier in the country than she had ever been in the city.

Trevor found it difficult to call her 'Mom' or even kiss her cheek. He didn't know her very well. All she did was talk to him about stuff like eating a nourishing meal and wearing a clean shirt and had given him three boring shirts for Christmas.

Her new husband was a big, homey fellow of a farmer, who talked just as little as his Dad. Trevor's half-brother, Gerry Junior, was a real pain in the neck. Gerry was just two and a half and threw temper tantrums at least a dozen times a day.

It became Trevor's favourite pastime to walk along the fallow cornfields or in the hills. At least he could get away from the house. He had discovered a gurgling spring between two vertical rock faces last summer. There he liked to sit on a flat rock and played with the pebbles in the water or he just read a book. But in winter it was just too cold for that.

Trevor much preferred the mild southern climate. The fragrant rose garden at Pemberton was his favourite spot. Here he would sit on a bench under the softly swaying birch trees and study. Even in winter.

When he became friends with the confident Chryséis Cromwell and Katherine MacDougal last year, they often sat together under the birch trees. The two girls never ragged him like some of the other girls. They were different. Sometimes, they just chatted while watching the colourful birds, flowers and dragonflies.

Oh yes, Trevor was glad to be back at Pemberton. He had arrived by bus in the morning and his short brown hair was still neatly combed.

Trevor had already spotted the two of them, but it would have been uncool to run and greet them now, in front of all the boys.

"Yeah, sure, I also can't wait for the baseball season to start again," he said instead. John LeGrange was going on about last season's highlights and he just couldn't shut up about baseball.

"I'd rather play cricket," said Ben.

Ben Harper from Rockingham, Australia was one of the wealthiest kids at the school. He carried on telling them every boring detail about some sailing trip, while Trevor watched the girls from the corner of his eye.

They waved wildly to each other. Katherine looked like a lady. Chryséis, on the other hand, had blonde pigtails and wore simple jeans and a pink T-shirt and. Pink was her favourite colour.

The Cromwells had named their first child after an obscure character from one of the Greek legends. The 'Tale of Troy'. The historical Chryséis had been a lucky maiden. Captured by the Greeks during the Trojan War and then given back her freedom.

This was unusual in Greek mythology, to say the least. The parents of the modern Chryséis had studied Greek and had been inspired by the story. Her younger siblings were named Jason and Cassiopeia, or Cassie for short. Also classical names.

Katherine and Trevor spent many a weekend in the town house of the Cromwell family. It was half hidden by an overgrown garden, in an area of town, where manicured lawns and straight flower beds were the order of the day.

Trevor had loved it there from the start. The family was so uncomplicated, and he loved Mrs. Cromwell's cornbread and gumbo.

They seemed to have so much time for each other and always talked during dinner. Inside, the house was bright and cheerful with loads of wooden furniture smelling of beeswax polish. There were framed pictures on the walls and all sorts of fascinating stuff was scattered around.

*

"Hi there, Katie!" Chryséis called and let go of her mother's hand.

Katherine started to run across the parking lot. But not without pinching the unsuspecting Trevor in passing.

That was unusually bold for Katherine and Trevor tried to playfully slap her arm. She was too fast for him, despite her stiff skirt and woollen twinset.

The white gravel crunched under their soles as Trevor chased her to the other side of the lawn. The two of them came to a halt in front of Chryséis, breathless and laughing.

"Hi there guys, good to see you'll again," Chryséis greeted them in her southern drawl.

"Hi there, girlfriend," Katherine laughed, still out of

breath. "Hello, Mrs. Cromwell!"

Chryséis's Mom greeted them and continued chatting to other parents.

"Hey Chris, did you get my last e-mail? I sent it off in Oxford yesterday before I left."

"Which e-mail, the one about Fred's tummy bug?"

Katherine nodded. "Yes, got it. Bummer."

Chryséis thought Katherine's two brothers were spoilt brats. Her younger brother Jason, on the other hand, was easy-going and played outside with his friends all day long.

"We couldn't do anything when we were in Marseilles. It was sooo boring." Katherine sighed at the mere memory. "Fred's such a nuisance. He always catches something when we travel."

Sure, his Mom's attention, Chryséis thought to herself.

Katherine still spoke in a pronounced British accent. According to some of the American kids, it sounded as if she had just arrived with the pilgrim ships in the New World.

"Read any interesting books during the holidays?" Chryséis turned to Trevor.

"What?" He was distracted.

Holly Benson, the class bully, stood nearby. Trevor hoped that she wouldn't notice him. He didn't like her much and it was unlikely that she had changed for the better during the holidays.

She had a pretty face under a mop of curly brown locks. It could have fooled somebody who didn't know her well.

For some mysterious reason, Holly Benson didn't like kids on a scholarship. She kept throwing back her dark curls and tried to appear disinterested as she inspected the newcomers in the parking lot.

Holly would have liked to be friends with Chryséis. Mr. Cromwell came from an old family in the area and chaired the Etheridgeville's Chamber of Commerce. Good family, Holly's Dad said.

The class bully stood just behind Mrs. Cromwell, who

was now talking to her parents. She had discovered the three friends laughing and sharing their holiday stories.

Why did Chryséis have to be friends with this Trevor Huxley character from Chicago? He was so common. How he had made the cut at Pemberton, she couldn't fathom!

Mr. Benson's company donated a proud sum of money to the school funds every year, and he certainly expected his daughter to be right up there with the best. And as for Katherine - well what was so special about *her* that Chryséis chose this English girl as her best friend?

"I asked if you've read any interesting book."

"Oh okay, actually I surfed more on the Internet," Trevor confessed.

"As always."

"This new website on astronomy is amazing. They have a screen saver with pictures of planets and galaxies and some info about black matter."

He was right at home, exploring the virtual world of the internet. Not to mention computer games.

"And what else?" Katherine asked.

Before he could answer, Chryséis said excitedly, "You've just got to read 'Distant Resonance'. It's a new book by Prof. Herbert Shelton. It's all about something that happens on one side of the planet and then somebody has the exact same idea on the other side and..."

Holly Benson had moved quietly next to her father, Harold J. Benson III. She now faced the three friends directly.

"Herbert Shelton? Read it ages ago. Good book!" she cut in with an air of self-importance. "Probably too expensive for you, Trevor." Trevor rolled his eyes and Katherine jumped.

"Whoa, where did *you* come from?"

Chryséis was annoyed. "Oh whatever, Holly. Nobody asked you anyway!" Holly never seemed to get it when she wasn't welcome. Prof. Cromwell noticed the icy atmosphere and came to the rescue.

"Hi Holly, nice to see you, darling. We'd better go now. Good day, Mr. Benson. Mrs. Benson."

She knew her daughter's quick temper and ushered the kids towards the stairs and the entrance hall, before Mr. Benson had a chance to lecture her about more pros and cons of holidaying in the Caribbean.

"Look, they prepared everything inside," she said.

Chryséis lugged a small, blue suitcase up the stairs with Trevor's help.

"Read Herbert Shelton ages ago… blahblah. Who did she try to impress?" she mumbled to herself. Chryséis had already had enough of Holly, and school had only just started.

Dr. Broadbent held his usual speech. "Good afternoon, ladies and gentlemen, good afternoon parents and other adults present..." Dr. Broadbent always addressed the students as 'ladies and gentlemen'.

He was a quick-tongued man in his fifties. With a receding hairline and a kind pink face, he was the picture of a school principal. Dr. Broadbent loved to spike his assembly speeches with little wordplays to keep his young audience on their toes.

Today his speech was comparatively lame. Eighth-grader Bradley Benson, a distant cousin of Holly's, pushed one of the smaller boys out of the way and Dr. Broadbent paused until order had been restored. At the beginning of the school year, he was still in a good mood. The entrance hall filled with more and more people.

"… and we find ourselves back in the hallowed halls of learning. An extended welcome to our teachers, who are no doubt in hiding somewhere in the building and - of course to our parents and the new students. May your stay at Pemberton be as fruitful—" Dr. Broadbent spoke for another ten endless minutes.

Afterwards, there were finger foods, before the parents left; mostly handfuls of sausage rolls.

Then Pemberton was back to business as usual. The relatively small private school had only two classes per grade. Katherine, Trevor and Chryséis were in the same class this year. So were Holly and her best friend, Natasha Manning.

"Oh joy," Chryséis moaned.

"Yeah well, nothing we can do," Trevor whispered.

"We'll see about that."

At least, Dr. Wilkins was their home-room teacher. A dedicated if slightly boring teacher, he had a kind heart. Unfortunately, he was easily thrown off balance. The grade-eights still giggled about a prank they had played on Dr. Wilkins last October. Apparently it had something to do with a whoopee cushion.

After a rushed dinner, rooms were assigned in the dormitories. Garments, books and personal items were sorted noisily from bulging suitcases into yawning closets.

The boys were in the east wing, the girls in the west wing. Soon the common rooms were buzzing with excited chatter.

"Did you see Vanessa? That new haircut!"

"I heard that Bobby's parents are getting a divorce…"

"No!"

"I'm taking Japanese this year…"

Chryséis shared a corner room on the second floor with Katherine and Sally Holfield, a new girl from Missouri. Being no early bird, Chryséis didn't like bright morning light and was pleased that their windows faced west. Thank goodness, Holly's room was on the floor below.

Trevor had put his things away earlier and sat reading on a bench outside. Leaning over the windowsill, Chryséis called out to him. "Hi there, Trevor!"

It wasn't very cool to call out to girls in their dorms. He waved back quickly and carried on with his book. 'The Dragonfly' by H.A. Humphries was a novel about a Chinese boy, who lived during the Ming dynasty. Only 74 pages left. He wanted to finish the book today.

Katherine gave Sally advice while putting away her

socks in the bottom drawer. Sally Holfield was nervous about going to such a famous school. She thought that she wouldn't keep up with the other talented students.

"New kids are sometimes targeted by the snobs here. So expect some hazing." She knew what she was talking about.

"Sounds scary."

"Only if you let them get to you. And we'll also be around."

"Trevor gave Holly Benson the cold shoulder last year until she gave up on him. He was hopeless as a victim." Chryséis grinned.

"Who's Holly Benson?"

"She's one of the popular girls in our grade. Stinking rich."

"Trust me, you don't want anything to do with her," Katherine said.

They wore their pyjamas, because it was lights out at nine. It was 8:37 p.m. according to the LCD clock on Katherine's bedside table. 'Lights out' was at nine sharp. They still had some time left.

Sally brushed her teeth and then sat in front of the dressing table the girls shared, to brush out her hair. "Why did Holly do that? I mean, why is she so nasty?" She asked the mirror. Sally wanted to be everybody's friend and who was this Trevor?

She combed her light brown hair into a ponytail only to brush bangs back in her face to achieve a sultry starlet look.

Katherine hung up a poster of her favourite girlie band 'Bliss Five' over her bed.

"Sally, do you mind handing me the sticky tape over there…?" She pointed to the table while holding the poster up against the wall.

"Holly's a spoilt brat, that's what!" Chryséis stated bluntly.

She usually just said whatever popped into her head and wasn't always diplomatic.

Sally gave Katherine the tape in silence and sat down in front of the mirror to put away her brush and hair clips. Chryséis moved into another yoga position on the carpet, putting her legs straight up into the air.

When Katherine had started at Pemberton, Chryséis had saved her from Holly Benson. That's how they had become best friends.

If Holly respected anybody, it was Chryséis. Somehow she found it hard to stand up to her and avoided fights with the quick-witted Chryséis.

Soon normality returned to the 'Pemberton Academy for Advanced Learning' and everything went its usual way.

Or almost everything.

▷▷▷ 3   WHAT, TIME TRAVEL?

"It has to work now, it has to!" Katherine was upset. Tools and bits and pieces of plastic lay in wild confusion all over her lab desk.

"What *am* I doing wrong?"

Katherine had come up with the idea to work on an endless energy source, based on the principles of quantum mechanics - her favourite subject. Professor Helbert had made it sound so logical in his book. She took a tiny screwdriver off her notes and read the formula again.

The formula was no problem, but when she tried to adjust the differentials, things hit a snag.

"Oh!!!"

She threw the screwdriver impatiently back on the desk. It spun off the surface and clinked onto the floor. Katherine rolled her eyes and bent down. Christopher Higgins slunk shyly past her. He was a stocky little chap with buck teeth and rather brilliant for his age.

Katherine suddenly reappeared behind the lab desk and startled him. His papers tumbled to the floor and he stared at her open-mouthed.

"Christopher!"

The fourth-grader scurried to pick up his papers.

"Sorry," he muttered and rushed to the far end of the laboratory. Katherine sighed. Now she surely had the reputation to be mean to the younger ones. Great.

She sat down and put her chin in her hand. She had everything to work with here, but the stupid vacuum battery just didn't want to do its thing.

The science lab was Dr. Broadbent's pride and joy. Thanks

to the generous donation from a past student, the school had been able to upgrade the facilities.

A certain Cecil Whitby had apparently cherished his memories of Pemberton in the sixties to such an extent that he left the school half of his considerable fortune five years ago. The money had been used to upgrade the science lab. It was henceforth called the 'Whitby Wing' and could now probably rival any NASA science lab.

Katherine saw Walt, the janitor, through the half-drawn Venetian window blinds. He instructed the two gardeners in the art of clipping hedges. The hedges looked just fine to her. Which was something that couldn't be said for her project.

"Need any help?" Katherine spun around. Suddenly Trevor stood next to her.

"Sorry, I didn't mean to scare you. You just looked ready to pull your hair out. I thought you might need some... help." He regretted his remark instantly.

"My word, Trevor, do you want to give me a heart attack?" Katherine flew at him. "And why would I need any help?"

"Actually," he said slowly. "I just wanted to see, if I could help. Okay, never mind, you have everything under control." Trevor knew that she didn't easily lose her cool, so this had to be serious. He waited.

"Sorry, I didn't mean to snap at you like that." Katherine drew her fingers through her loose hair, only to tuck it back behind her ears again. "But this thing is driving me c r a z y!"

She pointed at the jumbled mess in front of her and Trevor understood.

"Don't tell me it's Professor Helbert's vacuum battery. The 'endless energy source'. Not bad for a project, but nobody has managed to get it right yet."

"Well, count me in as nobody." Katherine glanced hotly at her obstinate creation. "I really want to smash the thing on the floor and trample it into a pancake."

"Ouch, Chryséis is already rubbing off on you?"

"Hmm," Katherine grumbled.

Professor Gaylord Helbert's theory for the vacuum battery centred - roughly speaking - around two poles touching in a vacuum, thereby generating endless power. According to the formula, different harmonic levels within a range of electromagnetic waves could be activated for all sorts of useful applications. Theoretically.

"Hang it. Chryséis is busy with another project. Some new theory about the time continuum. Black holes in space and so on. But I can't do it on my own." So there - she had said it. By now, black holes sounded more appealing to Katherine as well.

"Okay then, let's see. Did you check the vacuum? Let's have a look at these figures again…"

It hadn't occurred to her to ask Trevor. He usually worked on projects with the other boys.

"Are you sure?" She hesitated.

"Yeah, of course." He liked to solve problems.

"Very well, I downloaded the notes from the 'Q-Mechanics' website and it makes all perfect sense. The harmonics should be easy to tune now…"

They worked all afternoon on the solution and were proud of their respectable results. By the time the bell rang for dinner, the vacuum battery had already survived a series of tests. Katherine was in a much better mood.

"We should look at the outlet again. Maybe we can integrate an adapter," Trevor said.

"I guess it's our project now. If you don't have other plans, I mean," she ventured. Trevor nodded eagerly.

"Actually, I was supposed to work with Dan Atkins, but we couldn't agree on anything. He linked up with Ben Harper, I think. So yes, I guess we are project partners." They high-fived spontaneously.

"Good. Now we just need an application to demonstrate the battery."

"Let's not jump the gun. First the battery has to work properly."

"Yes, I know. There wasn't much on the 'Q-Mechanics' website other than the instructions. But we can start thinking about it."

"Hmm, okay. But I'm hungry now."

Christopher Higgins was busy tidying up his workbench. In the chemistry lab, Sophie Baxter, a grade 10 karate champ, poured some red liquid into a test tube and waited. She would also pack up soon. It was time to go.

"We could go to the library tomorrow and check out 'The Uses of Electromagnetism in Modern Science'. There was this one chapter... do you want to meet after class tomorrow?"

"Yes, we could do that." Katherine put her tools back into the drawer, locked it and crammed the notes into her schoolbag.

"That's almost too easy. How about starting a history project, when we are finished here? Early Chinese dynasties...," Trevor said.

"It wasn't that easy, Trevor! There's plenty of work left. Chinese history can wait."

The following day they met in front of the library. There was some kind of commotion underway in the lobby and the students tried to slink past the massive desk with downcast eyes.

"Mr. Booth!" The librarian's irate voice cut painfully through the usual quietude. "This is about taking responsibility!" She pronounced every syllable. "Two books in two weeks!"

Miss Eppelstein, affectionately nicknamed 'Apple' by all, paused for effect, "And you say they just - disappeared? I will have to report this. I'll simply have to. If you think you cannot expend sufficient care of school property...!"

Miss Eppelstein had earned her nickname from the students, thanks to her round figure and rosy cheeks. But sometimes, she could turn from a calm and helpful librarian into a furious book goddess, if her beloved books were 'lost'. And you didn't want to be in her way when *that* happened.

Samuel Booth, a scrawny sixth-grader with flaming red hair to match his ears, stood dutifully crushed in front of her. He was embarrassed and could feel everybody's eyes skewering him for being such a dork. But he had to admit that Miss Eppelstein was right. He had this stupid habit of leaving books lying around.

Apple wasn't quite finished with him yet. "Do you have any idea, Mr. Booth, how much the school pays every year for library books?"

Katherine and Trevor sneaked past the great desk in a throng of other students. Trevor didn't want her to recognize him. The same thing had happened to him not too long ago!

They searched for a rather large volume in the 'Physics' section. According to the record card, it was supposed to sit on the shelf under the letter 'B'.

"Look at this," Katherine pointed at a thin hard cover book.

"Have you ever heard of 'Extraterrestrial Intelligence' by Meredith Baker-Maitland? I wonder what *that's* all about —"

"A Nicola Tesla book is also in the wrong place!" She had read most books on Nicola Tesla, a famous 19th century physicist, who had been way ahead of his time. One of this maverick's achievements had been a light bulb that glowed without an electrical connection.

Unfortunately, nobody had shown much interest in his incredible inventions at the time. So the knowledge was lost. No scientist had since been able to figure out just how Nicola Tesla had made that globe glow. All they knew was that it used energy 'from around'.

"Ah, here it is," Trevor said. "'The Uses of Electro-magnetism in Modern Science' by Professor Thomas Barber,

1989 Pillory Press. Someone put it under 'D' instead of 'B'."

The heavy book thumped onto the low table next to the shelf. They sat down and began to page through the index. It was quieter now in the library. Miss Eppelstein's anger seemed to wear off.

"Enough already!" Katherine sighed. "I'm sure you can scrape the poor chap off the floor by now. I hope I'll never lose expensive library books like Sam. "

Trevor barely listened. He turned page after page.

"Okay, let's see. Where was it…? 'Gravitational Waves', 'Electromagnetic Waves'," Trevor mumbled. "…regular variations at a given point propagate to other points in space at the velocity c. It is the modulation, which enables information to be imposed on the carrier wave. We know *that* already…"

"I think this could be something: 'Harmonics in Electromagnetism'. Sounds about right. Chapter Thirteen," Chryséis said. They scanned the text carefully.

"Have a look at this, Katie." Trevor's finger stabbed at a complex-looking paragraph. He read aloud:

"*…At such a suitable location, preferably undisturbed by major electromagnetic fields, given a sufficient energy source, the space-time continuum may be accessed using such a device. Provided, that the source of energy be kept at a consistently high level… See table 11a… thus activating a time portal. A rotating vortex (!) representing a warp in the space-time continuum, bridges an often volatile overlap of periods in time. The factors time and speed may be stabilised by applying the following formula…*"

"Crikey, that means that time travel is at least *possible*," Katherine said in awe. "That's what you want to do with the battery?"

"Sure, if it's possible, why not?" Trevor said.

"As if you've always known that, Einstein!"

"For a while now."

"Ah, of course there's a hook. The energy source has to be continuous and *sufficient*. And it sounds like, ouch…!"

A corner of the heavy book had begun to slide off the table and bored itself into Katherine's thigh. She rubbed the painful spot and glared at the tome, but Trevor was too absorbed to pay much attention.

"That's true, I guess... sufficient... it has to be sufficient, but that's relative. All we have to do is increase the capacity of the vacuum battery and stabilize it."

"That's what it's all about," Katherine grinned and imitated one of Dr. Wilkins' favourite sayings. "Be daring, children!"

For a long moment they didn't say a thing, then the idea sank in. "What exactly are you saying, Trevor? I mean *time travel* and all that?"

"We can try to enter the space-time-continuum," he said slowly. "As long as we have an endless energy supply, we're already halfway there, aren't we?"

"Well, sort of."

"What's wrong with trying?"

"Oh, I don't know. For one thing, we have to present the project in about three weeks. And it's only...*time travel*! Crazy idea. We would need benchmark figures... then more information on existing devices...!"

"But I know we can do it. If we attach the vacuum-battery to the time portal finder, I figured out last year." He started paging through the book again.

"You figured out what?" Katherine was stunned.

And that's how Trevor told her about the lecture he had attended when he was nine.

One of Professor Barber's students spoke on aspects of the space-time continuum. Trevor had sat next to physics students for two long hours, eagerly scribbling down notes. He had read up on it the university library and built a timeportal-finder.

"What, and you never thought of telling me this?"

"Yes well, I thought you were gonna laugh. And I only tried it once," Trevor said. "And to be honest, I was scared of the flickering vortex. Well, I was nine."

"But that's still important... a flickering vortex, really?"

"Never showed anyone. The project on pyramids around the world seemed safer. Did you know that some are supposed to be buried under tons of sand in the Gobi Desert? I can't believe that a 150-meter tall pyramid was found at the bottom of the Sargasso Sea, though."

Katherine vaguely remembered his history project last year. "Trevor, you are changing the subject."

"Let's make a copy of this." He picked up the heavy book and carried it to the copy machine.

The thought of entering the space-time continuum and maybe never getting out again, sent a shiver down Katherine's spine. The thought of time travel was thrilling - and scary all at once.

Trevor didn't cease to amaze her. He had actually developed a time machine! What exactly was a time-portal-finder? Her head was spinning with all the new facts.

Time travel... what if it really *was* possible?

 **4**   **AN IDEA TAKES SHAPE**

"Are you kidding? How far are you then, seriously?"

Chryséis had just been told about the project and the possibility of a trip through space and time. She was intrigued by the idea. "Time travel with a vacuum battery - come on, really?"

"I honestly think it's possible. I haven't tested it properly, but the device has been in the works for a while now," Trevor said as if he had never talked about anything else. Chryséis was still not convinced.

"A time-portal-finder?"

"Yes. It detects irregular electromagnetic fields like time warps. They indicate a weakness in the space-time continuum, like a time portal, you know…"

"Right, of course."

"Seriously. We could even generate a vortex with the vacuum battery. The batteries I've used before were far too weak for that," Trevor said, keeping his cool. "I can test it after dark. Then we'll know more."

Faint croaking came from the far end of the pond. They sat under the birch trees by the pond with their feet in the water. The water was still too cold and they soon went back to sit on the bench in the rose garden. It gave Chryséis time to think.

"Wow. That's some project. You really think it can work – this vortex?"

"Yes."

"Well, then let's get going. I'm in." Chryséis's mind was already abuzz with all the possibilities. Maybe she would shake the hand of Socrates one fine day or meet Napoleon.

Okay maybe not Napoleon. Not such a nice guy.

"What about your assignment on black holes?" Katherine asked. "Aren't you terribly busy with that?"

"What, and let you have all the fun? I'm nearly done with it anyway. The planetarium in town agreed to lend me a video for the presentation," Chryséis explained. "I'm just waiting for some info from Texas on the musical note that black holes emit. The typing is easy."

She thought for a moment. "So yes, count me in. I can't pass up time travel for black holes."

After dark, Trevor slipped out into the school garden. That wasn't allowed, but he couldn't waste time with unimportant details. The trials weren't successful at first. Closer to the buildings, there was absolutely nothing. Maybe it was the interference that went along with electrical appliances and power lines.

Then closer to the golf course, he finally detected a modest shimmer. Just like before. But Trevor was not afraid this time. If this was a warp in the space-time continuum - a real time portal - then he had to know for sure. He moved even closer to the golf course and tried again.

Trevor pointed the device here and there and then at a random spot between a bench and an azalea bush. This time, the weak flicker turned into a respectable vortex. That was it! Without a second thought, Trevor jumped into the whirlpool.

But what was that? Trevor's eyes became wide with horror.

It couldn't have taken a minute and he landed again on his backside in front of the bench. The impact was cushioned by the thick lawn, but Trevor was stunned. He had seen something awful on the other side.

Big and covered in shiny green and golden scales... or maybe feathers... there had been steam. Had he seen long teeth? Then the thing had moved. Just a shiver that went through the scales. Just a slight wave.

Trevor didn't wait to find out what the 'thing' was. He

had pressed the reverse button and the vortex had swallowed him up again. Then he sat on the soft lawn. He was safe!

Alas, he didn't hear Natasha Manning open her window on the first floor.

"Mr. Huxley, I expected more of you. Wandering about the school grounds at this hour. What were you thinking?" Matron waved her arms in exasperation.

"I'm sorry ma'am. I needed some fresh air to think."

The white lie rolled easily off his tongue.

Like Walt, the janitor, Matron had a big heart for children. They often didn't know how to handle their own cleverness. Too clever for their own good. But rules were rules. If she made exceptions, there'd be chaos in no time.

"You know the rules, Mr. Huxley," the matron sighed and Trevor nodded.

For the next three days he had to sweep the back veranda and the path to the golf course after dinner and before dark. Much to Holly's and Natasha's delight: oh yes, the scholarship-boy had been put in his place.

"Hey, Huxley! Were you sleepwalking or did you meet someone special on the golf course?" Natasha guffawed and winked at Chryséis.

A few fifth-graders skulked close by, grinning broadly. A rare scandal!

Natasha was a carbon copy of Holly Benson. Although her hair was lighter than Holly's, it was permed into identical ringlets. She shook her curls and even talked like Holly.

Chryséis was fuming. Well, you just wait she thought hotly and shot furious looks at the girl. You just wait.

General attention shifted away from Trevor's misdeed when two other boys threw a baseball through one of the kitchen windows that afternoon. They were sentenced to cleaning the swimming pool for a week. It was Matron's favourite punishment for rowdy kids.

At last, they could discuss Trevor's adventure.

Everything had ground to a halt after Natasha had ratted him out to Matron. They had to be careful, though. Holly was capable of sabotaging everything, if she found out about the nightly experiment.

"And you are sure you saw scales?"

They sat in the common room on the second floor, keeping an eye on the door. Everybody else was still downstairs in the dining room. Chryséis demanded to hear the story for the umpteenth time, although it made her spine feel all chilly in delicious horror.

"I'm not sure. It was so dark. Could have been feathers or something." Trevor felt tired. The more he thought about it, the less he could remember. Maybe it had all just been a dream. But he still remembered turning round and round inside the vortex. No dream then.

"Sounds like a dinosaur to me." There, Katherine had said what the others were thinking.

"Maybe."

"That must have been a long trip then," Chryséis marvelled.

"I'm not sure. I just pressed the button and jumped in, before the vortex could disappear again." Trevor yawned. What was the big deal?

"Without choosing the time span?"

"Yes, without choosing the time span."

"We have to change that."

"Yes."

"And you say it was hot and smelled dreadful?"

Katherine couldn't let it go. If time travel was like that, she would stay behind for sure. Dinosaurs - just imagine!

"Katie, I don't know for sure. It took only a minute. Just drop it now." But his fellow scientists weren't ready to just drop the issue just yet.

"Hey, we missed dessert for this!" Chryséis protested.

"What happens if we travel into prehistory and meet face to face with a dinosaur or... a caveman?"

Better tackle the facts. "Or we land right in the middle of an ocean or in a volcano."

"What?" Katherine jumped.

She was busy eating a chocolate bar and played with the wrapper. It helped her calm her nerves.

"We don't have to go that far back. In any case, there are books about prehistory. And a cartful of DVDs."

Trevor perked up. "If it's supposed to be a bomb, we must at least go back a few thousand years. Otherwise, it's too boring. Let's do some research, guys. Will you stop it with that stupid paper already?!"

Katherine put the wrapper into her pocket.

"We program reference points in time. Not just the starting time." Trevor looked at the clock on the wall. "Sorry, gotta go. Walt's waiting with the broom for me." With that he hurried downstairs.

"We have to be careful. I'm sure that Holly's already watching us like a hawk." Chryséis pulled a face as if she had just bitten into a lemon.

"Or she has Natasha already spy on us."

"What are we supposed to do, sit around?" Katherine asked.

A group of fourth-graders walked into the room with their homework. They paid no attention to the older girls and soon studied their Japanese vocabulary.

"No, of course not. While Trevor sweeps, we'll visit our good, old library. Let's start with oceans and volcanoes," Chryséis whispered. They went to the library and took out a few DVDs to watch them later, then climbed the stairs to their room on the second floor to drop them off.

"Let's take a walk to the pond," Chryséis suggested. "At least we can be sure that we won't see Holly there. She hates water. "

On the water's edge, the two friends sat down and took their trainers off. "Dinosaurs are creeping me out." Katherine shook herself.

"I don't know, never seen a live one," Chryséis said. "I'm not sure if it makes any sense, but, why not check it out...well, why not..."

"What? Check what out?"

"Well, something to make us invisible."

"Right, invisible -" Katherine contemplated. "There's a thought. Wait, I think I read about that somewhere in a magazine."

"What magazine?"

"I remember... it was in the 'Science Today', December issue. Some inventor in Kansas came up with a clever idea. Bending light waves. Nobody takes it seriously, of course, but why not try it out?"

"It's definitely safer to go invisible when we need to..." Chryséis said. "Just in case some caveman wants to cook us for breakfast. Or some humongous dinosaur thinks we are too close to its nest..."

"Oh yes, don't wanna end up as caveman cereal. You got some imagination."

"I'm serious, Chris," Katherine said and felt gooseflesh on her arms. Chryséis stopped laughing.

"So am I. A virtual invisibility cape it is. I'll have a look at that issue of 'Science Today' magazine. Won't take me long."

They wiped their feet dry on the longish grass, picked up their shoes and walked barefoot back to the school building.

During the next few days, the three friends made good progress. They did research, and the idea with the 'virtual invisibility cape' had been quickly carried out. Chryséis offered to play the guinea pig. They just had to make sure that everyone else was on the back veranda for the afternoon snack. The ideal time for such an experiment.

"Calm down, you'll give us away with all that fidgeting," Chryséis said to Katherine. "Just now, Holly Benson will sniff us out!"

For Chryséis, there was only one thing that helped with

nerves. "Come do it like that."

Chryséis did the bridge on the carpet of their dorm room. One of her favourite yoga positions. Her face looked funny upside down as she spoke.

"No, don't feel like it," Katherine said. "How is she supposed to find out?"

"You know, when Holly is onto something, she's like a bull terrier. Where is Trevor?"

Somebody knocked on the door. Two long raps and two short ones. Their secret sign.

"Ah, there he is." Chryséis uncurled herself quickly.

"Ready you two?" Trevor whispered urgently.

He didn't feel like being caught in the girls' dorm and sweeping the back veranda or something for the rest of the year. "Let's get on with it. I don't want to miss dinner as well."

"Why do you always have to think about food?" Katherine asked irritated.

"I don't like chocolate."

"Stop arguing. Go ahead, Trev, we'll be there just now."

They met in a dead-end passage on the top floor, where sports equipment and old kitchen utensils were stored. Nobody would look for them here. At least not for a while, but they had to hurry.

"That's supposed to be the invisibility device?" Katherine wasn't exactly convinced.

"Yes, this inventor from Kansas gave an interview with all the details. It's the most logical design."

An aliceband with the box stuck on it and a button to switch it on and off. Ready for testing.

"Okay then, here goes."

Trevor put the prototype on Chryséis's head and pressed the button. She disappeared almost immediately. Katherine and Trevor caught their breaths. "Unbelievable."

"Well, get used to it girlfriend," a ghostlike voice said next to Katherine and made her eyes pop.

"You mean, when the dinosaur is ready to gobble us up."

Trevor snapped his hands playfully in the direction of the voice.

"Better safe than sorry is what I say," the ghost cackled.

"No nonsense, please Chris," Katherine warned her. "We'll see you at the lab in ten. Good luck!"

Katherine opened the door to the emergency back staircase. Trevor followed her. It was the quickest way to the 'Whitby Wing'.

"Nonsense! Would I ever?" Chryséis traipsed down the main stairs, carefully moving along the wall. Somebody might just decide to shoot around the corner and bump into her. The last thing she needed.

It went well. On the ground floor, Chryséis walked slowly along the passage. First past the library, then the school office. A couple of children were on their way to have their snacks before sports practice. Nobody could see her.

Chryséis moved more confidently now toward the teachers' staff room and slid through the half-open door.

Somebody spoke behind the bookshelves at the back of the long room. She heard soft laughter and whispering. Chryséis crept forward taking care not to make any noise. She peeped out from behind one of the shelves to get a better look. At that moment Mr. Hunter and Miss Gould, two student teachers, started kissing passionately.

Chryséis stepped back in surprise and bumped into one of the desks. The young teachers tore away from each other and Mr. Hunter stood protectively in front of an embarrassed Miss Gould. "Is there somebody?"

He walked a few paces forward and nearly collided with Chryséis. She turned around and fled.

Chryséis ran towards the door, thudding her big toe against the doorframe as she took the corner. It hurt an awful lot, but she bit her lip, trying not to make a noise.

Only when Chryséis had reached the top of the stairs, she checked if it was safe. Nobody followed her. Then she switched off the invisibility device at last. She bit her lip and tried to walk as normally as possible. Her toe throbbed with pain, but she managed to smile a greeting at Mr. Van Straten, who was on his way to the staff room.

Trevor and Katherine were waiting for her outside the lab. By the time she reached the Whitby Wing, Chryséis had recovered enough to tell her friends what had happened. She whispered her story in hushed tones, because other students were standing around. Not the best place to exchange secrets.

To add insult to injury, Katherine and Trevor could barely contain themselves. They kept chuckling and Chryséis threatened not to finish her story if they didn't keep it down. But then she had to grin as well. Imagine Mr. Hunter and Miss Gould!

Holly Benson shot stern glances at them from her desk inside the laboratory. Of course it was Trevor Huxley and his two girlfriends, she thought annoyed.

"Unbelievable! Can't you be quiet when we have to work?"

She looked around in search of support, but nobody else seemed to take any notice of them. She wondered what could possibly be so funny. Well, I'll find out, she thought smugly, and then they're in trouble.

But the day didn't end pleasantly for Holly.

In the evening, she found a slippery frog in her bed. Holly screamed blue murder, when her feet touched the moist, squirming animal. The blood-curdling scream could be heard everywhere in the girls' dormitory. She threw the blankets off and the horrified frog jumped up and down trying to escape, and quickly ended up in the flowerbed below, leaping toward the safety of the pond.

Holly was furious. She suspected now this culprit, now another. Two seven-graders high-fived in their room on the second floor and grinned. There was nothing the startled matron could do, except for shooing giggling girls back into their bedrooms. And Holly never found out who had played that ghastly prank on her.

It was lunchtime in the dining room and as Cook had promised, they ate a special Sunday meal: crayfish – and roast chicken for those with a shellfish allergy.

"So what's your IQ score then, Holfield?" Holly Benson smirked in the new girl's direction.

She hadn't been very friendly to anyone since the prank with the frog. Sally's face turned the colour of the red crayfish on her plate. She suddenly didn't feel hungry anymore.

"Leave her alone Benson," Chryséis snarled a warning without looking up. They all knew what Holly had in mind.

"What is it with you, Cromwell? Can't I ask a simple question without your approval?" Holly sulked.

It was such a bother with Chris and Katie, she thought. They always had to spoil a bit of fun with the new ones. Holly tried a smile in Sally's direction.

"Ahem 144," Sally breathed, fixing her gaze on a spot on the white tablecloth. She didn't want any trouble. Perhaps Holly wasn't as bad as Chryséis and Katherine had led her to believe. Look, she was smiling! Why couldn't they all just be friends? But Chryséis stuck to her guns.

"Listen here, don't try and make her feel bad, Benson. How about some small talk, before showing off your fabulous IQ score? Oh, I forgot... that's not your style." Chryséis's voice took on a silly breathless quality.

"What's wrong with talking about one's IQ? Pah!"

Holly knew from past experience that she couldn't possibly win this argument with Chryséis Cromwell. What a bore. Must be genetic, she thought hotly, just look at that odd mother of hers.

Others began to stare at them. Many of the kids thought that Holly was a terrible snob, but Holly knew better. Her superior intelligence went hand in hand with a little bit of arrogance, which was quite normal. Her Dad always said so.

They all continued to eat in silence until Dr. Broadbent announced an excursion to Carter Valley, planned for Saturday in two weeks time. Next weekend was reserved for the school's annual Sports Day. All-round cheering and some grumbling ensued.

Sport's Day, already! Katherine and Chryséis looked at each other. They had only just arrived back at school! The sporty students were, of course, delighted.

"Mens sana in corpore sano, ladies and gentlemen. Nothing like a breath of fresh air and aching muscles to tickle stale thoughts out of your grey cells," Dr. Broadbent boomed over the noise and launched into a brief speech praising the virtues of team sports.

Trevor didn't listen. His thoughts were far away. He was a good tennis player, but Sports Day was a nuisance right now. The time portal finder needed to be tested again. He no longer had to sweep the back veranda and the garden path, but cycle tests had been scheduled for every day of next week. And then there was Holly to consider. The project was due in less than 3 weeks.

Then he had an idea. The excursion to Carter Valley - it would be ideal!

On Saturday, it rained cats and dogs and the Sports Day had to be cancelled. All competitions and fun games were postponed to a weekend in April.

Students were milling about in their sports gear, not knowing what to do with themselves. Many lounged around in little groups on the back veranda and watched the downpour. Others watched TV in the common rooms.

Chryséis, Katherine and Trevor had visited the 'Paraguayan Coffee Shop', corner Church and Bailey

Streets. Dr. Naidoo. Their English teacher had agreed to let them wait in the coffee shop next to the movie theatre. All the other students and teachers went to watch the new movie 'The Caterpillar Club'.

The three aspiring time travellers had decided immediately to try out the virtual invisibility cape.

A bit risky perhaps, but they needed to observe the effect under different conditions. And the coffee shop wasn't too busy.

The girls had put on the alicebands in the dark foyer of the movie theatre and slipped through the door of the coffee shop right behind Trevor. They had left mysterious footprints on the floor, but it was impossible to tell them from all the other wet footprints.

Trevor settled himself at a bistro table by the window and ordered a hot chocolate and a piece of carrot cake. Two lonely daypacks sat on the other two chairs at the table.

"My two friends are on their way," he had told the waitress.

Trevor was supposed to wait for Chryséis and Katherine, but they almost regretted their daring plan. Somebody walked into Katherine, as the two girls made their way invisibly to the restrooms at the back.

A young woman stormed through the swing door dividing the coffee shop from the passage. Her hand brushed against Katherine, giving the girl a mighty fright. Katherine clung to Chryséis, who nearly dropped the muffin she had impishly picked up on the counter.

The woman looked up for a second. "Oh!" She looked in their direction, but could she see them?

Katherine's heart missed a beat. She was incredibly relieved when the woman just sat down at her table. They felt their way along the wall and squeezed through the open gap of the restroom door. Then they pressed themselves against the wall next to the hand dryers. They waited for two ladies to finish powdering their noses. Then the girls quickly de-activated the VICs.

"Phew, that was close!" Katherine's eyes were as round as saucers.

"Do you think that woman noticed something?!" she asked. Chryséis didn't answer straight away. She looked pale under her freckles as she started washing her hands, in case somebody came in.

"I don't think so."

"But what if she comes back to check?"

"Why should she do that?"

A girl, who needed the toilet desperately, walked in just as Katherine started to say something. The girls left. They could talk later.

In was in any case time to get back to Trevor. Katherine began to giggle as she sat down next to him and could stop.

"How did it go?" Trevor whispered and looked bewildered at Katherine.

"Just nerves," Chryséis sighed. "Somebody bumped into her by the swing door."

"Oh that's great, did he notice anything?"

"No, I don't think so. It was the lady over there..." Chryséis pointed slightly with her chin. The woman looked up at the waiter, who brought her the bill. Looked all normal.

"She seems okay," Trevor decided.

Katherine giggled some more as their order of hot chocolate was served. Bradley Benson walked past the window and Katherine stopped at once. He waved at them in an unusually friendly manner. They waved back half-heartedly.

"Don't tell me Holly sent him to spy on us." Chryséis creased her forehead.

"Who knows. But there was nothing to see." At least Trevor hoped so.

By the time they arrived back at Pemberton, Katherine had completely recovered from her giggling spell. They went straight to the back veranda, where a table was just being cleared.

Katherine snuggled into the comfortable cushions of the broad bamboo chair. There were jugs with iced tea and glasses on the tables that had been prepared for the Sports Day. 'Too good to waste,' cook Hadley had said in the morning. The students agreed. Cook's ice tea was even better than her famous lemonade. Katherine watched the relentless rain.

"Imagine all this water coming down in one great gush. Instead of slowly drizzling down," she said.

"It would be like a tidal wave. Sweeping away our beloved school and us in the process, girlfriend." Chryséis rolled her eyes. Katherine sometimes came up with these ideas out of the blue.

"Sometimes I am glad that nature just takes care of things."

"So am I!" Trevor agreed.

"Yes, like thanks to the rain I don't have to play tennis against all those champs today. Thank you, thank you nature—" Chryséis bowed mockingly toward the rain.

Like Katherine, she was no sports genius. The occasional swim or walk on the beach was okay - and yoga of course. But clobbering it out in a competitive match on the tennis court was not her cup of tea.

"I would have liked a bit of action for a change," Trevor said and added on a whiny note, "I've been working in the lab on our project non-stop for two weeks."

"Yes, we all have. We'll get plenty of action, trust me." Chryséis curled up in her chair and angled for her iced tea. "I'm hooked on this time travel idea."

"More than an idea by now," Trevor corrected her.

"Are you sure we won't end up in the future, when we get into the vortex?" Katherine shivered a little at the thought. "The future! Food shortages, wars, global warming and things like that. Yikes!"

More students came pouring through the open French doors and settled noisily around the low tables.

Katherine took a juicy orange quarter from the glass plate in front of her. She enjoyed these occasional downpours. They were much more pleasant than the endless drizzle on the British Isles.

Even so, it made her feel a bit homesick. She missed English food in particular. Luckily, her mother often sent food parcels with Marmite, mince pies, anchovy paste and Branston Pickle.

"Don't worry, the time spans are all set. In any case, it's a lot harder to travel forward in time than backward," Trevor said, stretching himself lazily.

He couldn't understand what was still bothering Katherine. Everything was under control. After all, he'd done it before. Trevor waved a brief impression of greenish, slithering scales aside and took a few hasty sips of iced tea.

"We can program the exact time of departure as a long-term reference point. Then we can take our time. Nobody will ever know we're gone. We'll just arrive back at the same time we left."

"We've two VIC-tests under our belts and the last TPF-test happens next weekend. Easy peasy."

"Alright, if you say so..."

"What's a Tippi Eff?" Bradley turned around grinning at them. That's all they needed!

Chryséis kept her cool and said casually, "Something to eat, smart ass. None of your business anyway."

"Okay whatever," Bradley said and took the glass jug to the kitchen for a refill. Katherine just managed to control another urge to giggle.

"I don't think he heard anything with all the noise around," Trevor said.

"Okay then, let's talk shop," Chryséis said in a soft voice. "The invisibility devices are sorted. And we've got the big experiment planned for the excursion. What do we take with us into the vortex?"

"Sounds scary: into the vortex. What if the vacuum

battery doesn't give us enough juice and we can't get out again? Will our skeletons keep spinning in it forever?"

"Oh rubbish Katherine MacDougal! The battery is working just fine. Don't get all scaredy-cat on us. What kind of scientists worry about something like that?"

"Yes, okay," Katherine said, but she didn't sound at all convinced.

"Stop going nuts on us, please, we still have so much to do," Chryséis said.

"Actually, we don't need that much. Just a few provisions. Food, sleeping bags. Stuff like that," Trevor said.

"Good idea. Chris, why don't you write down a list?" Katherine was back on track.

"Sure, why not." Chryséis scribbled on a serviette. "If it doesn't work out, we'll just try again some other time. At least we'll be all packed up."

"Not a chance. We're going in Carter Valley as planned." Trevor wondered for a second, if they would really manage to do it in such a short time. But then he relaxed. Sure they would manage.

"Okay then, next weekend then. We need some food, at least snacks and something to drink. Any ideas?"

The rain was letting up now and the sun broke through the thinning cloud blanket. Bradley Benson laughed out loud. He sat at a table with Holly and two other girls not far away. The three friends jumped, but Bradley didn't pay attention to them.

"He's making me all nervous," Chryséis said.

"Oh, just ignore him," Trevor growled.

"Talking about food provisions—," Katherine said, "I just received a food parcel from home. Fancy some toast with anchovy paste?"

"No thanks Your Royal Highness that's too British for me. I can do without yucky English food. How can anyone get used to that fish paste stuff and brown yeast spread and what not?"

"Thanks a lot! It can't be that bad, if so many people in Britain like it!" Katherine snarled back.

She fought an uphill battle to get her friends interested in delicacies from England.

"And in any case, what about yucky American food?"

Trevor stopped a full-blown argument about food.

"I'll get some chips from the tuck shop. What about you, want some? Thai Chili or Sour Cream and Onion?"

"Thai Chili for me, please." Chryséis rather enjoyed the occasional junk food.

"Okay, I'll have some Thai Chili, too," Katherine squeaked still offended. She mumbled something under her breath about ignorance and pampered American taste buds, but then she also enjoyed her potato chips.

Later at dusk, Trevor searched for another time warp in the school garden. He didn't tell the girls. They wouldn't like it after all the trouble with Natasha. But what if Katherine was right and things didn't pan out? He had to find out. By himself.

The warp was weak. He detected some faint vertical waves, but no sign of a vortex. Trevor managed to keep the waves going for half a minute.

Not a bad result so close to the school building. He was convinced that the device would do its job in Carter Valley. During the week, Katherine and Trevor were busy with last-minute changes in the lab, while Chryséis made a provisions list. On top of the list, she wrote plastic water bottles and cans of soft drink. They were useful even when empty.

Then emergency food like granola bars, peanuts, beef jerky and dried fruit. Chryséis wrote down lighters and matches; toothbrushes, water purifying tablets and aspirin. Something for stomach problems, antiseptic cream, lip balm, underwear and sandals. An old discman, which could also record and three music CDs. One CD for each of them.

A palmtop computer with memory stick (the vacuum battery could now be used for recharging) and a tiny digital camera. A Swiss army knife would come in handy and sunglasses, plastic bags and paper tissues. Then the smallest and lightest Sherpa sleeping bags available. She read the list again.

Was that overkill for a short trip? Maybe, but better safe than sorry.

A Frisbee maybe... no, a rainfly which could be folded really small... and moon bags. An electric stunner as self-defence might be good, or pepper spray. But they were too young to buy these at the shop. Chryséis wrote 'make a plan' next to these items. She trimmed and changed the list until it looked about right.

After dinner, they went over the list together and started packing in secret. The girls couldn't keep their activities hidden from Sally Holfield, though.

"Why are you packing so much stuff for a day trip?" their room mate wanted to know. Chryséis had to think on her feet. "Just to be prepared," she answered curtly.

"Prepared for what?"

Chryséis just shrugged her shoulders and stuffed a Frisbee into her daypack. Sally was puzzled. Gifted kids often did things differently, she thought, forgetting that she was also a gifted kid. So Sally kept quiet.

All the excitement had an undesirable side effect on Chryséis, though. She had one of her rare sleepwalking episodes. Getting as far as the passage window, she turned around, nearly mistaking a cupboard in the passage for the dorm room. Being sound sleepers, neither Sally nor Katherine noticed anything.

It was just strange that Chryséis lay sleeping on the floor rug next to her bed in the morning.

There was another more serious incident, however. Sally saw a pretty aliceband with a little black box on Chryséis's bedside table. The virtual invisibility device!

Admiring the fab hair accessory, Sally put it on in front of the mirror, stroking her light brown hair back for effect.

She was about to touch the critical button when Chryséis walked in. Seeing the horrified look on her room mate's face, Sally handed the aliceband over without a word and ran red-faced from the room. "How could I have been so stupid, Katie? On the bedside table!" she said to Katherine the next day. They had just finished lunch and were on their way to the lockers.

"Odd that Sally should touch your stuff like that."

"Do you think Holly put her up to it?"

"Nah, I think she just wanted to look pretty."

"Well, lucky nothing happened," Chryséis grunted. "We must be careful with Holly hovering and watching us and all. Anyway, where's Trevor?"

"Oh, he got a link by the golf course and decided to take a little trip on his own."

"What?!" Chryséis's eyes grew wide with surprise.

"Lighten up. It's a joke. Trev's in his room to change. He has tennis this afternoon."

"I thought for a moment... oh, don't do that to me. You nearly had me there." She nudged her friend playfully and they started laughing.

"Nearly? Hah…"

"Yes nearly. Think of all the green scales he'd have seen this time…"

Holly and Natasha passed them looking blankly ahead. Chryséis narrowly avoided Natasha's shoulder. Icy stares flew between them. "Wonder what they have to laugh about," Natasha said in a spiteful tone.

"Well, we'll know soon enough," Holly smirked. "Sally was a bit unhappy this morning. I'll speak to her later. I'm sure she's in for a bit of a deal."

She still suspected the girls of playing the frog prank on her and couldn't wait to pay them back.

"Good thinking, Sweet revenge—" Natasha hissed and they strutted away.

Trevor made sure that he was alone in the room when

he quickly packed his lot of the provisions. His room mates were fairly safe and more interested in a good game of chess or golf. But he couldn't take chances now.

Was underwear necessary? He decided that it was. Where had he put the camera Chryséis had given him? Oh, that's right, Chryséis had already packed it. They were still unaware of Natasha's and Holly's scheming.

By Friday evening, everything was ready and finally Saturday morning arrived. During the excursion everything worked without a hitch.

At last, the young time astronauts stood on the rocky platform right by the escarpment. The time warp was shimmering right in front of them and moved in waves. The wave motion began to accelerate and then churn. Trevor already knew the process and was proud that his calculations had proved correct. There was hardly any interference around.

"I'm going to activate the first time span now. Get ready."

Chryséis and Katherine grabbed each other's hand. Trevor had integrated time-spans ranging from 10,000 to 50,000 years, because that's how they had applied the formula. It was a giant leap. What they knew was that no monsters, volcanoes or oceans would wait on the other side. Well, quite sure.

Katherine tried to be brave. It had been difficult enough to leave her home in England. Never mind travelling back to an ancient past now. Her father had written a postcard from Lagos in Nigeria last week. That was also pretty far away, wasn't it? She consoled herself that she would be away for only a short while. In any case, they would arrive back in the present at the precise same moment they had left. But her courage left her, when the time portal made its appearance. Katherine stared at the swirling vortex that formed in front of the boulder now.

A real vortex!

Holly Benson watched how her three enemies vanished from sight between the rocks and away from the footpath. She pretended to have a weak bladder and had followed them off the path to the platform.

Of course, what else! She kept a safe distance, not to tip them off. Chryséis and her friends were clearly breaking the rule laid down by Dr. Broadbent, to stay away from the escarpment. They were way too close to the edge.

Gotcha! One to nil for Holly! She thought spitefully.

She ducked behind a large rock as Trevor faced her direction. He held something in his outstretched hand, but she couldn't see what it was.

Holly was so close now, she could have touched Katherine's arm had she wanted to.

Natasha knew of course, what Holly was up to. Sally Holfield would no doubt fill in the gaps later. She was about to turn around and alert one of the teachers, when something weird happened. Something *really* weird!

She couldn't believe her eyes. That was totally impossible: Trevor jumped into the rock!

"Oh no, no please I don't want to!"

Katherine grew rigid with fear and Chryséis had to pull her around and into the vortex. It was too late for a comforting chat. They had to go. Once inside the churning vortex, Chryséis couldn't utter a sound.

Holly just stood there with her mouth open. The two of them had also disappeared. Into the rock! Just like Trevor. A trembling went through the boulder. Then it was quiet. She listened out for the sound of voices, but all she could hear was the twittering of birds. Nothing else.

Seized by a circling motion that seemed to draw them ever deeper into the portal, they spun round and round. How long this went on, they couldn't say. There was a high-pitched rushing sound and then suddenly the time portal spewed them out again. Just like that.

Trevor sat stunned before the portal, staring in disbelief at the shimmering opening. His stiff fingers were still holding tightly onto the TPF. The electromagnetic waves oscillated further apart and grew fainter. Then they disappeared, and with them the portal was also gone. There was just a large rock in front of him. Just another ordinary grey rock.

Chryséis and Katherine sat not far from him. Good.

At first, it seemed as if nothing had changed. Same rocky platform and same grey rocks, Trevor jumped to his feet, but his knees felt like jelly and he nearly fell down.

He steadied himself and cried, "There must be a mistake - we should have travelled!"

But they had made no mistake. The time travellers looked around. Things weren't exactly the same. In fact, quite a lot had changed.

The rocky ledge had moved further out, extending the length of the platform. A clump of cedar trees and shrubs had not been there before and now blocked the view into the valley. It was also a lot warmer. That meant, they had definitely arrived at a different point in time! There was no other explanation.

"Wow that's awesome!" Chryséis marvelled.

"We did it. We actually did it!" Trevor was very pleased with himself. "And no monsters either."

Chryséis looked at her watch. Only seven minutes had passed since they had jumped into the vortex. Then she saw that Katherine's face was terribly pale. "What's wrong with you?" she asked.

"Let's go back please!" Katherine pleaded. "Please!"

"What? Katie, come on, we did it! We can't just leave without exploring a bit," Trevor said.

Chryséis stood up with determination. "We'd be some scientists, if we just left now."

"We just proved that time travel works. You should be proud of yourself. Our project's *the* bomb!"

Trevor looked at Katherine. She was obviously not feeling well, all that trembling. Her dark hair was stuck to her face.

"Are you okay, Katie?" Trevor began to get worried. "We'll be fine. We won't be here for long, anyway."

Katherine covered her eyes with her hands. Was she crying? Trevor knelt down and put a hand on her shoulder.

"There." He wiped her hair back with a brotherly gesture. "We'll be fine," he repeated confidently.

"It's awful that we're so far away. What if we can *never* ever go back?"

"Nonsense, of course we can go back. We are not that far away, we landed in the same spot. The reference point is stored. You know that. We can return anytime."

"Then let's go back. We've proved that it works. What more do you want? We don't know what we're letting ourselves in for," Katherine said vehemently. "Not even close." She looked as if she was going to burst out in tears.

"I'm scared," she whispered.

"Maybe she's in shock or something like that." Trevor looked helpless.

Was it a side effect of time travel? What now? His thoughts raced. She breathed too quickly. Too much oxygen made you pass out. Breathing into a paper bag helped, but they didn't have a paper bag. Would a plastic bag do?

"Katherine MacDougal, snap out of it!" Chryséis said impatiently. "All this was the idea right from the start. Everything's great. We just want to explore this ancient world a bit, take photos and so on."

"Yes, I know... but I never thought it would work."

"Oh really? Well, it did work. You can't chicken out now."

Chryséis realised that she had been too harsh. Katherine couldn't help it. She took out her water bottle and kneeling held it under her nose.

"Here, drink some water," she said in a gentler tone. "Yes, that's it."

Katherine took a deep breath and drank the cool water. Her colour returned and her breathing slowed. Trevor was relieved. "That's good Katie, breathe slowly."

Chryséis took deep breaths with her friend. It actually made her feel better too. My, it was warm here!

"Are you better?"

"Yes, much better."

"I'm taking my jacket off, aren't you guys hot?" Chryséis struggled to get her left arm out of the sleeve.

"Quite hot... maybe it's summer here."

"Actually, it should also be spring."

Katherine peeled herself out of her wind breaker and Trevor threw his anorak on top of his backpack. Chryséis stood up and stretched herself.

"I want to see what's behind those trees over there." She pointed to the cedars by the overhang. "Be right back."

"Wait, I'll come with," Trevor cried. "Probably looks the same as in Carter Valley."

"Be careful," Katherine said.

Chryséis mumbled something she couldn't understand. Then the two of them walked towards the trees, full of curiosity. They even didn't notice a fat, brightly-coloured lizard, basking lazily in the warm sun. It sat motionless on the rough bark of the cedar tree next to them as they peered into the valley.

"What?!" Trevor was speechless. He just stood there, staring mouth open and couldn't believe his eyes.

"No, come on now... that's impossible! I think I'm dreaming," Chryséis laughed in utter disbelief.

"What... what is impossible? Let me see!" Katherine wanted to get a look at the valley herself. What could be so sensational down there?

"Oh m y s t a r s! Come here." Chryséis stood rooted to the sport. "Shut up, shut up, shut up!"

Trevor had found his voice again. "Wow. Check that out!"

"Now come on, that's totally impossible!" Chryséis had trouble picking up her jaw.

"What? What's so impossible?"

Katherine pushed a few prickly twigs aside. The fat lizard was startled by the sudden activity below. It slithered up the trunk and hid on a higher branch.

Eyeballing a juicy, green fly, the lizard made its move and quickly retired to the top of its tree with its prey.

"There are streets down there... and houses. It's a proper town! Not a trace of the nature reserve," Trevor cried.

"Ha, ha very funny. Stop joking around. Let *me* see!" Katherine pushed between her friends... and nearly fell off the ledge.

The valley had definitely changed! No doubt, there was a town down there or at the least the image of a town.

Katherine pinched her eyes closed and opened them again. The houses and streets were still there. She tried rubbing her eyes. Same.

"Awesome! Maybe it's all just a dream," Trevor whispered.

"What, all three of us are dreaming the same dream at the same time?" Chryséis asked in awe.

Surrounded by the gently rolling hills they remembered, the valley looked now very much like a Mediterranean town!

The unspoiled landscape of Carter Valley, the nature park they had visited for years, was no more. Or not yet, depending on how you looked at it.

Where the marshland and the bird sanctuary had been with the winding country road and the occasional sign post, were now white and ochre-coloured villas.

Real houses surrounded by lawns and gardens full of flowers and shrubs. The town was arranged along broad avenues lined with blue and orange flowering trees.

The paved roads stretched the length and breadth of the valley as far as one could see.

To the right they dipped somewhat downward, towards what they knew was the direction of the seashore. To the left, they lost themselves in the distance. A few iridescent blue birds played a game of catch, chasing each other playfully around a marble fountain, trying to escape the watery spray. Much like sparrows would have done on a modern market place.

There was a fountain?!

"No, please, that can't be - a city in Carter Valley!" Katherine felt like laughing hysterically. Only a few moments, then she managed to control the urge. "That's totally impossible. Trevor, pinch me! Ouch, not so hard. Thanks a lot!" She glared at Trevor and rubbed a reddening spot on her forearm.

"Sorry, you said I should pinch you," Trevor said

absent-mindedly. He scanned the hills for familiar landmarks. The hills themselves looked more or less the same, just greener somehow.

"Look at the building against the hill over there." Trevor pointed to a smaller version of the Greek Acropolis. Just that it was a u-shaped building with pillars in a large courtyard. A huge water-filled basin with fountains gleamed in the middle of the yard. The basin could pass for an Olympic-sized swimming pool, judging from the distance.

A structure to the right appeared to be an amphitheatre. Two sports fields were right next to it and a row of smaller buildings.

"That must be a temple," Katherine said and corrected herself immediately. "But that's not possible! We are in... in America... discovered by Columbus." She sighed confused.

Chryséis stared at the supposed temple as if she could make it give up its secret. "I can't get my head around that one."

"People here sure seem to like water!" Trevor had discovered more fountains and artificial waterfalls in the town.

"Not even Pemberton can compete with that," Katherine said.

"No, not even Pemberton."

"Where are all the people in this place?" Trevor asked.

"Yeah, that's odd. Where are they?" Chryséis tried to detect movement. "I wonder if this town is for real."

"Do you think it's just in our imagination?"

"You mean like a hologram?"

"Why not?"

At that moment, they saw something move in the road. A woman in a long lavender dress walked through one of the gates. A little girl toddled after her. The woman picked the child up and carried her towards a yellow building inside plant-covered walls. The little girl tried to wriggle free and the woman put her down. She talked to somebody on her left, but the other person was hidden by a flowering tree.

The time travellers stared at the scene in fascination.

"Real enough for *me*," Trevor said.

"Yeah, they are real people."

The woman turned around and looked in the direction of their hill. They ducked instinctively. She laughed and turned around again.

"Look, houses come all the way up to the rocks below us," Katherine said weakly.

They cowered back into the cover of the bushes, peeping cautiously at tiled roofs and steep, rocky gardens a few meters from their ledge.

"Phew, what's all this? Where are the dinosaurs and cavemen?"

"Not here."

"I need some water." Katherine sat down on a rotting tree stump. She rummaged around her daypack and found the water bottle. After a long swig she felt better.

"You may want to go easy on our provisions," Chryséis cautioned. "We don't know how long it will take to find new ones."

"What about all the fountains down there?"

"Good point. There's plenty of water."

Katherine tied her hair back into a ponytail. Trevor squatted on the ground next to her and wiped his forehead with his sleeve. It was getting warmer as the sun continued to rise in the sky.

"What are we going to do now?" Chryséis asked. "We can't just waltz into town and ask for the way to the nearest youth hostel."

"Hah, just imagine," Trevor grinned. "People speak perfect English and give us directions."

"Oh great, and they won't notice our clothes and all," Chryséis said in an irritated voice.

"Hey, what's up with you?"

"We didn't think about that... how we should communicate."

"We'll find a way somehow."

"Do you think these people are Native Americans? We're still in America right?!" The three looked at each other.

"Probably," Katherine said. "Don't look like Indians to me, though. More like ancient Greeks."

"Where are ancient *Greeks* supposed to come from? Did we end up in a different country?"

"These houses are not exactly adobe either," Katherine said and her face lit up. "In any case, we are on the East coast, not the Wild West."

A light breeze blew fleeting cool air in their faces and they enjoyed the moment.

"Right. We're definitely not in Europe. I mean, think about it: the hills and the rocks. It looks still like the same place! "Chryséis tried logic.

"Sort of."

"You know what I mean."

"A parallel universe maybe," Trevor suggested.

"That's heavy."

"I also don't think so," Katherine said.

"Why not? We can't be sure about anything right now. How much do we really now about this era or about time travel?" Trevor stood up and began pacing the ground. He sometimes did that when he needed to think.

"What about... Atlantis?"

"Atlantis? No way, Trevor. The existence of Atlantis hasn't even been proven yet. Last time I heard, it was supposed to have sunk in the Mediterranean."

The three friends got really going now. They felt comfortable, having discussions like that. It somehow helped them in this strange place.

"But this town must have been colonised awfully long ago. There are no traces left in our time. And we are on our good old American mainland. No way that's Atlantis!"

"So we're back to the Greeks?" *What an odd discussion,* Katherine thought to herself.

"No, you're kidding. Imagine the headlines: 'Greek settlement discovered in Carter Valley from ... this and that millennium...'" Chryséis interrupted herself. "No they can't be Greek - wrong epoch."

"Which epoch is it then?" Katherine asked anxiously.

They hadn't thought of checking the time display on the TPF. "Let me see, I activated only the first harmonics level, so we should have arrived between 10,000 and 13,000 B.P. *Before the Present,*" Trevor said. "The display shows exactly 11,752 years B.P. Welcome to the past ladies and gentlemen!"

He changed his voice in a bad imitation of Dr. Broadbent. It wasn't that funny, but they broke up laughing anyway. "Wow, we've travelled that far?"

"Imagine Dr. Broadbent on a day trip to prehistory!"

They laughed some more. Then they grew serious again. 11,752 years. That meant they were *really* almost 12,000 years in the past.

Dr. Broadbent was so far in the future now with everybody else that they could barely imagine the distance.

The two other TPFs showed the same result. The writing 11,752 years B.P. gleamed on all the TPFs. So it had to be true. Phew!

"At least the TPFs are working," Trevor sighed.

"Way too early for the ancient Greeks and too late for dinosaurs. But might still see wild animals and some attractive cavemen," Chryséis joked.

"Fat chance. Cavemen don't live in villas."

"Yeah..."

"Wasn't there worldwide flooding? At the end of the Pleistocene, the sea flooded coastlands everywhere. Melting polar ice and so on," Katherine said.

"I think you're right," Trevor agreed. "Some say that meteorites hit the earth and caused a continental shift and flooding. Remember the doccie about the Blue Hole of Belize?"

The others nodded. The Blue Hole of Belize was an enormous, ancient cave, stalactites and all, sunk with land before the South American coast. Around about this epoch! They had still watched it on the Adventure Channel.

"It's quite hot here, that's for sure." Katherine tied her jacket to the straps of her backpack and put on the sandals she had brought.

"Okay, then let's wait for the big event, must happen any moment." Chryséis liked to hide her fear behind cynical remarks.

"You think we're in danger?" Katherine trembled.

"Relax, she's just joking!" Trevor thumped her shoulder.

"Didn't the floods start only about 10,000 years ago?"

"Probably. Good, then we've some time left."

"Yeah, a couple of thousand years."

"Exactly." There was a lengthy pause. They felt exhausted by all the weird things they were discussing. The reality of it all hit home.

"All right, having sorted that out, let's make a plan," Chryséis said.

"What kind of a plan?"

"I say we'll have a look at this town. Make sure it's not a *fata morgana*. If we meet somebody, we'll try to look as normal as possible."

"Ha, how do you practice looking normal?"

"Improvise. Maybe we understand the language a little. If it's Algonquin, at least." Chryséis had studied up on American Indian languages recently.

"Okay, you are the language expert. It's your job to translate for us."

"I can do that," Chryséis said courageously.

"Good. Let's get our story straight. We need one, in case somebody *speaks* to us and if we *can* understand them. Kids wandering around on their own are maybe not so normal," Trevor said. Another problem.

"Why didn't we think of stuff like that before?"

"How were we supposed to know what could happen?"

"I don't know. We'll just say that we lost our way and... that we are visiting with our parents... we are staying with friends... and we don't remember where that is."

"Yeah okay, let *them* figure out the rest."

"Before they find out what's cooking, we'll be gone," Trevor said.

Katherine was not so optimistic. "What if they are unfriendly? What if they don't care where we come from and just want to arrest us?"

"You mean we end up in some kind of dungeon?"

"For starters."

"Well, then we just turn invisible before they can lock us up. We run back up here and travel back," Trevor said.

"Then let's test the thingies - everybody switch on," Chryséis commanded. The invisibility devices tested perfectly.

"And... switch off." They appeared again one by one.

"Great, still works." Trevor picked up his daypack.

"Wait, I want to take a photo before we go." Chryséis took out the digital camera. "Can you stand over there? No, not against the sun."

Then Katherine took a picture of Chryséis next to the pine trees with a view of the valley. The slightly blurry temple was in the background.

"Now *you* two, by that tree over there. Yeah like that - smile." Chryséis squinted at the tiny screen. Click.

"Good, we'll document this trip like real scientists," Trevor said.

"What for? Nobody is going to believe us anyway." Katherine had a point there, the others thought..

"Hello, the project?! And anyway, scientists always document their experiments."

"Or...we could write a book about it," Chryséis said. Her eyes were all shiny.

"Exactly!"

"We'll can take turns and write about all those strange things here." Chryséis put the digital camera away. "That's what I brought the palmtop for."

The thought of 'strange things' was a bit unsettling for Katherine. Best not think about it too much. At that moment something soft and wriggly fell out of the tree above.

"Eeeyew!" Chryséis yelled and shook herself.

What was this green and red thing she couldn't shake off? Chryséis cried some more as a thin tail whipped her face. Katherine shrieked in sympathy.

The fat lizard had lost its footing on the high branch and now balanced on her shoulder, digging its claws in. Shaking didn't work.

"Sshhhh!" Trevor hissed. "Don't make such a noise!"

"Oh, that's so gross!" Chryséis closed her eyes.

"Hold still." Trevor stepped forward and pulled the defiant lizard off her. He put it down on the ground and it disappeared in the undergrowth. "It's only a lizard."

"Only a lizard? That's the most revolting lizard ever," Chryséis whispered angrily and wiped her shoulder as if that could remove her disgust.

"It's gone now. What's more important: did somebody hear you?" They listened, but everything was quiet.

"Are you sure it's gone?" Chryséis scanned the undergrowth suspiciously. Then she looked up, as if by magic the lizard might fall on her again. That had been fun!

What else waited here for them? Chryséis thought. Then she pulled herself together. This was an experiment. A scientific experiment!

"Yes. Can we go now?" Trevor couldn't wait any longer.

"We already said we would." Chryséis took a deep breath and picked up her things.

"Everything will be fine, won't it?" Katherine murmured.

"Yes, everything will be fine," Chryséis said and walked bravely ahead, down the rocky footpath.

The time travellers didn't have to walk far. Halfway down the hill, they caught sight of somebody under a pine tree.

A boy of about thirteen years! He was shaking pine nuts from their cones into a wicker basket. He jumped to his feet when he heard them approach, dropping his basket in the process. The boy had half-expected to see birds or squirrels, not people.

The children were just as surprised and stopped in their tracks. Should they turn around and make a run for it? Or activate the virtual invisibility capes? Too late for that.

"Shelanti – greetings good people. You startled me!" The boy said in a strange language and smiled.

The prehistoric boy spoke to them!

He gestured a graceful greeting with his right hand, touching his heart and then his forehead. 'Shelanti' meant 'I wish you everything I wish for myself'. It was a formal greeting used throughout the Known World.

What to do?! Was he friendly? Judging by his smile, he was. They didn't understand a word he was saying, so they just smiled back and waited.

The boy looked normal enough. At least not like a caveman. He wore clothes. A pastel-blue tunic with side slits and pockets over long trousers in the same colour. A turquoise line ran along the hems. He was tall for his age and nice-looking with light hair. His face and arms were tanned, which made his grey eyes appear very light.

"Oh dear," Katherine breathed. "A talking human."

They gaped at the boy. What were they supposed to do

now? The urge to run was still there.

"Shelanti," the boy repeated. "Don't be frightened. Where are you from?"

He thought it was strange that these children seemed afraid of him. And what were they doing on Shepherd's Hill in broad daylight? Weren't they supposed to be at school? Alun himself had been excused from lessons at the citadel school to help with his brother's wedding preparations. Kheton's wedding was in three days' time and there was still much to be done.

"What did he say?" Trevor whispered, while trying to maintain his smile.

"I don't know. 'Hello' or something," Chryséis whispered back just as softly.

Katherine dared to move at last and stabbed an annoying finger into Trevor's back. "Close your mouth!" she hissed.

"Ouch," he exhaled and closed his mouth.

"Let's greet him back," Chryséis suggested in a low voice. Good idea!

They clumsily copied the gesture they had seen the boy make, and said "Hello!"

"Elloh? Where are *you* from, children? Are you visiting?" He inquired curiously. "Do you go to citadel school here?"

He stopped himself. Too many questions at once! They weren't mute, but obviously not from around here. If they couldn't speak Alesian, he might be confusing them unnecessarily. Chryséis thought she'd heard the Latin word for school and started nodding. She hoped she didn't agree to marry him or something like that.

"I think he wants to know if we are going to school." She took a courageous shot at translating. They all smiled again, not knowing what else to do.

"I have never seen you at citadel school," the boy said. "You seem unfamiliar with our language. You are not from Alesia then?"

Trevor grimaced and gestured in what he thought was a universal language: palms up, he shrugged his shoulders with a puzzled look on his face.

"Where are we?" He asked in slow and clear English, while shrugging his shoulders. The boy seemed to understand.

"Oh, you must have lost your way."

They could only assume that he understood, so they nodded and pointed to the valley again, shrugging shoulders and all.

"Ah, mirá Vallé Cydonia!" the boy said proudly and swept his arm in the direction of the valley. "The southern suburb of our great city of Cydonia. The capital of the country of Alesia. I bid you welcome."

He bowed slightly. The children bowed as well. Alun hoped that this would solve their problem, but the time travellers were confused. Had the boy mentioned the name of this mysterious town?

"Did he say it's called Alesia?" Trevor asked.

"I think he said Valley Cydonia." Chryséis's head hurt with all that concentration. "The rest I didn't understand."

What if she had made a mistake and he meant something completely different? Bummer.

"Valley Cydonia?" She asked the boy, waving her arm at the valley just as he had done.

Alun nodded delightedly. So these children may after all speak a dialect of the 'Known World'. Odd, that they didn't understand Alesian then.

"Why are you here on the hill?" He asked slowly and clearly.

This was complicated. Chryséis listened hard, but she didn't understand at all what he was saying. At least the boy didn't seem to mind speaking to females, she thought. A good sign, right?!

"What did he say?" Trevor asked impatiently.

"No idea."

"Great."

"I offer my help to you good people. Kindly accept," the boy said and looked at the ground.

"What do we do now?"

"What's with the staring at his feet?"

"Don't know."

"Just do the same."

The time travellers did the same, but they didn't understand what it meant. Of course, they didn't know that Alesians were a cultured and hospitable people, always prepared to help others out. Lowering one's gaze was a non-threatening gesture.

When they didn't answer, the boy looked up confused and pointed to his chest in another age-old gesture. This one was not difficult to understand.

"Alun," he said, then added his birth place. "I am Alun of Cydonia." It was the custom when speaking to foreigners.

They were overjoyed. At last! Trevor followed his example and introduced himself as 'Trevor of Chicago', Katherine as 'Katherine of Oxford', then Chryséis called herself 'Chryséis of Etheridgeville'.

Alun repeated all the names as he understood them. He struggled with the pronunciation of Katherine, Oxford and Etheridgeville, which sounded more like Kathín, Oxfol and Ethigevee to him. It was cool that somebody who lived such a long time ago actually tried to say their names. They nodded and repeated the boy's name.

"Alun of Cydonia... Shelanti...?"

The boy called 'Alun of Cydonia' seemed satisfied with this display of civilised behaviour and they felt more relaxed. They could communicate! Even Katherine who was standing behind her friends no longer saw a need for invisibility capes.

"If you are lost, I will offer you hospitality." Alun pointed at the town. According to custom he was obliged to offer them the shelter of his home. It was just one block away from the bottom of Shepherd's Hill.

That was too complicated.

"Valley Cydonia," Chryséis said.

"Yes, in Vallé Cydonia," Alun confirmed.

Chryséis looked up proudly. It was settled then. But first Alun had to finish his job. He had set out for the hills this morning to gather herbs and pine nuts for the roasted ptarmigan stuffing and raspberries for the pies.

That's exactly what he intended to do up here. Alun pointed to the ground and placed a few raspberries back in his basket. They understood. This was getting better by the minute!

"He wants us to help him," Katherine said needlessly.

They began to shake pine cones, just as Alun demonstrated. The work gave them time to adjust to the new situation.

The heat wasn't so bad in the shade of the pine trees. Soon they were all picking raspberries from brambles on the other side of the footpath.

The basket was filling up quickly. Katherine picked a good-sized dark red raspberry and put it in her mouth. It was sweet and aromatic and tasted divine. Definitely not supermarket stuff.

A squirrel with a bushy tail sat nearby, munching on pine nuts that had dropped to the ground. For some reason the little animal reminded her of Pemberton. After a while, Alun decided that it was time to leave. He had enough pine nuts and raspberries and placed the herbs on top.

"I will take you to my father's house now, athenai." He pointed to the sun, then downhill and waved for them to follow him. The meaning was clear, but the time travellers hesitated.

"We can't just go with him," Katherine warned.

"Why not?"

"What if we do something to change the future?"

"Do what?" Trevor demanded to know.

"Oh, I don't know, like squishing an insect by mistake."

"I don't think that will change the outcome of evolution."

Alun waited patiently, while they discussed the matter

in hushed tones. They came to an agreement. What could possibly happen?

The friends nodded and followed Alun down a slightly different path to the one they had taken on the way up almost 12,000 years later. Things looked familiar, even if there was no longer an inn at the bottom of the hill, nor a parking lot with cars.

Alun now noticed the odd clothes his new friends wore. Two of the children were undoubtedly girls, to judge by their hairstyle and behaviour. But all three of them were clad in similar breeches, made of a heavy, blue fabric and shirts with long sleeves. Too warm for the Alesian spring. They had wisely taken off the thick jackets and tied them to their backpacks.

They looked foreign alright and their satchels were full. Runaways, perhaps. But runaways from what?

In Alesian society, unhappy children were extremely rare. And they were certainly not giant *Gabari* from the uncivilised northern territories. They were too small for that.

It was more likely that their parents stayed in the neighbourhood. If someone from foreign parts had taken lodging in Alesia, they would be found, no doubt. Alun's older brother Kheton worked on citadel hill and would report the incident to the Lady of Cydonia. Her maidens would surely locate the parents soon. No - he decided, they were just lost. Separated from their parents by some coincidence.

They walked onto a road paved with large flagstones. The colour of the stones was almost white in the glaring light.

Soon they passed a small park where four roads met. Like some kind of traffic circle. Just that there was no traffic.

Chryséis imagined carriages drawn by horses driving around. But they had already established that this wasn't ancient Greece. In fact, this Valley Cydonia must be so ancient, that horses were probably still unknown in America.

"That's so awesome," Trevor said.

"Yeah. Look at that!" They passed a curious water feature that gave off a pleasant cool spray. Hewn blocks of dark rock looked like an open seashell on top of a half-moon-shaped boulder. Water conduits made of the same dark stone aimed at the shell from different heights.

The water splashed and gurgled. It was the only noise around. Emerald and burgundy lawn covered the ground. The two colours created simple patterns and exotic plants grew in the rocky crevices and all around the park.

Alun always felt proud when he saw the water feature. His father had it specially made in honour of the *Nereids*, the water fairies, as thanks for a successful sea voyage. The Nereids were daughters of the god *Nereus*, the 'Old Man of the Sea' and especially revered by the seafaring peoples of the 'Known World'.

Alun wanted to tell his new friends all about this, but decided that they probably wouldn't understand.

During the midday siesta, most people remained indoors. Only a handful of Cydonians walked about in the streets. They were all dressed in a similar fashion: soft-flowing, pastel-coloured garments and strappy sandals.

Some wore long tunics with buttons down the front and some women seemed to prefer dresses. They tried not to stare and didn't notice that they were causing a small sensation.

Curious glances shot at the strange youngsters from under lowered eyelashes, but nobody gaped openly or stopped to question them. It would have been incredibly impolite. And after all, the children were with Alun.

Katherine nudged Chryséis and said, "Awe, look at the baby!"

A rather dark-skinned mother walked past with a sleeping baby on her back. The other prehistoric people they saw had an olive complexion and high cheek bones, their hair in shades of blond and brown. Chryséis noted the details and would record them as soon as she got a chance.

Alun led the little group towards a walled corner property painted in a warm terracotta colour. The walls were edged with rows of flowers. Blue ball-shaped flowers on long, elegant stems and fleshy red cannas.

Most of the arched opening was covered by a bougainvillea with reddish flowers that grew vigorously into a nearby tree. Some of the shady trees along the road had blue and orange blooms. Long cypresses and broad cedar trees grew in the space between houses.

They marvelled at everything they saw. Houses, plants, people. Everything.

Katherine had seen similar streets in northern Italy, where she sometimes holidayed with her family. But the flowers here were so large and bright.

They entered the courtyard through the arched portal. A large walnut tree spread its canopy in front of a double-storey house. Lending its shade to two older women and a mother dog, suckling her two honey-coloured pups.

They sat on facing benches, chatting and preparing vegetables for cooking. Red and blue striped baskets were placed on the ground and vegetables and grains on mats around them.

A few geese clucked and pecked at morsels here and there. The paving was sparsely covered with green walnut buds that cracked softly underfoot.

Alun pointed to colourful decorations that hung from branches, windows and doors. "It is my older brother's wedding ceremony soon," he explained.

The children from the future didn't understand a word he said. They just assumed that the red and turquoise colours around the yard had to do with some festivity. They smiled politely at the women, who looked up curiously.

The big dog sniffed the air lay down to snooze and the

women continued with their work, wiping their hands now and again on brightly cultured towels. Alun walked up to the benches in greeting.

"Shelanti, shelanti!"

There were these greeting movements again.

"Shelanti." The visitors copied the greeting as best as they could.

Like Alun, the women were tanned and had strong features and grey eyes. They wore pastel tunics with a bright red stripe along the hem. Polite words were exchanged and the women smiled at the guests.

The three visitors were completely clueless as to what was being said.

The two matrons didn't seem to notice that and patiently listened with knitted brows as Alun told the story how he had found the threesome wandering around by themselves on Shepherd's Hill.

Their hearts went out to the poor children. They had been separated from their parents!

The women nodded consent when Alun suggested that his home be offered as a refuge until their missing parents were found.

"Áhó, áhó," they murmured and nodded.

Nodding was good, Trevor thought. They could relax. This was obviously no prison.

The aunts were pleased with their young nephew's handling of the situation. They smiled approvingly, while their hands never stood still for a moment.

Alun led the way into the house. The door was broadly framed with blue tiles and red fabric garlands that hung down on both sides. They stepped into the entrance hall and onto a mosaic floor.

Their very first prehistoric house!

In the mosaic blue and green fish wriggled around a bearded man in a purple tunic, who held up a large three-pronged fork. Ships, dolphins and mermaids looked out from between chopping waves.

"That's lovely," Katherine whispered.

The entrance hall led to two spacious rooms on the right. Doors with curved tops like butterfly wings stood wide open. Opposite the entrance, a staircase swung gently upwards with two closed doors underneath. A roomy kitchen was to their left. The black and white checkered floor of the kitchen shone with cleanliness. The walls of the hall were painted in a creamy colour and sparsely decorated.

Chryséis lightly touched the wall. It felt cool and smooth, almost like marble.

The walls were somewhat rounded and ceilings gave the illusion of movement in waves and spirals. Katherine remembered that she had seen ceilings like that in a picture book about architecture in Barcelona.

"Awesome!" Trevor muttered, then said in a normal voice, "just look at those ceilings."

"Ssshh," Chryséis hissed. It seemed wrong to speak in here.

"Okay," he mumbled and was quiet for a while.

But that wasn't all. The wall next to the staircase was

covered in a mural. A moonlit landscape with a river flowing into a glittering lake. It was so life-like, one could almost smell the freshness of the water.

The delicious aroma of baked cake came from kitchen. There were unusual things about this kitchen. The cooker was operated with concentrated light waves.

The oversized 'cooling cupboard' functioned cleverly with alternate condensation and evaporation. Without the use of electricity.

Unaware of this, the time travellers followed their new friend into a big room to the right. Alun seated his guests on two facing sofas and gestured 'eating' with his hand and chewing movements. He went to the kitchen, but they could still see him through the open door.

"That's really nice of him," Trevor declared and settled into the big sofa.

"Yes, really nice. I'm starved"

"I wonder what these people eat," Katherine breathed.

"That we'll find out just now," Chryséis said.

"The two women outside were cleaning a mountain of vegetables."

"Vegetables are better than fried spiders."

"Chris!"

"Yeah, much better than fried spiders," Trevor grinned.

Alun placed his basket on an oval kitchen table. He rummaged among platters of food in the cooling cupboard, and put a plate of snacks together.

A neighbour, who helped out with the cooking, unpacked the basket and said something. She shooed Alun away from a large cake in the middle of the table. It was intended for the wedding. The entire household was abuzz with preparations for Kheton's wedding that was only three days away.

Chryséis looked around the room. Double-winged butterfly doors led to another room that faced the front of the house. A slight breeze drifted through open veranda doors opposite and the tiled floor extended into the backyard. By the sofas the tiles were covered with a thick, maroon-coloured carpet.

"Wow, this is so…modern. Who knew! That they have real houses here, not just huts or caves."

"Fantastic."

"Without Alun of Cydonia we'd never have seen this house on the inside," Trevor marvelled.

"Maybe if we made ourselves invisible." Chryséis studied the decorations in the room. "Did you see these wall hangings and the sofa covers?" Some of the patterns looked Middle Eastern, others were made of colourful patchwork.

"They are quilts," Chryséis said excitedly. "I saw quilts at an exhibition in the town hall. Takes ages to make them."

A row of small windows got Trevor's attention, just below the ceiling letting in soft daylight. "Just look at those windows. You think they're glazed?"

Chryséis looked up. "No way!"

It was pleasantly cool thanks to a small indoor fountain that was fitted on the opposite wall in the living room. Boxes with ferns surrounded the small basins and water trickled down the tiers with a soothing sound.

"They put huge shells on their walls." Trevor pointed to an illuminated nautilus snail, mounted to the wall.

"Is that supposed to be a lamp?" Asked the otherwise rather quiet Katherine.

"And we thought we'd see cavemen in loincloths," Trevor said with a grin.

"*Some* kind of cavemen!" Chryséis giggled.

"Perhaps we shouldn't be in here at all. If we change something important…"

"Oh not now, Katie, let's just explore a bit."

So they looked around a bit more. In the front room stood a low table and cube-like stools. The walls shimmered softly, as if they were covered in mother-of-pearl.

There were more of those large wall-mounted snails.

The broad table had a row of water-filled squares right down the middle. Ornaments and vases with flowers were arranged on a low, curved shelf against the wall. Plates, bowls and platters were stacked on the lower shelf board.

"Must be a temple there in the front."

"A water temple?" Chryséis asked jokingly.

"They have a thing about water here, that's for sure."

"That table could be an altar."

"C'mon a temple in a home like that?" Trevor wasn't convinced at all.

"You saw the Neptune mosaic, right? How many homes you know have something like that?"

"You think? A water cult?"

"Look, there are also shelves next to the sofa," Trevor interrupted the chitchat about water and temples. Katherine craned her neck to get a better look.

On the shelf were books stacked on top of each other, if they were books at all. Rectangular pieces of thin metal foil were arranged in holders next to small rolls in sockets. The top shelf was decorated with large, shimmering seashells and snails. Trevor was itching to have a closer look, but he could hardly rifle through Alun's things. After all, they were guests in a prehistoric house not in the Cromwell town house.

"What are those metal foils for and those rolls?"

"Who knows," said Chryséis.

"Wouldn't you like to know?"

"Sure. Maybe we'll find out later."

"I don't know. I can't get rid of this funny feeling," Katherine said. Was she starting again? Chryséis and Trevor rolled their eyes.

"What feeling?" Chryséis asked.

"That these people here are long dead and forgotten. Long before our time. And now they stand there in a kitchen, making food for us. Don't you think that's weird?"

"No, not really."

"I'm sitting here in their no-longer-existing house. It's just creepy."

"You can't think like that, Katie," Chryséis pleaded with her. "Don't go all nuts on us now. This is a scientific experiment."

Katherine looked at her crossly. "I'm not nuts!"

"Just think about it. It's like visiting another country. Morocco maybe," Trevor suggested.

"Right. Morocco," Katherine mocked him.

Alun still pottered around in the kitchen and they watched him through the open butterfly-door.

Katherine took a deep breath. "Alright then."

"Alright what?"

"I'll do my best not to think about it," Katherine said bravely. "We don't really belong here, but I'll try not to think about it." Her friends were relieved.

"Good on you." Trevor made a thumbs-up sign. "We are only here to get enough material for our project. That's all."

They watched Alun warm a plate of flat bread in a longish box. Soùmi was important at all Alesian mealtimes. Pieces of the bread were torn off and used to scoop up food. Spoons were used to dish up and to eat soups, but forks for the purpose of eating were unknown. Steaming flat bread came out of the box.

"Looks a lot like a microwave," said Trevor.

Chryséis was not in the mood for jokes. "Get outa here! A microwave!"

"What if they *do* have technology?"

"Come on, have you seen any mobile phones yet?" Katherine threw in.

"That doesn't prove anything," Trevor defended himself. "They could have... different technology to us. Maybe they don't need mobile phones."

There was suddenly movement in the room. Honey-coloured movement. "Oh look at that!" Katherine pointed at the door.

One of the puppies they had seen under the walnut tree had sneaked in and made its way toward the sofas. The little dog took a shine to Katherine and sat down in front of her. Eyeing the gentle stranger, it lay down on the carpet and started to lick her toes.

"Oh look, he's so cute!" Katherine's heart melted.

"It's a *SHE*, rather," Trevor corrected her. "I think she wants to be your friend."

"What if the dogs aren't allowed inside?" Chryséis was worried. "Should we take her outside?"

"No, let Alun to do that when he comes back with the food. We might offend him, if we do something like that." Trevor wanted to be careful.

"Aren't you adorable? Yes, you're so pretty," Katherine cooed.

She pulled her feet up and settled back into the soft cushions. The little dog tried to climb onto the sofa and Katherine padded the soft fur.

The food was nearly ready. It smelled so good and suddenly they felt very hungry.

▶▶▶ **10**   **A GIANT SURPRISE**

Alun carried a tray with food into the "water temple" and deposited it on the low table. Then he went to fetch his guests.

"Tepi, what are *you* doing inside?" He laughed and picked up the puppy.

He said the dog's name again and gestured 'naughty', shaking his index finger in front of the puppy's black nose. They laughed together and Katherine gestured that she liked the dog. Alun pointed invitingly to the adjoining room and took the puppy outside.

"Why are we eating in the water temple?" Trevor asked.

"Don't know. Maybe food is holy to them?" Chryséis said.

"It's not a temple, you bright sparks, it's a dining room." Katherine pointed to a picture of a water pitcher and a bowl dripping with fruit.

"Nice." Trevor felt stupid.

Alun motioned for them to sit down and help themselves to the snacks. Sitting on the cubic stools was unexpectedly comfortable.

He demonstrated how to eat with your hands, tore a piece off a flat bread and made a pocket, scooped a dip from one of the small bowls into the pocket with a white spoon, added a choice of toppings and put the bread pocket into his mouth.

There were marinated white anchovy fillets, grilled vegetables, a variety of shelled nuts, sliced hard cheese and tender olives. A shallow bowl with pieces of sweet green melon, purple pears and black mulberries next to the plate stacked with flat bread.

Trevor tried to copy his host and used his hands to eat.

"What a good idea. Saves plates and cutlery!" he said while he chewed.

"I am pleased you enjoy the food, friend Trevór. This is called Aioli!" He pointed to the bowl full of the tasty cream.

"Garlic mayo," explained Katherine.

"Aioli," Alun repeated slowly. "I apologize for the lack of a cooked meal, athenai – friends. Auntie is busy baking for my brother Kheton's wedding and doesn't need me to be under her feet." They didn't understand him, but kept smiling politely while they chewed.

Alun showed them how to pick up baked vegetables with a bread pocket and they copied him nimbly. Soon, Alun served a fragrant herbal tea with a minty apple-like taste in small drinking bowls. The bowls were shaped like fat snails' houses without handles.

Trevor wasn't exactly fond of herbal teas, but for the sake of science, he had to get used to prehistoric drinks. He tasted the cooled tea - not quite his favourite coke or iced tea, but not bad at all.

Alun tried to make conversation now. He asked questions that even Chryséis barely understood. So they gestured a lot and spoke very slowly. There were strange cultures in the Known World that Alun had not yet learned about. Despite the many dialects in the Known World, there were only three basic languages. So most people could communicate a little.

"Tell me more about where you come from," he encouraged them to speak about themselves and made hand movements to that effect.

He got some answers that left him puzzled. Apparently, the beautiful girl with the dark hair came from over the Atlantean Sea, if he'd understood her correctly. Prydhain was beyond the Atland Archipelago. Beyond Atland, the old continent. She looked quite civilised for a Prydhanian, Alun thought to himself.

"Do you mean Prydhain, Kathín?"

"Britain, Britain," Katherine repeated loud and clear.

"Áhó. Yes. Prydhain, Prydhain."

"Maybe that's the same thing," she sighed.

Alun struggled to follow her speech. The fair girl called Chryséis and the boy Trevór both pronounced their places of birth much clearer.

"Etheridgeville." Chryséis pointed to the ground.

That had to mean that Ethidgevee was in Alesia. Strange, he had never heard of it before. Trevór pointed in northerly direction. Bizarre, since the northern parts of the continent of Patala were cold and almost uninhabited... unless he was from Edfun.

Alun must have misunderstood. No, he did not strike him as a barbarian or Gabari. His parents must be stationed at some outpost on the Edfunian border.

"I wish I could understand you better. We must find your parents."

Although they were safe in Alesia, parents always fretted. The sooner they could be found, the better.

"We don't understand you so well, Alun," Chryséis said and tried to say the same in Latin without much success.

"Oh yes, I'm sure you must be anxious. I would also miss them," Alun said. "The Lady of Cydonia has already given instructions to search for the foreigners, whose children were lost by Shepherd's Hill. She will surely help you! Tonight you may sleep in the cottages at the back."

All he got were confused stares. Perhaps he should take them to the Cydonian testing station for agriculture in the fertile region west of Cydonia tomorrow. Alun's father Harun worked there as a scientist. He knew that a group of foreign scientists had arrived to study the improvement of indigenous food plants in their country. Perhaps the parents were among them.

"We will go to my father's place of work tomorrow," he gestured.

"Knitting?" Chryséis was confused.

"Working with plants, athenai. Plants. Alesian agriculture is famous all over the Known World. My father has travelled east beyond the Atlantean Sea, to a country aptly named Su Mâr — Over-the-Sea," Alun told them proudly.

"Frequent flooding has turned stretches of fertile soil into marshland. My father flew there to advise which crops would be better suited to the saltier soil." He moved his hand through the air.

"Wheat could no longer be produced. So tests were done and a solution was found. Rye and barley. Father's voyage was inscribed on the citadel wall, for everyone to read!"

Alun was so enthusiastic, he was unaware of the confusion his flood of words caused. Yes, it was a good idea to go to the station. The animal breeding project alone was worth a visit. And in any case, he wanted to get some silk worms to keep at home.

One of the aunts they had met in the yard, called Alun. Something urgent that couldn't wait.

"Will be back just now," Alun said and went outside.

"Did *you* understand that, about growing plants and flying?" Katherine asked. "And writing on the wall. Did that make sense to you?"

"No, not really. It had something to do with his father."

"He seems to work with plants. Maybe he's a gardener or farmer."

"And he went somewhere or flew."

"Yes strange..." It was pretty clear that they must have misunderstood.

"I can't believe there are no Indian legends about this Cydonia," Chryséis said suddenly.

"Maybe there are legends we don't know about."

"Too long ago for legends!"

"Archaeologists wouldn't even think of digging in Carter Valley. Why should they?" Trevor said, "Look, Cydonia may not even have existed."

"What, why not?

"You mean like a parallel universe?"

"Not again," Chryséis groaned.

"Perhaps there is simply nothing left to find," Trevor cast aside the idea and Katherine agreed with him.

"I think you're right. Imagine, thousands of years of flooding and wind and earthquakes. What's left to be found?"

"There were loads of lost civilisations, or not?"

"Hmm."

"I read that scuba divers found ruins of giant buildings back in the sixties. There are paved roads and walls out in the sea around Bimini. And what do we hear about it?" Chryséis said.

"Nothing."

"That's random! The houses here aren't gigantic."

"True."

"I tell you, archaeologists wouldn't believe this Cydonia even if they found it. And —" Chryséis's jaw dropped. A hulk of a man entered the entrance hall and moved toward the staircase.

"A giant!" Katherine cried and quickly put her hand in front of her mouth.

"Ssshhh, he can hear you."

Katherine looked at Trevor in horror. The giant lumbered up the stairs and was gone at once. "Huh!"

"We have to tell Alun. What if he is dangerous?"

"The giant must belong to the household." Chryséis opted for logic.

"You're probably right. The women in the yard would have screamed."

"Or he killed them before they could scream."

They peeped anxiously out of the window. Alun was still talking calmly to one of his aunts. Relieved, they sat down again and found their bearings.

A few minutes later Alun returned. The guest rooms had been prepared. Chryséis understood sort of what he said and they followed him across the backyard past a bubbling fountain. It one was covered in a blue and golden mosaic. Long-fronded palms in terracotta pots were posted along the house walls.

It was afternoon and the sun prepared to dip behind a neighbour's tiled roof. It wasn't nearly as hot as before.

A short passage along the house led to the far side of the garden. Three rooms with blue doors faced the back wall of the garden.

"Pretty garden," Trevor whispered.

Alun opened the first door. The room was very clean and fitted with carved beds, wooden cupboards and chairs. Fresh clothes were laid out on the beds. Calf-length trousers and short-sleeved tunics. They were surprised that the waists had elastic bands.

Alun pointed to the sun and said, "Surya," while wiping his brow. Blowing air, he pointed at the new clothes and added "Meshor, better!"

The clothes seemed better suited for warm weather. What they saw next left them in shock: a blue bathroom with enamelled tub and flush toilet! The fittings shone with a mother-of-pearl glow. Alun didn't seem to notice their astonishment and opened the second cottage. "Make yourselves comfortable. I have much to do and must go, athenai," he excused himself and disappeared down the passage.

"Did you see those toilets?" Katherine gushed excitedly as soon as he was out of earshot.

"How can they even have *bathrooms*?" Katherine said. They had to take a closer look!

"Are you sure we didn't travel to the future by mistake?" Chryséis asked in awe.

"Yes I am," Trevor said. "Pretty sure."

"This is even nicer than the bathrooms at home!" Katherine stroked the cone-shaped washbasin. "It feels like metal."

"Maybe it *is* a parallel universe," Chryséis said.

"I don't even know how to program the TPF to find a parallel universe."

"You're right, we must have travelled in a straight

timeline."

"What else?" Trevor knocked here and there against the basin. "The pipes are see-through," he said.

"That's definitely not glass."

"Well, blow me down with a feather," Katherine said. "If I didn't know better, I'd say this is synthetic!"

"Gosh!" Chryséis was stunned. "Plastic?"

She switched the tap on and off by touching the yellow metal on top. They had figured out that much. Clean water started swirling into the basin and down the see-through pipe. Chryséis washed her hands and wiped them on her jeans.

"Totally crazy!"

"Imagine someone from the Middle Ages seeing this. Thinking *he's* the modern guy?"

"Bit far-fetched," Trevor said.

"You guys have no imagination," Katherine said crossly.

Her friends ignored the remark. "If that's plastic, what happened to it? There should be tons still lying around," Chryséis wondered.

"Could be biodegradable. Just falls to pieces after a while," Trevor said.

"Possible, but too advanced."

"Just think about it: 12,000 years. That's enough time to degrade."

"Yes, that's a long time."

"I've heard of ancient cities with flush toilets on a Greek island. What was its name again? The one where the volcano exploded." Trevor couldn't think of the name.

"In Greece maybe. But here almost 12,000 years in the past?"

"And what about Western India? Harappa. The whole area is covered in ruins of prehistoric cities. They found sewage systems thousands of years old."

"Really? Never heard of it."

"You should pay more attention in history, Chris!"

"I think it's just awesome." Katherine was distracted by

the carved cupboards. Only shelves inside.

Blue tiles covered the walls of the room and there were again these small windows under the ceiling. Just as in the main house, they could be opened and closed with strings. Trevor climbed onto the one bed and reached up, tapping against a window pane.

"Wow!" he cried.

"What?" Chryséis jumped next to him on the bed and knocked on the window. "That's not glass either!"

"No." Chryséis remembered that they wanted to document everything. "I'd love to take a sample of this."

"But we can't just break a window," said Katherine

"No, of course we can't." She climbed down from the bed. A nautilus shell was hanging next to the bed. It seemed to be a lamp with a short white bar inside. On closer inspection, it wasn't connected to any cables.

"Let's see how that works,"

Chryséis searched for a light switch on the wall. None. She tried clapping her hands. Nothing. Finally, Katherine discovered a tiny dip-switch right on the shell. It worked.

"But there's no cable. The lamp's freely suspended."

"Tesla!" Chryséis whistled in admiration.

"What's next?" Katherine said and switched the shell lamp on and off.

"I'm beat," Trevor said. "I'm gonna take a nice cool bath in my archaic tub and then a nap. See you guys later."

"Alright, later then."

The girls went to the room next-door they would be sharing. Chryséis couldn't resist taking pictures of their bathroom. She would write down a few notes after they had bathed and changed into the new clothes. They examined the lotions, powders and soaps on a low table.

"And here we thought that we're the height of technology. Then look at all this!" she said. "I just don't get it."

"Who says you have to understand everything?"

"And that's coming from you!"

They chatted about clever Nicola Tesla before taking a well-deserved nap. An hour later, they sat clean and refreshed in the long shade of a tulip tree on the lush dark-red lawn. Chryséis was dressed in reed-green trousers and a short-sleeved tunic in the same colour. Katherine's suit was a soft lilac.

When Trevor appeared wearing a suit in a rusty colour, Chryséis was already typing away on the palmtop computer. He yawned and went over to join the girls.

"Hi there, feeling better?" Katherine greeted Trevor.

"Yes much," he said. "Nice that Cydonians like hygiene."

"Why do boys always take longer than girls to get ready?" Chryséis mumbled without looking up. She had decided to put together a list of new words they had learned. Words she sort of understood. Chryséis hadn't figured out yet, what the word Alesia meant, but just added it to the list for now.

Katherine felt her lilac sleeve. "I like this material. I think it's silk. It's so soft and light."

Trevor was puzzled. "But it's not shiny."

"Trev, silk doesn't have to be shiny satin, you know." Katherine couldn't believe his ignorance.

"Phew lucky! Just imagine me as the disco king in white satin!" The girls chuckled at the thought. Boys!

"The tunics don't have stripes along the hems. Perhaps the stripes have some kind of meaning," Chryséis said and scribbled it down.

"What happens, if these people realize that we lied about our parents?" Katherine asked.

Trevor didn't see a problem. "We never actually said that, Alun just assumed. If it's an issue, we move on to plan B: *back up the hill and beam ourselves back to the future.*"

Chryséis stopped typing for a moment. "I'm almost sure Alun wants to take us to his father's farm tomorrow. It would be great to explore this Valley Cydonia, before we leave."

"So you think the inhabitants of Cydonia are farmers?"

"Can't tell for sure, yet."

"We must learn some of this language," Katherine said.

"Already onto it! I've started a glossary. How would you spell 'surya'? I think it means heat or sun or something like that," Chryséis said. Trevor gave her a likely spelling.

"Yep, that's how I wrote it." Chryséis saved the file and closed the lid of the little computer.

"Perhaps I should stay here tomorrow. I can start typing the journal," Katherine suggested.

"Not a chance. We *must* stay together," Chryséis said. "Just think about it. If we have to go back quickly, we must go together. Or do you want to stay here by yourself?"

"No, of course not." Katherine breathed a little faster. She really didn't want to drown in a flood or end up trapped alone in prehistory. Chryséis was right! They had to stay together.

A few roller birds settled on the small tree next to them. They fluttered up and down, their light blue feathers shining in the setting sun. Katherine watched them in fascination.

The experiment was going well. The Cydonians were friendly, and they had already discovered so many awesome things today! Soon they would return home.

"Okay then, let's have a look at this farm tomorrow," she said just as it got really dark in the garden.

A light spring rain drizzled on Cydonia that night, bringing welcome relief from the unusual heat. An earth tremor rippled through the northern parts of Alesia, but the townspeople in Cydonia didn't feel a thing.

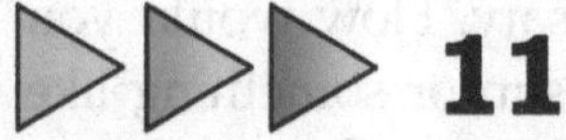 **11**   **THE VIMAAN**

"It is time to rise, athenai, friends!" Alun's excited voice rang through the pleasant remnants of Trevor's dream.

He was sitting on the shore of a beautiful lake in the twilight, somewhere in the Minnesota Boundary Waters. Just the way it had looked last summer during the week-long canoe trip. Should he take a swim or not? Then he heard the rapping on the door of the cottage again.

What was all that noise about?

"Time to get up, Trevór, Kathín, Chryséis. The family is waiting!"

To Alun's disappointment, mother had returned late yesterday from an errand at the citadel. Too late to call the children back into the house.

"The poor things must be exhausted, son. Leave them be. They will be presented to the assembled family on the morrow."

Mother's word was law. Like most Alesian women, she considered all children to be *her* children and would do anything to help. Her husband Harun had once done his citizen's duty after a skirmish on the north-western border with Edfun and found an orphaned *Gabari* child. The border region was in constant need of protection.

In the past, a number of citizens along the border had been killed or carried off by the giants. The cruel Edfunians strove to punish those who had left their homeland and now sided with Alesia.

The boy's parents had belonged to the true Gabari line and their crime had been to leave Edfun for the safer neighbouring country of Alesia. The boy Túvar had escaped, his parents had not. Alun's mother could have delivered the young Gabari into the care of the 'House of

Life', but instead she had raised Túvar together with her two sons. He was almost grown now and towered over the rest of the family.

Túvar did his adoptive parents proud. He loved working with plants and animals and father took him daily to the testing station. There he helped with the planting and harvesting and showed talent in talking to animals. He was training to become a scientist like his adopted father Harun.

Now it was morning at last and Alun could wait no longer. He started knocking on the door of the second room.

"Athenai, friends! Get up, it is time!"

It took Trevor a few moments to realize where he was and that he would not take a swim in the lake just now.

Then it slowly dawned on him that he had time travelled with Katherine and Chryséis! It had to be morning, judging by the sunlight. He opened the door and his sleepy head appeared.

"What's the noise all about, Alun?"

"Trevór, the time has finally arrived to meet the family!"

Alun waved towards himself and then to the house. Trevor understood that he was to report to the house immediately. He also thought he heard the word 'familia'. Trevor nodded and got dressed quickly.

The girls were already waiting outside. The morning air was cool and fresh from the nightly rain and the grass felt moist under their feet.

"Could sleep another week!" Chryséis yawned unashamedly. She rubbed her eyes and pouted. "Past or not past, I'm still tired."

She was none too happy to rise at such an early hour on what felt like a holiday to her. On top of that Chryséis felt homesick.

"Come on, Chris, let's go. We can't just laze about and annoy our hosts." Katherine was determined to make a good impression. "Alun seems excited about something. Let's find out what it is."

"He'll probably want to go to that farm," Trevor said.

"Yes, right, the farm."

Katherine and Chryséis had chatted till late and recorded the events of their first day in Cydonia on the palmtop.

"Why are *you* so bright-eyed and bushytailed?" Chryséis snapped at Trevor as he joined them on the lawn.

"That's such a great adventure. Better than any computer game!" Trevor said enthusiastically and by now wide awake. Chryséis wasn't in the mood for computer games.

"Yeah well, suit yourself."

"Stop being so grumpy, that's not like you at all. You're acting as if it's my fault that we're here. Yesterday you couldn't wait to see this prehistoric farm, remember?"

Chryséis pulled herself together. "I know. Sorry, Trev. It's not every day that I wake up in the past. I needed to let off some steam. Time travel isn't as easy as I thought." She yawned again.

"Then let's go to the house already," Trevor said.

They reached the fountain and saw Alun already waiting impatiently by the back door. He waved them inside. A group of people of various ages stood around the sofas. They faced the young guests curiously.

The two ladies, who had sat under the walnut tree yesterday, were also there and gave them a little smile. A rather large youth with unkempt blond hair towered over everybody. This must be the giant whose back they had seen in the hall yesterday! He couldn't be much older than Alun.

The woman from the kitchen walked in hastily and joined the group. The family was assembled. Only Kheton, Alun's brother, was not present. He had to attend to an important matter this morning, before setting off for work at the citadel courts.

Chryséis took the lead. "Oh hello, good morning."

The visitors gestured politely as they had learned yesterday. "Shelanti!"

"Shelanti!" The assembled folk answered with the same

gesture. Shelanti was truly a magic word.

The man next to Alun had to be his father. He looked young with his closely trimmed beard and bright eyes. Alun resembled him much.

Alesian custom demanded the formal reception of guests into the household, no matter how long their stay. As the head of the family, Harun carried the formal greeting.

"Be welcomed to this humble abode, athenai. May your visit be agreeable."

The time travellers understood the friendly gesture and smiled. However, that was all they understood.

"Thank you," Chryséis said.

Harun now addressed Alun. "My son, you say these foreign children wandered about Shepherd's Hill yesterday? Their parents' whereabouts are not known and they do not speak our tongue?"

"Yes, father it is true," Alun replied respectfully.

"What are their names, son?" his father inquired. Alun pointed to the children one by one.

"Father, I present to you Kathín of Oxfol, Trevór of Chicagó and Chryséis of Ethigevee." He was proud to have remembered their names so well. The three time travellers tried to smile.

"So, they all come from different locations? And none of them from Alesia?"

"That is not established yet, father. I don't understand them very well."

"Mmh, that's curious. The Lady of Cydonia has been notified, but nobody has inquired. Perhaps their parents can be found among the group of Mittanian scientists we are expecting at the testing station today. They arrived from Ruta Ynis yesterday."

"Yes father." Alun didn't mention that he had thought of this himself.

Ruta Ynis, a large island to the north east to the harbour of Aztlan, had been inhabited by fauns, elves and satyrs since the *First Time*. An ancient forest embraced the southern part of the island.

Birds from the tiny kolibri to the enormous moa and other animals inhabited the forest since times unknown.

Sought-after medicinal plants flourished on Ruta Ynis and nowhere else. Fauns and elves tended to the unique plants of their subtropical home and didn't like to share the plants with other nations.

They also didn't see eye to eye with the satyrs in the western part of the island, the dry Meropis savannah.

The Mittanian scientists had been lucky enough to obtain the elf queen's permission to collect a number of rare plants. The fickle queen had to be won over with unusual presents first, and the price had been a precious Mittanian headdress made of rare feathers. The Mittanians were now in Cydonia to study Alesian agricultural methods.

The land of Mittani was in sore need of help. Long-term irrigation with brackish water was turning rich farmlands into a salty desert. Just like those in Sû Mar. Wheat, the staple grain of Mittani did not grow well under such conditions.

Next, the scientists would visit the testing station of Tollùn on the Southern Continent. After devastating floods there, farms had been moved to higher regions with great success. Harun's team experimented with indigenous crops from Tollùn, in order to increase their useful properties.

Recently, large grains on a cone-shaped cob had been successfully improved. The grains came in different colours and experimental plantings promised to yield an excellent harvest. They had also managed to remove toxins in an otherwise nutritious starchy root from Tollùn. They could now simply be cooked to make them edible.

It was quite possible that the Mittanians had been too busy to notice the absence of their children.

Harun now introduced each member of the household by name. There was Alun's mother, whose name they simply didn't understand. Then it was chachi Monia and chachi Karna's turn. They were Alun's aunts and the lady from the kitchen. And lastly, Túvar and a great Uncle with white hair. The children tried to repeat each name. With a bit of luck, they would remember some of them.

"My son, you showed good judgement and consideration. As much as you are needed to prepare for Kheton's marriage ceremony, the children must be reunited with their parents. After breaking the fast you will take our guests out to the testing station in the vimaan."

Alun beamed with pride. Alesian parents believed in praising their children where praise was due.

"Should the parents not be among the Mittanians, you must meet with Kheton after the second court session at the citadel. He will accompany you to the Lady and request her valued advice in the matter." Harun was unworried whether the three guests understood his speech. He didn't mean to be rude, but he said what had to be said. Important test results had to be analysed this morning and it was time to leave.

"Yes father, thank you. We will be at the testing station later."

"Túvar, my son, come we have to be on our way. Shelanti!"

With that he was out of the butterfly-winged door. Túvar smiled a shy goodbye and shuffled dutifully after his adopted father.

Soon the other members of the family dispersed and busied themselves with their various tasks. One of the portly aunts brushed closely past Trevor on her way to the backyard and he jumped aside. Alun's mother stayed behind. She was a tall, good-looking woman with long, dark hair. She lingered for a moment and tried to learn from her son about the children's background. It was obvious that they did not yet speak enough Alesian to have a meaningful conversation. So they had to use a lot of gestures,

"They seem all confused, poor things. Sit down and eat, children!" She gestured toward the dining room table. "Alun, I think you should teach them how to speak at least some Alesian. Point to objects and repeat their names."

"Yes, mother, I shall do so."

"Good. Shelanti!" She smiled and bustled towards the

kitchen.

The time travellers tried to fit in as much as possible, but the customs of the 'Known World' were still too confusing. What did she say? A Shelanti on their lips, they stared after Alun's mother.

"Phew, I'm glad that's over," Chryséis said. "I'll never remember those names."

They followed Alun's example and helped themselves to breakfast from a large, yellow plate. Alesians believed that in the morning, cheerful colours had an invigorating effect on the mind.

Katherine was not particularly hungry, but soon she also scooped chickpea pâté with pieces of soùmi bread into her mouth. There was minty herbal tea in snail-shaped cups again. This time the tea had a lemony taste.

Chryséis had understood that Alun was supposed to bring them in a *vimaan* - and the *vimaan* turned out to be a vehicle. A sturdy vehicle with an aerodynamic, red body and a transparent bowl on top. Two other vimaans were parked next to it. Excuse me?! A horse-drawn carriage maybe, but that?

"These people have *cars*?" Chryséis blinked a few times.

"I can't believe it," Katherine breathed.

Was there no end to shock surprises?

At Alun's command, the bowl-like top opened noiselessly. The see-through material felt almost as hard as metal. It had to be the same hard plastic the windows and pipes were made of. Inside were three seats in the front and three seats at the back. It was a family car!

The time travellers stood there open-mouthed and Alun had to usher them into the vimaan. The clear top closed with a soft thud, allowing for a panoramic view. They looked at each other with big eyes.

"What next? Just look at this!" Chryséis knocked on the cover from the inside and Alun looked at her in obvious confusion.

"And here we thought plastic was a modern invention."

Sitting in the vehicle was amazingly comfortable. Almost as if the seats were filled with gel. Alun operated a half-moon-shaped bar and the vimaan lifted effortlessly into the air. About a foot or so above the road surface.

"It's not a car, it's a plane!" Trevor cried.

"Well I never!" Katherine said.

The vimaan swiftly negotiated the space above the road, making no noise in the process.

"I'm sure there's no engine in here. Must be another propulsion system," Chryséis decided.

"Anti-gravity device. An electromagnetic field," Katherine said. What else?

"Yes, magnetic levitation or diamagnetic repulsion." Trevor was all scientist again. "Fascinating!"

What the time travellers had seen was far removed from their naïve idea of prehistory. At least it felt like getting a better grip on things, if they could explain what they saw.

"Do you have the TPF?" Trevor whispered.

"Yes." Chryséis nodded and felt the device in her pocket just to make sure.

The vimaan avoided a tree and responded quickly to Alun's steering manoeuvers. It had to be fairly safe if kids were allowed to fly such a vehicle.

"I wish we could do that... back home."

"Just imagine!"

Chryséis's heart missed a beat when she heard the words 'back home'. But the flight was so exciting that she soon forgot her homesickness.

"Why didn't we see these vimaans yesterday?" Katherine wondered.

"No clue." They didn't know yet that most Alesians rested during siesta time.

"I think Alun's taking us sightseeing," Chryséis said. Alun seemed to take a bit of a detour and occasionally said something in his language. They moved through neighbourhoods and around a really large park in the centre of town.

Tall buildings that looked like longish cones, stood out between other odd-shaped structures. Much smaller box-like houses in different colours were clustered together against a hill. There were washing lines between the house walls and children played in narrow lanes as in any modern town. They saw shops and stalls and more vimaans in various shapes and sizes.

Instead of passing through busy pedestrian traffic, Alun raised the vimaan above the heads of people to a safe height. Way better than the noisy and smelly traffic in modern times. If there were any traffic rules for vimaans, it was to always follow a road on the left-hand side. And to fly with consideration. They never saw a traffic jam or a vimaan flying recklessly.

After a while, they were heading for the countryside through a rural area roughly west of the city. The spaces between houses became bigger and a number of smaller settlements flew past.

The temperature inside the vimaan was quite pleasant and they leaned back into their seats. Now and again Alun slowed down, pointed to an object and pronounced its name slowly and clearly. "Drachat - tree." "Agricolan - farmer." "Svinis - pig." "Phalam - fruit."

They repeated the words after him to their best ability. Not so simple. They didn't mean to be rude to Alun, but it wasn't easy not to laugh when they struggled with the sounds.

"Wait let me take the knot out of my tongue first!"

"Did he point at the fruit or the leaves?" Katherine asked seriously and scribbled something down.

"Let me put my teeth back in. Drekat, Drakat… I give up!" Chryséis laughed.

Alun thought his new friends rather untalented when it

came to learning Alesian. It was a dialect of the Akkadian language group and it should be easy to communicate. At least for civilised people of the Known World.

"What do you call your language athenai?" Alun asked.

They didn't understand his question.

"Sorry, Alun, that was too fast," Trevor apologised.

What tongue *did* these children speak? Alun wondered. Perhaps he should try to learn some of this outlandish gibberish. Yes, he would ask them later to teach him! But then he forgot all about it.

"Did you see that huge pig over there?" Katherine pressed her nose against the see-through dome.

"That was no pig."

"What else?" But then they had already left the animal behind.

The closer they got to their destination, the more the landscape changed. Cypress and poplar tree avenues crossed the broad main road where roadside stalls offered fruits and preserves. A couple of vimaans were parked next to the stalls, the drivers browsing through the wares.

The strangest thing were the animals. They grazed peacefully on grassy fields or frolicked about in fenced-in paddocks.

Some of them looked a lot like hairy pigs with short trunks and squirrel teeth. Others were an unlikely cross between llamas and buffaloes with rather long necks.

They lifted their heads and bellowed plaintively as the vimaan passed close by. A herd of small, fat farm animals with smooth olive skins and strong beaks, pecked incessantly at the ground.

Olive and fruit trees and vineyards draped in fresh new green hugged terraced hillsides. A flock of bee-eaters settled on a fence as the vimaan passed, preening their golden-green feathers. It was so peaceful and beautiful and exciting all at once.

Then the rolling, green hills gave way to a fertile plain.

Plants covered the fields in endless rows, where the soil was rich and dark and gave off an unpleasant smell.

The children in the vimaan didn't notice a Wildman family of four, hovering between some rocks in the low foothills.

The Wildmen were well-disguised. There was no need for clothing, because thick dark fur covered their sturdy bodies. It was almost too warm in the lowlands, since the sun had begun its summery journey in the sky.

Just the other day, the dome-headed Konks had woken up from their winter sleep in their snug cave stuffed with hair and leaves.

Every spring they trekked down from their cave dwelling in the highlands in search of green spring vegetables and succulent roots. A welcome change from their fare of nuts and dried berries they had collected in autumn.

Alesians tolerated all Wildmen and even looked after them in times of need. Konks led a placid existence in the mountains and were rarely seen. They took only what they needed in the valleys and disappeared again without bothering anyone.

Konks were not interested in farm animals anyway. They tasted funny to them. It was far better to hunt small rodents on the way back to their hearth.

The dome-headed Konk family soon made their way back up the slope. Their leather pouches filled with bushels of fresh roots and greens and early fruit.

▷▷▷ 12 KHETON AND LELANI

A misty veil still lay over Cydonia in the morning as Kheton left his father's house. He would miss the formal introduction of the three young guests Alun had told him about. Well, that couldn't be helped.

Kheton strolled down the road by the river, a longish packet in his hand. The rising morning sun painted the sky over the city an orange hue. The road was quiet and he enjoyed the leisurely walk.

Kheton served as an assistant judge at the citadel. After only two years of legal apprenticeship at the 'House of Wisdom', he had been chosen to join Alesia's diplomatic corps. Civilised countries such as Alesia were governed by strict laws. Even so, all sorts of quarrels and disputes kept the citadel courts busy. Like all judges of the 'Known World', Kheton was bound by a strict code of honour. Every apprentice could recite the beginning of the code by heart:

'If you are a leader of men, who controls the affairs of others, seek to do good wherever possible so that your conduct may be seen to be blameless. Great and lasting in its effects is justice, unchallenged since the First Time.

If you are a leader of men, with far-reaching authority, listen patiently to the speech of one who pleads. Do not stop him saying what he has to say. When a man is in distress, he needs to pour out his heart to someone who will hear whether or not it will win his case. Not every plea can be granted, but a good hearing soothes the heart...'

For the next two years, Kheton would take over the position of 'Honourable Junior Delegate' in the island state of Atland.

Atland meant the 'Old Land', but many still called it *the Motherland*. The 'House of Nations of the Known World' was located on the main island of Atala. This important council administered the affairs of all civilised nations of the Known World.

He would board a ship with his wife Lelani in Aztlan, the biggest Alesian seaport, shortly after the wedding. The ship was bound for Atala, but they would visit other islands on the way. They were remnants of a large landmass that had once existed in antiquity. Many of those islands formed an archipelago around the main island of Atala. They were connected through boardwalks and suspended bridges. Complex structures that were the pride and joy of Atala's skilled engineers.

Atland sounded so grand that the young judge couldn't wait to see it for himself. Apart from sports events and the occasional family visits, he had hardly ever left Cydonia.

Kheton was handsome and gallant with golden brown hair and a clean-shaven chin.

He was eighteen and his build had not yet filled out, but he was already as tall as his father. His sparkling hazel eyes reflected his happiness at the imminent marriage. Kheton's face lit up, as he thought of Lelani.

Lelani - with her graceful beauty and bright, soulful eyes. Quiet and diligent, this young man had ignited her heart the moment they had laid eyes on each other.

The morning was Kheton's favourite time of the day. Before nature burst into life with noisy birdsong and frantic activity. He walked on with a swing in his step and ducked instinctively as a flock of small flying lizards screeched past overhead.

Swarms of insects were the lizards' sought-after prey at this hour. What a nuisance, Kheton thought slightly annoyed. The flying lizards were so unpleasant compared with the little blue roller birds on the other side of the road. They chirped and twittered close to a fountain, fighting for crumbs on the ground.

Kheton drew his breath and walked faster as he neared his destination. Proper custom demanded that the *Earthmother* be thanked for her blessing at the 'House of Worship' today. Generations of betrothed Alesians had done this before him.

The *Earthmother Aïma* watched over marriages, fertility and an increase in prosperity. He had carefully chosen cinnamon incense for the occasion. Kheton reached the little temple and unwrapped the fragrant incense. He lit a fistful of thin sticks in the golden bowl before Aïma's image.

"Goddess your blessing is needed today. I am giving thanks for my good fortune." Kheton watched the rising smoke. It was done. The incense carried the simple prayer to the Earthmother. Everything would be fine.

The flowers he had picked off the bataleia shrubs by the river gleamed red and pink before the gently-smiling image. Yes, Aïma would be pleased and aid him in his errand today.

The entire Known World revered the Earthmother under many different names. When the time for sowing arrived, the spring festival was held in her honour. It had just been celebrated everywhere.

Other deities had to be considered too. *Nereus* and his daughters, the *Nereids*, protected travellers by sea. *Ankh Els*, the flying messengers of old, assisted the sun god Rais. The small image of an Ankh El adorned the front of each Alesian vimaan. Other nations had gods for wind and rain and the like, but in Alesia this was seen as pointless.

Kheton adjusted his white robes. The turquoise stripe along the hem proclaimed his office at the citadel. A red stripe would be added shortly, showing the status of marriage.

He left the shrine and set off for the Monsan district nearby, just as all the birds in the area seemed to burst into song. The air had warmed to the golden sun rays and the mist over the river melted away.

Kheton reached the purple bougainvillea bush at entrance to Lelani's home. Purple was a portent for good luck, he thought contentedly.

Lelani had been chosen at the age of fifteen, to attend to the Lady of Cydonia as an apprentice-maiden. Maidens acted as officials to the Ladies of citadels and had to undergo careful training.

Besides guarding the eternal flame, their duties included healing of the body and mind as well as teaching pupils at the citadel school and overseeing ceremonies. Maidens also carried out various instructions of a Lady.

To have a maiden in the family was a great honour. The women were required to live a life of chastity, detachment from worldly possessions and desires. This meant devotion to their new family - the community and nation. For this reason, an initiated maiden in the service of a Lady was forbidden to marry.

There had been a secret courtship between Kheton and Lelani. At first, they had tried to avoid each other, then they made up their minds. Lelani's father consented to their request for marriage without further ado.

He knew better than to argue over this issue with his headstrong daughter. Such cases of marriage were rare, but the young people would not be reproached for their choice. On the contrary, having been an apprentice maiden for almost two years would enhance Lelani's status among other matrons.

Her advice was almost as valuable as that of an initiated maiden. Of course, Lelani had to leave the service of the Lady of Cydonia, when she entered into marriage. This was the law.

Kheton's sandals scratched over the flagstones, as he crossed the short distance to the front door, decorated with garlands. Lelani's mother, clad in her best clothes, was awaiting the arrival of the young man. By tradition, no other person was to be present this morning. The formal visit served to begin a cordial relationship between the mother of the bride and her future son-in-law.

"I have done my duty by the Earthmother," Kheton announced formally.

"Then enter and be welcome in this home," Lelani's mother answered.

He walked over the threshold and respectfully handed over his gift of incense and flowers.

"Wash yourself and be rid of the dust of yesterday." She offered Kheton the ritual bowl with scented water and warmed towels, so he could wash his hands and face. Then the portly woman led the way to the sitting room, where refreshments were waiting.

Between the two sofas, an ebony table with intricate whale-tooth pattern was heaped with delicacies. Carved room dividers made from fragrant sandalwood were placed by the sitting area, giving off a pleasant scent. The walls were covered in paintings with scenes from Alesian legends.

The aroma of hot chili-chocolate and freshly baked sweetmeats reminded Kheton that he had not eaten breakfast.

"Help yourself to the modest offering I have prepared with my own hands." As expected, Kheton praised the food politely.

Lelani's mother heart warmed and she urged him to eat more. She was not displeased with her daughter's choice. However, she would tell Kheton how much her daughter had given up by choosing a husband.

It was crucial that he understood Lelani's worth. According to Alesian law, a married woman could own land and items of value and her opinion in family matters was considered. As a husband, Kheton would be treated with the respect that befitted the station of a wedded man.

Family, in every sense, was at the centre of Alesian

society. Young adults were instructed early on in all aspects of community and family life. Every rite of passage was marked by a specific ceremony, however simple. The wedding ceremony joined two families and this was valuable to the whole community.

"Kheton, everything has been prepared for your journey," the matron said.

The newlyweds would spend two phases of the moon together. It was an Alesian custom.

Everything had been carefully planned by the family of the bride. The safely guarded coastal reservation of Kalkan was a perfect choice. Kalkan was close to the border with Edfun and sufficiently secluded. Young couples were left to their own devices in a comfortable tent house.

"I thank you and compliment you on the beauty of your home. Surely this has contributed to Lelani's pleasant nature," Kheton said. Flattery in this regard was expected.

Kheton's thoughts wandered to present court matters. The practice of black magic by some individuals of Edfunian origin, gave cause for concern. Alesia battled such tendencies with the necessary means.

The young man caught himself. This was neither the time nor the place for such thoughts.

Careful attention to Lelani's mother was called for. Kheton was determined to win her approval. And the matron was pleased with her future son-in-law's impeccable manners.

"May Aïma bless the union of our families," Kheton said and spilled some juice on the tiled floor in honour of the Earthmother.

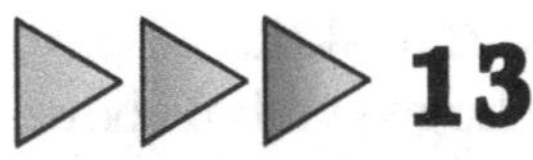 **13** IN THE COUNTRY

At about the same time, Alun's vimaan turned noiselessly into the agricultural testing station. The building was set back from the main road and resembled other such institution in the Known World.

"Looks like an airport," said Trevor

"Without planes?" Chryséis scanned the surrounding area. Just a few flying cars like Alun's.

A marble statue next to the entrance held up a dark stone tablet. An upturned conical fruit basket was engraved on top of the plate. With lines of text underneath. With the other hand, the statue pointed towards the entrance of the building.

The façade consisted of large windows. They were presumably made of the same hard material as the top of the vimaan. Furrowed fields spread to the left and behind the buildings. They were covered with patches of young maize and bushy flax plants.

Foliage crept along the ground in rows and tight heads of green lettuce and cabbage dotted the dark soil. Pulses and gourds grew on stakes, leaning together like wigwams. The irrigation canals seemed well planned and were lined by tall fruit trees. To the right mowed lawns and neat hedges shielded the fields from the road.

This was definitely no airport!

"Looks more like a modern farm to me."

"Interesting," Trevor said. "Wonder, if all farms have sculptures like that."

"Maybe it's their farm god."

"Could be. The writing looks a lot like *Sanskrit*,"

Chryséis mused. Sanskrit was an ancient language of India. Sweeping characters connected with bars on top. Unfortunately, Chryséis didn't know any Sanskrit.

"Nice building." Trevor studied the large symbol above the entrance. He had seen it around the city: A circle divided into a half-sun and a half-moon.

Alun 'parked' the vimaan and the top of the vehicle opened with a smack. They climbed out stiffly and Alun led the way inside. See-through doors slid apart and they stood in a spacious hall. Young plants grew under soft lights in transparent containers filled with a blue liquid. The raised containers were arranged in parallel rows.

It was warm and a little humid in the hall. People in orange coats checked on the growing plants, applying something here, adjusting the temperature there. This had to be a laboratory.

"Ah, you are here, son. Shelanti!" Alun's father looked up from behind a bulky machine. "I will be with you in a short while."

He worked a few shiny buttons and a round cover closed. Then the contents of a small drum started rotating. Faster and faster.

"Shelanti, athenai," a young woman greeted them. "I am Nunika of Eris."

"Shelanti." They introduced themselves.

"Nunika, kindly show our young visitors around until I am able to join you," Harun said to the apprentice scientist. She smiled encouragingly at the children. There was a thin turquoise stripe on her faintly orange-coloured tunic. *Perhaps that means something,* Katherine thought.

"I'll show them our farm with pleasure, Harun."

The young scientist assisted Alun's father on his latest projects. She also worked on upgrading a laser beam device. Such devices were used to keep rodents and vermin away from the fields. She guided Alun and the visitors past rows of the transparent troughs. Nunika knew that the foreign children did not speak Alesian and explained with simple words and gestures. They began to repeat her expressions and haltingly asked questions. "K'yah-hé? What is this?"

Astonishingly enough, Nunika and Alun answered.

"A hydroponic trough with nutrient liquid."

"These are food plants."

Of course, they couldn't fully understand the answers. The gestures and sounds that accompanied the words were often hilarious. But at least they communicated.

In this way they learned that the plastic-like material they had admired was called *'têrakhon'*. Trevor wished he could ask for the formula or its manufacturing process, but he lacked the words.

Nunika showed them tomatoes and eggplants with small white fruit. Green pear-shaped fruits resembled tiny avocados.

"They are called *'Auacáté'*. They grow on trees and have been sent for analysis from Tollùn."

She showed them how plants were 'improved' in the sterile section. They watched scientists through a window at work in the lab. The scientists were dressed like modern surgeons in silvery suits and masks, and they handled tiny green leaves in clear dishes.

"No way, I'm having kittens! Gene technology 12,000 years ago," Chryséis said in awe. This was no ordinary farm!

"No, that's impossible!" Katherine agreed. "They don't even have mobile phones or computers and then something like that."

"If we stick around long enough, we might just find out why not," Trevor said. "Maybe there's a reason for it."

"Look at *this* plant..." Katherine stared at a longish lettuce with red leaves. She received an answer without even asking a question.

"Makes a good sleeping potion," Nunika said in Alesian and gestured 'sleep' with her palms together. Katherine was surprised. How did Nunika guess her question?

In the herb section, they were allowed to rub leaves between their fingers and smell the spicy scents. They wondered which one of the plants was used for the apple-mint tea. But again, they didn't know how to ask. Alun's father joined them outside the sterile laboratory.

"Would you like a tour of the silkworm farm until the Mittanians arrive?"

"I believe it would be very interesting for our guests, father."

"Son, just reach for the wooden box over there, please. I will give you some silkworms to tend at home. It will take another week before they spin their cocoons. Feed them well with mulberry leaves. We will put them back with the other parent moths once they have hatched."

Alun found silkworms fascinating. He loved to watch the silkworms fatten until they started spinning their downy cocoons.

They walked through another sliding door. The doors closed automatically behind them. The new hall was bright and full of chest-high tables under a transparent domed roof. Large trays with layers of dark leaves stood on the tables. The packed leaves were moving with thousands of voracious silk worms.

Katherine held the wooden box, so that Alun could help his father spread a load of fresh leaves from baskets into an empty tray. Helpers picked up wriggling worms from another tray, gently pulling them off the leaf skeletons.

Nunika pointed to pictures on the wall that explained all about silk-making. That's how Alesian school children were taught when they came to the farm.

Different colours of silk were obviously achieved by feeding the worms different kinds of leaves. Beetroot leaves gave the silk a dusky pink colour, mulberry leaves shades of white, yellow and orange. Ready-spun cocoons were then taken to another section. A bath of hot water killed the chrysalis inside to prevent it from hatching.

"Unfortunately, this cannot be avoided," Nunika apologised.

Some of the cocoons were saved. The hatched silk moths laid then eggs - the next generation of silkworms.

The pictures showed how the silk was processed. The thread was unravelled and taken off the reeler. Then stretched on a wooden frame, rewound and spun together on a quilling wheel. The weavers then produced the fabric. Nunika didn't have to explain much.

"How did they figure out how to make silk? It's so complicated," Katherine whispered in Chryséis's ear.

"No idea. They are just clever."

They also learned that a new plant was tested in Cydonia. It produced long smooth fibres in a seed capsule. It was already used in the country of Ta Mery to make clothes.

Trevor studied the picture. "Hey, that's cotton!"

"Really?!" Katherine said.

They detected Túvar through the large windows. He worked behind the building in a field with other helpers. Some of them were Gabari like himself. Túvar saw them and waved as they stepped out into the open. The children waved back.

Nunika excused herself as she was needed inside and Alun led them to a large emerald field. Beautiful white horses pranced around jauntily. But it wasn't so much the white horses that caught their attention.

A light brown horse looked rather odd. As it came trotting toward them, they saw that the upper body of the horse was that of a man with arms! The time travellers' jaws dropped.

"Gobän of Cydonia," Alun said. Gobän was without any doubt - a centaur. It was Túvar's job to look after the horses with the help of horse minders, who were centaurs. He could communicate with animals in an extraordinary way, just like centaurs did.

The horses were from Túvar's native Edfun and the herd had been rescued a long time ago. He often brushed the magnificent animals, until their silky fur shone. In turn, they adored Túvar and had learned to tolerate the young giant on their backs.

Chryséis fumbled with her digital camera, but her hands trembled so much that she couldn't get a proper shot of

Gobän. Alun was already walking over to the experimental farm's animal section and she had to hurry to keep up. As if the sight of a centaur wasn't enough, Chryséis nearly fell over when she saw the farm animals in one of the pens.

The stocky little occupants burrowed with loud grunting noises through a heap of grass and leaves. They looked much like turkey-sized reptiles with short tails. Their scaly skin was covered in black-rimmed red and brown patches and they had red beaks.

"What on earth is that?" Katherine asked flabbergasted.

Up close, they looked very much like dinosaurs. Impossible, Trevor thought.

"Harpees," Alun said, expecting the question and pointed to the enclosure. "They make a good roast, lay big eggs... and eat a lot," he explained, gesticulating wildly. The children nodded bewildered.

"Okay, they are good to eat. Oh, and they eat a lot of food themselves... and they obviously lay eggs," Chryséis translated haltingly.

"Yes, obviously." Trevor had a look at the artificial nests along the fence. They were made of baskets lined with straw and contained several bluish eggs. About twice the size of a hen's egg and sprinkled with tiny black dots.

"Reptiles. They must be reptiles or..."

"... or... dinosaurs?" Trevor completed Katherine's sentence.

"No, that's not possible, Trev. They are clearly reptiles."

Harun spoke to the animal keeper for a while. The new tests were introducing grains into the harpees' diet. It was not quite a success yet. The harpees still preferred masses of fresh plants, which presented a problem.

"Harpees!" Trevor just could not believe his eyes. "There are no dinosaurs left, or what?"

"Well, birds are actually distant offspring of dinosaurs. But these harpees are definitely reptiles," Katherine insisted.

She leaned over the fence to inspect the clucking animals more closely.

"Sure, whatever." Trevor was in no mood to argue.

"Amazing, they have teeth in their beaks." Katherine leaned over a bit more.

"Have you seen any chickens yet?" Chryséis asked.

"No. Maybe harpees taste better."

Suddenly, a squeaking male harpee shot forward, stood up on its hind legs and expanded a signal-red collar. The collar made it appear larger. In a second, the male charged at Katherine and sunk its teeth into her hand. Oh, these harpees had needle-sharp teeth! Then it let go. Katherine was so astonished that she lost her balance and fell backwards.

"Katie?… Katie!!" Chryséis cried.

Somebody pulled Katherine back onto her feet and away from the enclosure, while farm workers shooed the agitated animals into a far corner. The harpees quacked and squealed and the noise was deafening.

Túvar had come over to join them and reacted quickly. He carried Katherine with long strides to a nearby feed box and sat her down.

A silver disk on a chain dangled around Túvar's neck as he leaned forward. Katherine noted the disk and then her hand started to burn badly. Tears shot in her eyes and she couldn't see anymore. Trevor and Chryséis ran after them. Chryséis carried the invisibility device that had fallen off Katherine's head. They struggled to get through to their friend. The incident had attracted a number of spectators.

"Is she all right?" Chryséis asked out of breath.

"She'd better be."

Túvar stepped back and a scientist knelt down by the feed box. The man moved some device over Katherine's bleeding hand. The bite marks healed within moments. What had looked like a nasty wound moments before, had simply disappeared.

Nunika urged Katherine to drink a watery liquid, called *recutis*, from a cup. Recutis tonic was made from chamomile flowers and had a calming effect. The scientist told everybody to go back to work. Nothing more to see. Chryséis and Trevor finally managed to push through the crowd and knelt down next to her.

"Let me see your hand!" Chryséis demanded. "Where is the wound?" She asked startled. "I saw that harpee bite you. There was blood."

"And it hurt hellishly! That man moved something over the wound and it just disappeared," Katherine said in wonder. "I thought this only happens in movies. Look, not a scratch."

"It disappeared? How did he do that?"

"I just told you, Chris!"

Nobody else seemed surprised about this. Harun clearly tried to apologize, though. His explanation was not so clear, but he tried nevertheless. A harpee bite could be very painful. Harun knew this from experience. The usually mild-mannered animals were more aggressive than usual. The new diet was plainly not working.

"What is wrong with those stupid harpees?" Trevor was still upset. "Farm animals aren't supposed to be that dangerous!" He glanced over at the enclosure. The hot-headed harpee male stood meekly at a distance from the herd. Its collar now all pale and deflated.

"Did I provoke them?" Katherine asked.

"I don't think so." Trevor checked Katherine's hand. The wound was really gone. Apparently, this was completely normal for Alun and Harun. "No wonder they are no longer around. Not my kind of chickens."

Nunika walked toward Harun and said softly, "The delegation from Mittani has arrived."

"Ah, that's good news. Let's hope the parents of the children are among them."

But Harun's hope sank when he saw the dark-skinned scientists approach. They were rather tall with finely chiseled features and obviously no relation to the abandoned children.

The Mittanians showed sympathy for the 'orphans', but

wondered quietly how parents could not be looking after their offspring. Unless something unspeakable had happened to them. They seemed genuinely concerned, but it was time to get back to work.

"My son, I think it is time to consult the Lady," Harun said after a short while.

"Yes father, we will be on our way."

They said their good-byes and Harun walked back into the building, the Mittanian scientists in tow. Soon they were deep in conversation about soils and crops and the like. Alun was looking forward to having his new friends around for a bit longer. Never mind their strangeness. They followed him to the parked vimaan.

"Can we go home now?" Katherine asked. "We've seen the city here and the country. I don't feel like more surprises."

"I'm actually starting to have fun here."

"Trevor, that wasn't fun just now! What if something like that happens again?"

"Come on Katie, it wasn't that bad."

"Easy for you to say," she sulked.

"Let's stay a bit longer or are you scared to miss school?" Chryséis said with a grin.

"Sort of —"

"What? Come on, we'll return at the same time we left, you know. Nothing to worry about."

"But we might forget what we've learned until then. Exams are coming up, you know."

"We'll catch up easily."

Katherine gave in. She didn't have much of a choice.

Nunika gave each of them a purple pear. "Shelanti athenai, please honour us again with your visit. Here, something for you to eat."

They nodded and Alun thanked her properly. Then they were up in the air and moving along the main road toward the city.

"He is taking us to the main temple, I think," Trevor said.

"To be sacrificed?" Katherine asked anxiously.

"Oh, please! Katherine, you've got some imagination. To meet the ruler there, I think," Chryséis said.

"That should be interesting."

"Better than being sacrificed…" Katherine held the wooden box with the silkworms on her lap. She lifted the lid and looked at the striped worms. Some of them rested on the leaves, heads in the air. Others chewed ferociously on the green leaves.

"Which ones are the females?" Chryséis wanted to know.

"No idea," Katherine said. Zoology was not their strong point and they didn't know how to ask Alun. He was rather quiet on the way back.

They paid more attention to the farm animals this time. Some of these creatures looked a lot like dinosaurs! Large hay-coloured animals slowly lifted their heads as the vimaan passed by. They had ducks' bills with teeth.

Katherine was still convinced that they were simply reptiles, but decided that it was impolite to argue in English in front of Alun. Perhaps they were mixed forms of reptiles and dinosaurs or reptiles and mammals. There was so much they still had to find out. She leaned back and watched Chryséis as she tried to take pictures of the animals.

There were also sheep, buffaloes and hogs, happily feeding together with the supposed dinosaurs from heaps of ferns and hay. They didn't seem to mind the strange animals. Maybe they really were dinosaurs, those dumb harpees, Trevor thought. 'Jurassic Park' on a farm. Did carnivores like Tyrannosaurus Rex still exist? Hopefully not!

But then it wasn't impossible either. Coelacanths were prehistoric lungfishes and had been found just recently off the South African coast. Allegedly extinct for 70 million years. Trevor felt goosebumps rise on his arms. A visit to the country had turned everything on its head.

And that was only the beginning.

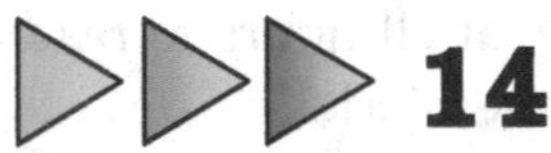 **14**   ON CITADEL HILL

They reached the town just after 11 o'clock. Chryséis had checked her watch. Alun flew straight to Valley Cydonia, where the citadel overlooked the quiet suburb. A canal separated the citadel complex from the villas.

They passed people, who made their way up the hill and over the bridge on foot. A paved footpath led from the parking area to the courtyard. White pillars on both sides of the gate were topped with female statues in flowing tunics.

The statues held stone plates with writing against their stone bodies. The arch between them was topped with a large round plaque, painted with the 'half-moon half-sun' symbol. One of the statues held a scale and had her eyes covered with a stone scarf. The goddess of justice. The other statue had an upside-down basket with falling stone fruits carved down the folds of her gown.

Sparse rocky terrain surrounded the citadel grounds and behind the perimeter walls, a stark cliff offered suitable protection. Rows of tall columns ran along the front of the building. The citadel was a town hall, hospital, court of law and school rolled into one. A big city like Cydonia needed a big citadel.

They stepped onto the paved courtyard. The citadel buildings were larger than they had looked from the other side of the valley. A small hall with large windows was to the left. It was the *prytaneum,* where the maidens of the citadel kept the sacred flame burning day and night. Fire was believed to have cleansing powers and symbolised civilisation.

All official buildings of the Known World had a prytaneum, even if it was just a fire bowl or lantern. The public visited the sacred fire and came at all hours to read the inscriptions on the western wall of the citadel.

People sat chatting on the broad rim of the fountain basin. Children played happily in the water or balanced on the rim between the adults. Food could be bought from stalls by the gate. The smell of fried mushrooms and freshly baked bread wafted through the air.

"Stop staring at the food!" Chryséis hissed and Trevor sighed. He felt hungry after the eventful morning.

"Today is court day," Alun tried to explain as they passed the doorway to the courtroom's waiting area.

The litigants were ushered into an outer sanctuary, where they waited until called upon. A carved stone plate inside the waiting area reminded them of the principles of justice in the 'Known World'. It was inscribed with the three main statutes of civilised law. They read:

1. Close not your heart against the Voice of Truth
2. Keep your anger balanced as the Scales of Justice
3. Remember the Path of Truth is often stony and clothe
  your feet in the Sandals of Courage

The 'Hall of Audience' itself was a long room. The panel of judges, two court orderlies and the scribe entered through a small door at the back of the hall. The opposing parties had to walk twenty paces, before they faced the dais. This was necessary for the judges to assess the supplicants.

Judges had to use their learning as much as listen to the wisdom of the inner voice. There were no lawyers. The presiding judge held the scarlet feather of truth in his hand throughout the hearing. He was required to close a case with the words 'I weigh my scales with the feather of truth and pronounce my judgement from the knowledge of my heart.'

"I wish I could tell you more about this, but perhaps you also have courts where you are from?" They understood. The symbols of justice were still in use. They nodded and Alun walked on satisfied.

People sat outside on benches and waited for relatives or friends, who were in the 'Hall of Audience'. Some visitors whiled the time away by walking around the gardens.

Colourful flowers and shrubs were planted along a maze of footpaths. Wooden benches invited them to rest by fish ponds or under trees. There was also a small platform where musicians entertained with flutes and harps. The herb and vegetable patches faced east on softly terraced slopes to make the most of the morning sun. Women in white tunics busied themselves with weeding the gardens. They were maidens of the citadel.

A group of school kids listened to their teacher as he held up a yellow flower, explaining its use in herbal medicines. A ball game was in progress on one of the sports fields. The upper stories of the main building were called the 'House of Wisdom'. Here the Lady of Cydonia and her administration staff worked tirelessly for the good of the community. Kheton waited at the bottom of the inner stairs. He was dressed in the turquoise robe of a judge.

"There you are, Alun. Shelanti. We must make haste. The presiding judge requested my quick return to the chambers."

Kheton was the assistant judge and needed to be present during the hearings. It was his task to search the hearts and thoughts of the involved parties with his 'inner voice'.

He looked at the three foreigners. "Shelanti athenai," he said and the time travellers answered. "Shelanti." Then Alun introduced them.

"The meeting with the Mittanians did not lead to a reunion then?"

Alun shook his head. "No brother, they were unknown to each other."

"Take heart Alun, we will seek advice from the good Lady. She is awaiting us." It was a formal but unusually brief welcome. Kheton was in a rush. This morning, a panel of three judges had heard four cases. The court was in recess now.

As Kheton climbed the steps he thought back to the first hearing this morning. A man had accused his childless neighbour of weaving a spell to steal his children's affection.

The allegations were unfounded and the truth was soon revealed, as the man with the children had a jealous heart. He was ordered to visit his neighbour and observe what it was that attracted his children's friendship. Then learn to be his children's friend, also.

'Become your children's and your neighbour's friend and your unhappiness will depart.'

The presiding judge's sentence was above reproach. The second case had been that of a mother, who refused permission for her only son's marriage out of selfishness. Then a couple requested that their bond of marriage be severed. A property dispute had been the last hearing before the break.

They reached the last flight of stairs. A young woman dressed in a long white tunic greeted them and asked their business. Kheton answered in the same formal tone, giving their names and the reason to see the Lady.

While they waited to be summoned, two novices in grey tunics with long braids down their backs, served tumblers with fruit juice. The visitors thanked the girls, who withdrew, all smiles.

"Are there no men here?" Trevor demanded to know in English. Of course, neither Alun nor Kheton understood a word of it.

"Do you feel outnumbered?" Chryséis whispered.

Trevor just shook his head. It was clear by now that the ruler of Cydonia was a woman. Kheton hadn't paid much attention to what they were saying. He was mulling over the property dispute that still needed to be concluded and Alun was too excited to chat. He would be introduced to the Lady!

Katherine, Trevor and Chryséis waited patiently, sipping their juice and looking at the decorations in the lobby. So far things had gone way beyond their expectations. Now they would even meet the queen of Cydonia. Not bad for their first time travel experience!

After a while, a maiden in a white tunic took them to the Lady's quarters. It was obvious that Kheton blushed, when he looked at the young woman. Alun had done his best to explain to his guests about the wedding, and they understood that Kheton was Alun's brother and to be married soon. They looked at the girl with interest. *This had to be Kheton's bride*, Katherine thought.

Lelani was rather pretty with slightly slanted blue eyes that were in stark contrast to her wavy auburn hair. The maiden moved gracefully.

She came up to Kheton's chin and beamed a smile at her fiancé before opening the door. Lelani then ceremoniously announced the group and stepped back.

A very formal Kheton put the situation to the Lady of Cydonia and asked for her wise counsel in the matter.

The Lady was as tall as him. Her golden brown hair was streaked with grey and tied into a loose bun. This seemed to be the preferred hairstyle of Alesian women.

Her face looked kind and younger than they had expected. Her translucent grey eyes held the sparkle of intelligence. She wore a simple mother-of-pearl necklace and matching earrings. Apart from polished gemstones, pearls were the only type of jewellery they had seen in Alesia so far.

The Lady wore a flowing silk robe with a golden sheen. Instead of a turquoise stripe, they had seen so often, a purple double stripe adorned the hems of her robe. This was reserved only for the highest-ranking individuals in Alesian society.

She listened carefully, then asked Alun to wait outside and gave Kheton formal leave to resume his court duties. They left the Lady's quarters, saluting respectfully.

The time travellers were alone with the ruler of Cydonia.

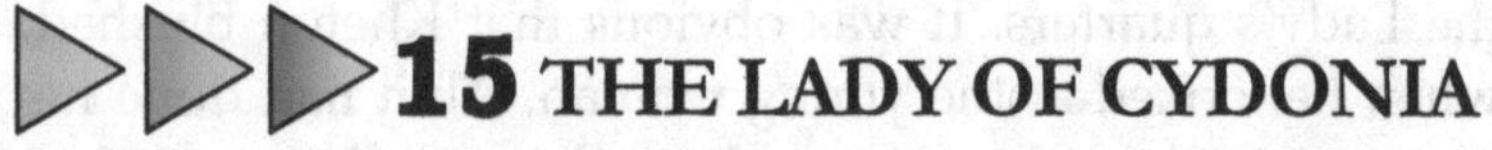

▶▶▶ 15 THE LADY OF CYDONIA

After a moment's reflection, the Lady ordered the youngsters with gestures to sit down in upholstered chairs. Then she sat down opposite them.

"Shelanti and welcome to Cydonia, athenai," she gestured the customary Alesian greeting. "I am the Lady of Cydonia."

"Shelanti," they answered politely.

The Lady seemed to contemplate the circumstances of their visit. They waited patiently for her to begin the conversation. Finally, the Lady spoke softly but with an irresistible authority.

"So, you have decided to visit our world. I take it that you did not travel here to Alesia by accident?"

The children gawked at the Lady open-mouthed. No way! She had asked in clear and modern English with only a slight accent.

"Why now?" she said easily. "Did you think you were the only ones to travel through the portals of time?"

They were stunned. Of all the things they had experienced since yesterday, this had to be the most mind-blowing.

"I see you are speechless," the Lady continued. "Then let me tell you that travelling through time and space is not unknown to the initiated of our culture. And not new either."

A green pet-iguana changed position on the gnarled branch he was resting on. His domicile was a finely-worked metal cage, open at the top. There was gravel at the bottom of the terrarium, a water bowl, food and small potted plants.

Mesmerised, they followed the animal's slow, rocking

movements. The Lady noticed their interest.

"A tame pet," she said. "The ones I encountered on my own journeys to the remote past were not so tame. Some rather large lizards in our time are still of threatening appearance. Luckily, they are safely contained in remote places - in the 'Outer World' - far from human settlements."

"I am glad to say that they are not as gigantic and numerous as in ancient times. Our ancestors certainly had their hands full." Remote past? How much more remote did human history get?

The Lady stroked the tame iguana lightly on his scaly green back. The reptile lifted its head slightly, used to her touch. They still couldn't speak.

"This one is only an adorable miniature version." The Lady looked up. They stared at the scene in fascination.

"I saw the remote past, and garnered much from the wisdom and foresight of our learned forefathers."

Right. Knuckle-dragging lummoxes then? Chryséis thought.

"I saw those as well. But no, I am talking about Titans. Forefathers of our now frightfully ignorant Gabari," the Lady answered as if Chryséis had spoken. "They are much smaller now and alas some have kept some undesirable traits."

"How-?" Chryséis began flabbergasted, but the Lady of Cydonia continued.

"There were other men too in the past. Much advanced. They taught me what would be called white magic in our time. All this will be forgotten by the time your generation comes around. Oh yes, I have also visited your world in the future."

The future? This was getting better by the minute. Trevor couldn't figure out why the Lady seemed so familiar to him. She reminded him of his late grandmother. The Lady wasn't nearly as old, but maybe it was her voice or her eyes. Granny did have grey eyes just like that.

Astonishingly, Katherine was the one to pluck up her courage first. "Lady, how is it possible that you found out about the time portals in this distant past?" She asked in a trembling voice. "Do you also have a vacuum battery?"

Her friends were surprised that Katherine was so brave. She was always the shy one.

"Why, our culture is not primitive, as you may have noticed. We have better things than your vacuum battery even now. Only the initiated among us, mostly Ladies, have insight into the nature of things... and know about the secret of time travel."

The children listened carefully. There were more of these Ladies around?

"For us this is no fun experiment. We must carefully consider what improves our way of life. How we must prepare for the future and guide our people."

The Lady poured tea from a copper pitcher into round têrakhon cups. She pointed to a plate with food on the table next to a small water feature. A polished stone sphere spun on a column of water in a white marble bowl. The trickling water had a calming effect on the nervous children.

"This kind of knowledge might be harmful in the hands of the unwise," the Lady said. "The consequences of misuse are severe. This is one of the lessons I *did* learn in your future times."

"Not how to gain the knowledge is of importance, but how to use the knowledge with care and wisdom in the best possible way." She smiled.

The children couldn't eat. They just wanted to listen.

"I saw giant Titans build their enduring settlements with such ease. How cleverly they laid out streets and harbours. Much has been lost with land and continents. Some constructions have lasted well into the future."

They sat spellbound.

"Titans held the wisdom and skills of the forefathers in

high esteem. They knew how to transport boulders and rocks 'through the air' with the power of sound. They perfected the art of softening the stone just enough to mould the boulders against each other."

This conversation was taking a totally unexpected direction. But then of course, the Lady already knew that there were no mysterious parents to be found.

"A knowledge, even our generation has not yet reclaimed. In time perhaps. We develop technology to make our existence more pleasant and meaningful. For the good of all. Not for personal gain. Ah, but I can see that you must feel overwhelmed by all this talk."

She was right, it was near impossible to digest everything she said in the blink of an eye. The Lady walked over to one of the mosaic-framed windows and looked out, giving the children a chance to take a look around.

It was the first time that they saw their hill from the other side of Carter Valley. No, it was Valley Cydonia now.

There was an oval-shaped table with thirty chairs on the far side of the room. The walls were painted in shades of green and the painted plants gave the illusion of a midsummer garden. The fourth wall was a landscape that seemed to end on the horizon.

When the Lady moved away from the window, Trevor had recovered somewhat from his initial shock.

"Dear Lady," he said hoarsely. "We have never met anybody like you... believing in time travel... and you speak English... and you travel through time portals yourself..." His voice sounded a bit squeaky.

The Lady had to smile as she saw the two girls reach gingerly for some snacks on the platter.

"Of course you were surprised. You expected cavemen and dangerous animals. Never this." She made a sweeping gesture with her hand. "It must have taken skill and courage to come so far." She looked at them with praise in her crystal grey eyes.

"I have met here in Alesia only once with a scientist from close to your times. He was a bit odd, not to mention - unwashed. He kept mumbling about divine wrath and the devil's work and the like."

The Lady sighed at the memory. "Poor man. There was no time to cure him of his mental ill. He insisted on leaving us after two days. We had to secretly adjust his energy generator. It was not sufficient to take him back to his own time." She creased her forehead and took a sip from her tea cup.

"Dear Lady... this time traveller you mentioned..." Trevor began shyly.

"I believe our eccentric visitor mentioned the year 1678. He was a physician from the island of England. It corresponds roughly to our country of Prydhain, although now it is still joined to the mainland."

The friends looked at each other. 1678 was close to the 21st century from the Lady's perspective, but ancient history to them.

"Our good doctor had found a secluded spot in Virginia in the United States. 'Tobacco Land', as he called it. This is now of course here on the continent of Patala. Not far from here, actually. He said that the authorities of his time were not in favour of his research and gave him a hard time."

"Really?"

She answered Trevor's next question before he could ask. "I believe his name was Gunniva." She lifted her eyebrows and looked at her visitors, but the name Gunniva didn't ring a bell.

"Unbelievable that he had found a way to harness electromagnetic powers with the very primitive means available to him. He had been lucky indeed that he had not landed in Edfun." What was Edfun?

The Lady of Cydonia shrugged her shoulders and

changed the subject. "It would also be to *your* benefit, if you allowed us to make changes to your own device. To ensure that any time portal you choose at any place will take you safely back."

That would be a great... but they weren't so sure about handing over their TPF. They had only just met this astonishing Lady. Could they trust her enough?

"Don't be fearful children. I mean well." She smiled winningly. "I've known about you since your arrival on Shepherd's Hill and was contemplating how to help you."

She walked back to the window and sat down on the broad window sill. *She'd known about them since they'd arrived in Cydonia? The Lady has to have telepathic abilities!* Chryséis thought.

"How else would I know about your secret? Indeed, how else would I be able to offer good advice? You have much to learn!"

She turned around to face them again. A small flying lizard landed on the windowsill behind her.

The Lady jumped in surprise, then laughed out loud. The children gaped at the squeaking lizard. It was mustard yellow, holding a dragonfly between needle-sharp teeth. It eyed the woman and took to flight again.

"Don't worry yourselves. The telepathic abilities of an untrained person are minimal. Most people can only pick up on good or bad intentions. I guess you could call it intuition. To use mind-reading in the right way, one must learn the skill. It is part of the training for judges and citadel officials."

This might be an explanation for the lack of telephones in Cydonia, Katherine thought to herself. Imagine - if people in modern times could do that!

A faint melody carried up from the gardens. Somebody played the flute. The Lady listened for a moment.

Did Kheton also have this mind-reading ability? Trevor wondered.

"Of course Trevor, but he could not read your minds precisely. It is Kheton's role to 'read' plaintiff and defendant and to transfer his findings to the presiding judge. It is the judge's function to weigh up the truth and then make the judgement."

Trevor was taken aback. He had to be careful, and not share his thoughts so openly. This telepathy began to creep him out.

"Enough of this serious talk. How do you enjoy your stay in Cydonia so far?" The Lady asked.

Grateful to be able to talk to somebody at last, the children told her of all the things they had discovered during their short stay.

They chatted for a while. Then the Lady of Cydonia said, "Dear young visitors from future times, you seem more capable than Mr. Gunniva to grasp our culture. Perhaps you would like to see more of our ancient world and travel awhile?"

The children fell quiet. What, travel?

"You may decide and I shall understand if you would rather return to your school life and your families."

She stroked her pet-iguana lightly with her index finger. Trevor felt uneasy. The memory of a huge scaly, steaming 'thing' still fresh in his mind.

"Iguanas make good pets. Their minds are blank and do not interfere." The Lady poured water from a crystal pitcher into the iguana's bowl.

"I will assist you no matter what your decision. Should you choose to remain here, I shall garner the support and protection by other Ladies of the Known World."

Travel - they weren't prepared for such a decision.

"Dear Lady, may we discuss this briefly amongst ourselves?" Katherine asked timidly.

"Of course, child. Such a thing is not to be taken lightly."

The three friends put their heads together and debated

the advantages and drawbacks. Going back was not an option yet. That much was clear. This place was just too interesting. Even Katherine agreed.

"What if it's too dangerous to travel?" Trevor worried.

"It would be safer to stay put," Katherine said.

Chryséis was more excited about the idea. "We could study other continents. Should we pass that up? Can it get any safer than this? I mean, all these Ladies will protect us. Just think about it..."

"I'm dying to see this Prydhain," Katherine said.

Trevor and Chryséis couldn't believe the change in her.

"So we do it?"

"I say we do it." Katherine said. "Hang on - what if we make a mistake and change the future?"

"Okay, we'll ask her what she thinks," Chryséis suggested.

"Okay." They turned around and Trevor spoke on everyone's behalf.

"We've made a decision. We'd like to accept your offer."

"I am glad that you chose to remain in our epoch a while longer," the Lady of Cydonia smiled. Of course, she knew already.

"We just have a few questions... err... what do you want in return?" Chryséis asked. She was a businessman's daughter after all. There was no such thing as a free lunch, right?!

"You are right to ask. I do understand that you come from a time when nothing is given for free," the Lady said. "It is different in our time. We want you to learn about our civilisation and hope you might put it to good use for the benefit of future generations."

The Lady of Cydonia leaned back in her chair and folded her hands. "So much knowledge has already been lost. But there is hope that mankind will advance with better comprehension."

"I see," Trevor said.

"As to your next question... you should not worry about

changing the future through your presence here." They were surprised, but of course the Lady could read their thoughts.

"There is a good reason for your journey to our time or it would not have been possible. There is more to it than a mere school project."

They would have liked to ask more questions, but the Lady began to speak about the plans for their journey.

"Two weeks after their wedding, Kheton and Lelani will leave by ship for Atland. Atland is the *Old Land*. Kheton is a promising young man. He will take up a post as 'Honourable Junior Delegate' from Alesia in Algebras, the capital of the main island of Atala." They didn't understand what that meant. Old land and an island with a capital?

"I will explain this later," the Lady said. "What's important is that you will accompany them on this voyage. A letter of recommendation will be issued, addressed to Ladies of citadels in civilised countries. In case of a problem, you will seek their assistance at once. By thought transfer, if necessary. For this purpose you will have to learn telepathy."

This sounded exciting. They would learn telepathy!

"When can we start with it, Lady?" Trevor asked eagerly.

"At once, if you wish."

This Lady meant business.

So the time travellers took their first lesson in telepathy, while Alun waited patiently outside.

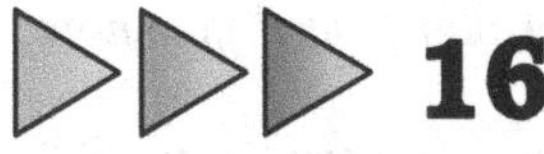 **16** **MIND POWER**

Katherine stood on a long patch of lawn in the citadel gardens with her eyes tightly shut. She pinched her mouth into a thin line and tried to concentrate on Trevor's face. Just as the Lady of Cydonia had demonstrated to them minutes earlier. *The grass is red, the grass is red*, She kept thinking over and over again.

Trevor stood next to Chryséis. They were on the other side of the lawn. He concentrated as well, trying to see Katherine's face with his eyes closed.

They were supposed to practice relaxing their minds and sending thoughts to each other. But that wasn't half as easy as it sounded. He wanted to read Katherine's mind, but there was nothing. Not a twitch.

"Katie, don't try so hard. You have to relax, remember?" Chryséis reminded her. Katherine squeezed her eyes a little. 'The grass is red, the grass is red.' She repeated the same words in her head and tried to send them to Trevor.

'Clear your mind of unwanted thoughts, chattering away incessantly,' the Lady had explained to them. 'Then picture the other's face. Lower your thought into your heart and concentrate on the words. Intense but not desperate.'

After giving them basic instructions, the Lady of Cydonia had let them out through a hidden door into the top part of the garden. The Lady's private meditation garden, enclosed with flowering hedges. They would be able to exercise here for a while, undisturbed by maidens and visitors.

Chryséis looked on impatiently. It was *her* turn next.

Wading through a sea of thoughts and unable to swim in it was totally uncool. She had to suddenly think of red grass. *Red grass? Nonsense! Go away thought, I don't need you now*, she grumbled.

"I can't get it!" Trevor was disappointed. "What *did* you think about?"

"The grass is red, Trevor! You are not relaxing enough."

"I'm hopeless. What, if it never works?"

"The grass is red, really? But I had to think of that. The grass is red!" Chryséis cried triumphantly. "Do you think I could've picked up your thought?"

"Seems like it."

"That's not supposed to happen." Trevor felt jealous. Why couldn't he get it, was he simply too stupid to do it?

"No way! I didn't send the thought to you. I definitely saw Trevor's face in front of me." Katherine walked over to her friends.

"At least we know now that something did work." Trevor's frustration lifted. "Maybe it's just a matter of practising more often."

"Yip, let's do it now."

Chryséis couldn't wait to try it again. The Lady of Cydonia had told them that thoughts were not sensed in a particular language, but rather the meaning of it.

"Let's get the focus right. You don't want just any bystander to receive our message. Okay, relax your facial muscles…"

At the end of the session it was still only Chryséis, who could receive thoughts. But the telepathy bug had bitten them and they had many questions for the ruler of Cydonia.

The afternoon sun covered the valley in a veil of gold. Even the Lady's quarters were magically transformed by sunlight slanting through the windows, casting a golden glow.

The Lady tried to ease Trevor's worries.

"Not everybody learns at the same pace, Trevor. It has nothing to do with intelligence."

It still unnerved him that she knew what he wanted to say, even before he had a chance to say anything.

"What, if I need help and I'm all upset?" Katherine wanted to know. The Lady smiled at her eagerness.

"A call for help is made with an intensity that doesn't go unnoticed. We practice relaxation even in situations of distress. An inner calmness is more helpful than a turmoil of thoughts."

It made sense, but how to do this in a real situation was another story.

"It will happen in time. Continue to practice daily and the results will show." The Lady knew what she was talking about. She had mastered telepathy rather well.

"Mankind has all but forgotten about the power of thought in future times. You must reawaken your natural abilities."

"What happens, if you don't know the other person's face?

"Then you concentrate on the name, clothes, the location or such."

Something else suddenly crossed Trevor's mind. "Lady, is it possible to protect oneself against bad thoughts?"

"It is indeed possible to protect against harmful or negative thought forms. You shall learn more about this, as soon as you have made some progress in simple thought transfer." Then Katherine asked something completely unrelated. "Lady, hmm, I don't know what else to call you. Don't you have a name? I mean like ours?"

"No, my dear girl. 'Ladies of the Citadels' give up their personal names. We become just 'Ladies' of our respective realms."

"But the maidens who work for you, do they get to keep their names?"

"Yes, a maiden keeps her name. If they were all called 'Maiden', what a confusion *that* would cause!"

They all laughed. There was a knock on the door. An urgent message had just come in - telepathically. The Lady of Cydonia had to attend to another matter.

The three time travellers left. They now had an ally! No,

they actually had *many* allies all over the Known World in the 'Alesian Epoch'. 11,752 years ago. Their trip back in time had become more of an adventure than they could ever have imagined. It was like being locked in a sweet shop, eating all the sweets they wanted.

When they were outside again by the stairwell, Alun wanted to know why it had taken them so long to talk to the Lady of Cydonia. But all they told him was that the Lady had offered them help. Even if they had wanted to tell him more, their knowledge of Alesian simply wasn't enough.

"So, there is your answer why people don't have mobile phones here," Trevor said to Katherine when they climbed into the vimaan. "...and why their technology is so advanced."

"Well, knock me down with a feather," Katherine said.

"Yeah." Chryséis didn't feel like saying anything more.

After dinner, they had recovered enough and talked for a while in their guest cottage. "How could the ancestors she told us about have been so clever?"

"Do you think these huge Titans really existed?"

"Why not? Just look at Túvar and the other giants..."

"All we wanted to do was explore the town a little. Now suddenly all of *this* happens. Giants, flying cars and dinosaurs," Chryséis said.

"Off the wall!" Trevor said.

"Yes, but we are totally lucky to have somebody like the Lady on our side. We'll be fine. And they were reptiles."

"Whatever. It's a real adventure now. Wonder what this land of Edfun is like."

"Must be north of here. Didn't the Lady mention Virginia?" said Katherine.

"I'm going to sleep now. See you all in the morning." Trevor sauntered off. The girls still wanted to update their travel journal. Trevor was soon asleep and dreamed of dinosaurs and black spiders.

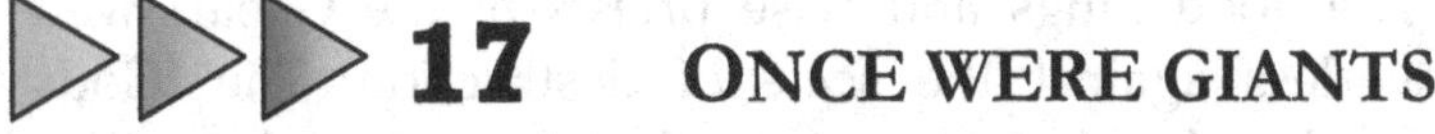

▶▶▶ **17** ONCE WERE GIANTS

Edfun, the vast country on the continent of Patala, had been the home of the 'Gods' many sheaves of years ago - during the *Golden Age*.

The Titans, the 'Great Ones', had been a noble Edfunian race. The chosen allies of the 'Gods' in the uncharted world of the young planet. Taught by the 'Gods' how to harness the forces of nature. Famous were their cities of black lava-rock, their harbours and ships.

The Titans revered the moon they called *Zarpa Nitu*. In Titan legends, Zarpa Nitu had once been the home of their glorious ancestors. Their offspring, the Gabari, still called themselves the *Chandravanshi* in the ancient language.

The 'Children of the Moon'.

But then one fateful day, things had changed forever. Natural disasters struck the thriving mother planet. The Earth trembled under the unrelenting onslaught. The Dark Age began.

Floods engulfed great coastal cities and flourishing farms. Continents sunk amid molten rock and mountain ranges were reduced to lowland. Where once gentle valleys had stretched, now towered jagged peaks.

Sâkadwipa, famous continent in pit of the south suffered the cruellest of fates. Few were able to flee when once fine and temperate lands disappeared in a grave of insurmountable sheets of ice. Banished to the realm of legends, Sâkadwipa survived only in the hearts of its survivors.

When the trembling Earth came to rest at last, the face of the planet was devastated. Ancient nations had disappeared in the blink of an eye in Earth history. The great civilisations of the Golden Age were no more.

The good kings and wise priests of the Gabari were powerless against the scale of destruction. The 'Gods' themselves had left. Gone were the times when the nations of the 'Known World' had praised the noble Titans. No longer were they called 'the Great Ones' - giant in stature and knowledge.

The caves of the 'Gods' with their hidden treasures of the ancient and priceless records of civilisation were destroyed or no longer known. Their kingdoms fallen into ruin, Gabari blended with other nations and soon lost their gigantic stature. An era of darkness followed.

Wisdom and kindness made way for greed of power and cruelty. Self-styled rulers seized control of the country of Edfun. In the wake of destruction on the injured planet, non-giant nations maintained the values of the 'Gods', while the greatest nation of them all was embroiled in warfare.

Alesia became one of the realms of renewed and righteous civilisation. A happy realm that was now dedicated to the sun and the moon.

The royal Gabari of old, still true to the ancient teachings, tried in vain to resurrect the nation of the 'Great Ones' to its former glory. In vain they strove to reunite.

Superstition and black magic had swiftly gained the upper hand among the new humans in Edfun. Warlords increased their status and material belongings. The seizure of slaves turned into popular pursuit.

In times of peace, challenges were held to the amusement of ribald spectators. It was a test of physical strength and endurance of frightful competitors. Losers were put to death to the roaring laughter of a screeching audience. Cruelty had become a virtue and pitiless revenge was meted out where barbarous new laws were disregarded.

Many of the learned true Gabari perished while resisting the new sovereigns, who attempted to gain the ancient knowledge of the 'Gods'.

The survivors, believing in fair and peaceful rule, were contemplating escape from their beloved homeland. When Goma, a stronghold of the true Gabari, was burned to the ground with great loss of life, the time had come to leave behind the forces of evil in Edfun.

In the cover of darkness, a steady flow of refugees was led through harsh terrain. Always in disguise, changing their routes and timing, the true Gabari trickled across the border into Alesia.

The neighbouring country gladly received the refugees. Known for their knowledge of 'White Magic' and high morals, the true Gabari were most welcome in the growing nation of Alesia.

Settlements sprang up on the coast and along the border. The Alesian border was secured against the cruel warriors from the north, but the royal Gabari stayed shy of the main cities at first. For fear of detection.

That's how the ancient traditions lived on beyond the reach of wicked Edfun.

Generations came and went, but the Edfunians had not lost their inclination for warfare. Within its borders, Edfun's rulers and sorcerers maintained unmerciful oppression and the civilised nations were often forced to intervene. The peaceful ways of the new civilisation had to be preserved for the good of all.

There had been no incidents for a very long time.

▶▶▶ 18 NIGHTLY EXPLORATION

Katherine woke up with a start. Had she heard a noise by the door or was it just in her dream? She checked on Chryséis. The bed was empty, but the watch Chryséis always wore was still on the small table she had moved next to the bed.

It was 2 o'clock in the morning.

Chryséis was not in the bathroom either. Had she gone for a walk in the garden? Had she been kidnapped? Panic gripped Katherine. She went to the other cottage and knocked on Trevor's door. The bright moonlight cast shadows in the garden, but no sign of Chryséis.

"Trevor, wake up. Trevor, Chris is gone!" Katherine called in a shrill whisper. If she carried on calling him like this, she'd wake the people in the house. She knocked. Trevor was a sound sleeper, so Katherine simply opened the door. It took some shaking and cold water to wake him up.

"What the —!" Trevor was annoyed.

Who was shaking him so roughly? Then he saw a frightened Katherine standing by his bed. He was all wet. Trevor was awake in an instant.

"Katie? What's the matter, did anything happen? A flood?"

"No, Trevor, of course not! Chris is gone. I woke up and heard a noise by the door. I *think* I heard a noise. Then I saw that she was gone."

"Slow down... gone?" He tried to shake off the stupor of sleep.

"Yes Trevor, gone! Maybe something happened to her?" She began to sob.

"Katherine MacDougal! Do you want to solve this

problem by crying?"

Trevor was not in the best of moods. The logic of his harsh words was compelling though and Katherine stopped abruptly, wiping her eyes.

"I just don't know what to do," she moaned. "Why should somebody want to take Chris? These people have been so nice to us."

Trevor ran his fingers through his hair. "Maybe Chris wasn't kidnapped at all. Think about it. The moon shines bright tonight. She went for a walk, that's all," he tried to convince himself and Katherine.

"But why would she walk around by herself in a strange place like this, in the middle of the night?" Katherine was now more angry than worried.

"I don't know. We have two choices," Trevor said. "We go back to sleep and see if she comes back - or we try to find her."

"Oh Trevor, let's please look for her," Katherine begged.

"Okay, I'm awake now anyway... and wet." He wiped his face. "We might just as well go and look for her. I'll get dressed. Get your invisibility device."

It was best to use their virtual invisibility capes, before someone caught them traipsing around the garden. They had, however, forgotten about the dogs sleeping inside the entrance hall. The mother-dog started growling when she heard them stumble over the crackling walnut buds in the yard. Katherine and Trevor hurried through the gate and the growling stopped. The dogs had recognised the children by their smell. Nobody seemed alarmed.

"Phew! Let's go," Trevor said.

"Wait—" Katherine whispered urgently. "How do I know where you are?"

"Here, take my hand. I'm right next to the gate. No - on the other side." Katherine groped through the air and caught hold of Trevor's outstretched hand. They walked hand-in-hand to the next corner and peeped cautiously around a hedge. Nobody was in sight, just the murmur of voices nearby.

They followed the sound of the voices and heard faint singing coming from the other side of the road.

"Do vimaans fly around at night?" Katherine asked anxiously. Trevor shrugged his shoulders. If they did, there weren't any around now. They decided that it was safe to cross the road and as they walked on, the chanting grew louder.

A secluded park lay in front of them. Slightly higher than the road and below a small hill. It was a lovely park, with gurgling fountains and statues made of gleaming white stone. The pleasure garden was enclosed on all sides by dark hedges and there were also hedges between lawns and flowers and several benches. Topiary trees pruned into ball-shaped lined the raked path. The full moon bathed everything in a soft, silvery light and the scent of flowers still lingered in the warm night air. Could Chryséis be here somewhere?

Close to the back of the park, half-hidden by a clipped hedge, a group of rather tall people moved rhythmically to muffled singing. One of the giants raised his arms in what seemed to be a greeting to the moon.

Like the others he was clad in a white robe. But on his grey hair he wore a silver crown. A silver disk framed by silvery ears of wheat. It looked a lot like a headdress of Egyptian gods. Katherine and Trevor watched from behind the low hedge with bated breath.

What were these giants doing? It looked like some kind of ritual that involved dancing and singing and talking to the moon.

"You think, they're wizards?" Katherine asked.

"Ssshhh - don't know."

The giants looked harmless enough, bouncing around towards the stone table and away from it.

"Ayam rātris purusah candra masam

sanātanah jyotir nivartate…" they sang.

"This night the supreme moon planet
returns the eternal light…"

The dance became more rhythmic and the giants swayed sideways around the stone table.

Katherine suddenly squeezed Trevor's hand. "Look at that!" He had already seen. "It's Túvar!"

"Do you think Chryséis is here as well?" Katherine whispered. Trevor was so enthralled with the dancing Gabari that he had sheer forgotten why they had come - to look for Chryséis!

"Maybe, she's with them by the table," he whispered back.

They moved closer and looked around. Chryséis was nowhere in sight.

They didn't dare speak - so close to the Gabari. What now?

The singing stopped abruptly and the grey-haired leader held up a broad silver bowl with a clear liquid in it. The group started to hand the polished bowl from one person to the next, taking small sips of the liquid to soft humming.

Ranef spoke in a gentle voice as 'the mirror of the moon' was handed around, invoking the strength and wisdom of 'Father Moon'.

"Zarpa Nitu, dwell in our midst on this night of reunion."

Soma, the mildly alcoholic drink in the silver vessel, reflected 'Father Moon' in the starry sky.

It helped the true Gabari to connect in thought with their giant brethren of the righteous path. On this night, many Gabari in exile were engaged in moon worship.

These ceremonies were quietly tolerated in the Known World, provided that the peace was not disturbed. The true Gabari drew their strength from the silvery rays of Zarpa Nitu for their common cause. To counteract the dark forces of Edfun.

One day the giant race would reunite in noble spirit once again!

Túvar was a child of the royal line. He was being trained as Gabari leader in Cydonia. The hope of many rested on his young shoulders. Ranef was growing old now and the vigour of youth was needed in their midst.

It had come to their attention that Edfun's dark forces were on the upsurge once again. In the morning, a formal missive would be sent to the Lady of Cydonia. Tonight they celebrated.

There was no reason why Trevor and Katherine should stay. They crept gradually backwards, then turned around and walked silently on the lawn towards the street. Suddenly, Trevor bumped into an invisible wall that began cursing under its breath. He somehow managed not to let go of Katherine's hand.

"Chryséis, is that you?" Katherine called softly after the first shock.

"What on earth are *you* doing here? You gave me a heart attack!"

"Well, what do you think we're doing here?" Katherine felt relieved and angry at the same time. "How could you just run off like that?"

"Guys, keep it down. You'll get us into trouble!"

"They can't see us, Trevor," Chryséis said.

"Right, okay..." he said. "Why are we standing around here - invisible - and yelling at each other?"

"Let's go back to the house then," Katherine suggested crossly. "I'd like to shake you, Chryséis Cromwell and look at you while I'm doing it."

"Phew Katie, don't be so cross. I was just taking a walk and you were sleeping."

"Told you so," Trevor said. Katherine ignored him.

"You could have been kidnapped. I was worried."

"Sorry."

"You can apologize back at the house! Now move," Katherine said in the general direction of Chryséis's voice and pulled on Trevor's hand.

"Ouch," he complained.

"Hey, how do I know, I'm not running into you again?" Chryséis asked meekly.

"Give me your hand," Trevor said. "And don't you dare fight on the way back!" He groped through the air and got hold of Chryséis's wrist.

A lone vimaan with light bars in front and the rear illuminated the street and passed the park in silence. The children hid behind a hedge, forgetting that they were invisible. Once they were back at the house without seeing anybody else, Katherine flew at Chryséis.

"How could you just sneak out like that?" She had tears in her eyes. "You could have at least left a message. This isn't summer camp you know."

"Hold your horses, Katie. I'm guilty as charged," Chryséis tried to defend herself. "I know it's not summer camp."

"So why *did* you go for a walk in the middle of night?"

"I was sleepwalking. Don't know why the invisibility device was switched on. Lucky," Chryséis admitted. "I woke up outside in the street and saw Túvar, the giant boy. He was on his way to the park. There was singing and I was curious and followed him. Sorry," she closed her defence-speech.

"You were sleepwalking?" Katherine remembered finding Chryséis on the rug in their room at Pemberton.

"Yes, I sometimes sleepwalk when I'm stressed. It started when Mom had Jason and Cassie in hospital. I was little and missed her so much."

"Why didn't you say something before?"

"It's embarrassing."

"*That* could give us some problems here. Can't you control that? An expedition isn't exactly stress-free," Trevor said.

"I don't know. Maybe."

"We could ask the Lady of Cydonia. Perhaps she can help," Katherine suggested.

"We can try." Trevor changed the subject. "What were the giants doing in the park?"

"They must belong to some cult. It was a ceremony to do with the moon. Fascinating, don't you think?!"

"The neighbours didn't seem to mind. You can't tell me that nobody heard them singing, except for us."

"Who knows?" Chryséis shrugged her shoulders. "Let's go to sleep, I'm beat."

"Yes okay, we'll talk tomorrow."

*

That night, far to the north beyond the Alesian border, a group of other giants were performing a different kind of ceremony. They were Edfunian warlords and had everything but good intentions.

Drums boomed deeply and rhythmically within the cold fortress walls of Shuruk. The bare yard was illuminated with the dancing flames of torches planted around the altar.

Their ruler, the terrible Highpriest of Shuruk, brandished the ritual knife dripping with blood. The sorcerer's headdress was made of red copper.

His forehead under matted hair was tattooed with a black spider, his back hunched under a heavy leather armour. Tattoos on his arms were almost covered by the sleeves of a black tunic. Although the copper disk reflected the moonlight, these Gabari did not worship 'Father Moon'.

The black bull on the altar stone writhed in the last throes of death. Blood, the symbolic life force, ran down a stone groove into a bowl of beaten copper.

The Highpriest dipped a crude copper chalice into the blood and handed it to one of his towering apprentices. It would be kept for later use.

The moon shed cold white light on the malevolent scene. The torches flickered in a sharp gust of wind as the Highpriest invoked *Xipe Xolotle*, the fierce planet Mars. He presented the life force of the powerful animal to the merciless red god of warfare.

Pronouncing a terrible spell meant to intercept the silvery forces of 'Father Moon' and to tear apart the treacherous alliance of Gabari exiles.

'Father Moon' was after all only a feeble old man of a god. He was revered by the equally weak Gabari traitors in enemy lands.

Zarpa Nitu was unfit to aid the leaders of Edfun in their righteous endeavour to gain power. The merciless force of the Red God was what they wanted.

"Forgive us 'Lord of Warfare'. This poor sacrifice is unworthy of you," the sorcerer apologised. "We'll soon have better fare."

Edfunian spies had reported the arrival of three young and strong foreigners in Cydonia yesterday. Their origin was Unclear, yet they seemed to hold extraordinary importance to the Lady of Cydonia.

This status imbued them with a most desirable energy. The timing was perfect.

Just as Ranef, the leader of the Gabari in Cydonia, the Highpriest of Shuruk chanted in the ancient dialect of the 'Great Ones'. It had been used in rituals since the remote Golden Age. Suddenly, the sorcerer's voice rose in a booming invocation.

"Adhiyajñah katham ko 'tra
 dehé asmin
Jñeyah asi Prayāna kāle?"
"Lord of sacrifice, how can you be
known in this body
at the time of death?"

The giant warlords, who were looking on, answered with a blood-curdling war cry.

"Ari-sūdana!"

"As killer of enemies!"

The fearsome giants shook their mighty weapons above their heads and bellowed in triumph. The sorcerer's assistants swiftly cut the carcass into pieces. Then the bloodied meat was carried to the drawbridge in an eerie procession.

Small stone igloos stood on either side of the bridge. Large female tarantulas were housed in the two dolmens, tasked with guarding the fortress of Shuruk.

Pieces of meat were heaped in front of the dolmens. The monstrous spiders didn't lose any time. They crawled over the sacrifice and started spinning.

The brutal faces of the warlords were mere grimaces in the flickering torchlight. The giant tarantulas pulled the white parcels into their stony igloos.

The torches flamed higher and brighter as if to mock an unwilling moon. It had been done. The Red God had accepted the sacrifice! Their undertaking would be blessed by *Xipe Xolotle*!

Again the thunderous battle cry rose and like-minded Edfunians outside the fortress walls joined in.

"Ari-sùdana!"

Xipe Xolotle would be even more pleased tomorrow. Three innocents were just what were needed for their purpose.

"Ari-sùdana!"

"Ari-sùdana!"

▶▶▶ 19 THE INCIDENT AT THE MARKET

Without delay, the Lady of Cydonia had given orders to abandon the search for the foreign children's parents. Harun and his family did not quite understand why, but did not question the ruler's wisdom.

They would take care of their young guests then, until they left with Kheton and Lelani. It would be an honour.

After the wedding, the time travellers had to report for a medical examination at the 'House of Life' before they could attend the citadel school for two phases of the moon.

In the meantime they tried to stay out of the way. The wedding preparations at the house had reached fever-pitch.

"Why not explore the citadel grounds some more?" Chryséis suggested.

"Okay, let's go to the amphitheatre, then. I've always wanted to see one."

"Okay," Trevor said and lifted himself lazily from the bench. They were busy watching a children's choir rehearse in the citadel garden, when Katherine's virtual invisibility device slipped. She touched the button - and disappeared!

"Katie!" Chryséis hissed.

"What?"

"You're i n v i s i b l e —"

"Oh dear..."

Lucky that nobody had noticed the sudden vanishing of the foreign girl. Something like that could be mistaken for dark sorcery or *'obeah'*. Bad news in Alesia. They had learned that much.

"Wow, good you were standing behind that azalea bush!" Chryséis said.

They were walking over to the amphitheatre, where some orchestra was practising.

"I'll say."

"Just remember to always use your left hand to steady the VID. The button's on the right. Steady left, button right."

"Okay, I'll remember."

After a while, they went back to Alun's house. They took the path through the back garden.

"It's probably better to leave them in our daypacks under the bed anyway," Trevor said, when they were alone in the girls' room.

"Do you think it's safe without the VIDs?"

"Why not? The Cydonians only have a problem with us, if we do something weird like disappearing and so on."

"I think we should take them with."

"Okay, but be careful. Steady left, button right."

"Sure thing."

They practised some telepathy and this time Trevor even managed to pick up a thought from Chryséis.

Soon, they were summoned to the Lady's quarters. Pomegranate juice and walnut cookies were already on the table. This time the Lady of Cydonia told them her own adventures as a time traveller in the future. She had managed to travel into the future! Thousands of years... they were stunned.

During one of her trips, she had travelled to medieval Italy with her friend, the Lady of Algiras.

After sharing their views on poor living conditions of the people with professors and students at the University of Padua, the women had been accused of witch craft. Cruel punishment was threatened as they were taken to the dungeons. The two women didn't lose any time.

"It caused quite a stir when the two witches all of a

sudden disappeared on their way to prison," the Lady laughed.

"But, wasn't it dangerous?" Katherine asked. "They could have tortured - or killed you!"

"We had to speak out. Their opinions were just so wrong. Imagine our planet is flat and education is only for rich men! Everybody else is inferior."

"But... they could have taken your time travel device away."

"Our devices are very different to yours. The guards would not have known what they were looking at."

They listened in fascination as the Lady of Cydonia told them how she had also made the acquaintance of Red Indians. At first, the tribe had been frightened of the strange woman in the shiny dress, who appeared and disappeared at will. Eventually they had reluctantly welcomed the Lady as a supernatural spirit.

After this, she had travelled many sheaves of years farther into the future. In the year 1967 in the city of New York, love and peace had seemed to be rather important values.

"Twenty years later, the pursuit of money and power was clearly more important, despite an improved technology. Yet there is hope for coming generations. In the year 2034..." The Lady stopped herself abruptly.

"Yes—" Chryséis couldn't wait to hear it.

"Oh, I must not get carried away with my story..."

"Why not?"

"To talk about your own future would do you no good."

That was all the Lady of Cydonia was willing to say about the children's own future, no matter how much they begged her to reveal more. They were disappointed. The Lady would also not say, how time travel into the future worked.

"Everything in its own good time," she said.

Later, Chryséis made secret recordings of musicians

playing in the hall at Alun's house. There were two flautists and a harpist, who also played the lyre. A drummer with two tablas and a bard. Apparently it was his job to tease the bridal couple with banter.

Katherine listened to her favourite girlie band on the lawn behind the house through her earphones.

She was humming to the songs while she jotted something down on the exam pad. The pen with the fluffy green feather cheered her up. It was a present from her Aunt Trudie, Mom's younger sister. Katherine remembered that Aunt Trudie liked science fiction movies. She'd surely find Katherine's trip into the past real cool...

Trevor came to tell her that Alun's mother needed a few things from the market. Alun had to purchase this and that at the Moti Market in the centre of town.

"He asked if we wanted to come with him."

"Okay sure. Let's go," Katherine said.

This time there was no sightseeing. The centre of Cydonia was ultramodern with its glistening, conical towers. A park circled the curious buildings, separating the inner city from the suburbs. Four main roads crossed the green and the segments were connected by pedestrian bridges. Paved footpaths made it easy to walk around the lakes. One could also play sports on one of the fields or simply rest on a bench.

No vehicles were allowed in the park and Alun landed his vimaan close to the inner edge right by the market place.

Alun showed his new friends quickly a special attraction right next to the sports fields. A number of large footprints, called 'Giant's Leap'.

Millennia ago a Titan and a dinosaur had run next to each other on soft sand. The footprints had turned to stone. They were found under a layer of limestone when the city was built. Scientists were sure that they had tried to escape an erupting volcano.

Alun tried to tell the story with lots of gestures and they could sort of follow the exciting story. Unbelievable. School kids were swarming all over the rock, touching and standing in the three-toed dinosaur footprints.

Then Alun led the way across a bridge to the domed buildings at the market square. Outdoor stalls were arranged around a large fountain.

Just as they passed a cake stall, the shoppers burst into merry song. Alun did not seem in the slightest bit surprised. He explained to his startled friends that one of the customers was simply praising the taste of a particular cake. So everyone had started singing a popular song about baking a cake.

At least that's what they understood.

The market was busy. Alun moved swiftly between throngs of people. The time travellers tried to keep up with him. There was not much time to explore the fascinating sights. Many people bought candles, incense and little fish-shaped oatcakes for an Alesian holiday. Typical offerings to Nereus, the god of water and his daughters, the Nereids.

Alesians still thanked the gods for the rescue of their ancestors from the salty waters, when Atland had broken apart and sunk to the bottom of the sea.

In one of the market halls of the 'Moti Market' the floors and walls were made of polished, beige stone. Much like a fancy train station. The transparent têrakhon dome let in sunlight onto a floor inlay. The half-sun-half-moon symbol of Alesia.

The Lady had told them that it joined the sun sign of Alesia with the moon sign of the 'Children of the Moon'.

Shopping was done in no time and just as they were on their way out, they heard screaming nearby. A young man stuffed under his shirt tried to run away with it. Stealing in Cydonia? Why? The shoppers were confused and amid much pushing and shoving a strange thing happened.

Strong hands grabbed the time travellers and lodged themselves onto their faces. The children moved through the air towards the open doors. Alun stared in shock and pointed at them, unable to speak. Nobody else seemed to take notice. The thief on the other side of the building was the centre of attention.

Everything seemed to go according to plan for the giant kidnappers. But they had not counted on an angry Chryséis. She bit hard and the big hand flew from her face with a groan. Chryséis started kicking and screamed as loud as she could.

"Aaaaahhh! Let me go, let me go…Aaahhh… Let me go!!"

Her high-pitched cries carried over the general confusion. High up in the air, they were already close to the entrance. People coming to their aid were flung aside.

At last, more heads turned and everyone took notice of the foreign children, hanging limply in the air, flying towards the exit. Obeah at work! Theft was despicable enough, but who would want to harm innocent children with black magic like that?

They got ready to help the children. The Edfunians quickly checked that they were indeed still invisible. The amulets they wore around their necks were still there, so everything they touched should disappear as well. But obviously those rotten Alesians could see the foreign children!

They had been ordered telepathically to abduct them. The intense blue eyes of the cunning Highpriest of Shuruk had left them no choice. The children were needed as sacrifice for Xipe Xolotle, the cruel 'Red God of War'. Now this!

A wall of Alesians gathered around, too many to fling aside. And now the heavy têrakhon doors were being closed before them. The mission had to be abandoned! They had failed their Highpriest, their country and their god. But the Alesians would not find out the truth.

The henchmen took to flight. The large invisible hands

holding Chryséis loosened their grip, and she dropped onto the polished stone floor.

Chryséis cried out as a stabbing pain shot through her ankle. Then the other two children dropped to the ground. They rolled to the side, but seemed unharmed. A flash outside was the last sign of the kidnappers.

The Alesian onlookers were stunned. *Obeah*, black magic! Here! Was this the work of Edfun? Peace had prevailed for many sheaves of years...

A protective circle formed around the children on the ground. A woman sat with Chryséis until a medic arrived.

"There, there, it'll be fine. Help is coming," she kept saying.

Market guards tried to locate the culprits, but they had long fled the scene. In any case, the guards were trained to control the proper use of weights, tender and the quality of products. Chasing after invisible kidnappers was not exactly part of their job description.

A medic arrived and examined Chryséis's ankle, which was just sprained. She was treated on the spot with a healing device. A calming drink of recutis restored the three children soon.

Alun was questioned by the guards, but could only state the obvious. "The children moved through the air - towards the doors. Then Chryséis screamed and they all dropped to the ground," he stammered.

A report needed to be sent to the citadel administration. Three of the children were obviously foreigners, under the protection of the Lady of the citadel. The older boy was from Cydonia. Mysterious, the whole thing.

Shoppers were thanked for their support. Everyone went about their own business. But the air was still buzzing with questions. Why had the abductors been invisible? What could they possibly want from foreign children? Was Edfun behind the incident?

Yes, Edfun had to be right here in Cydonia! A ripple of unease went through the crowd. Cydonians would have to be on their heed from now on.

The hapless thief was apprehended on a street corner not far from the market hall. He turned out to be a young scribe in the service of an Alesian merchant. He had been sent to the market to purchase oatcakes and incense for the festival. He looked bewildered when questioned about the theft.

"I have no need for a statue of the Earthmother!" He was embarrassed to be accused of stealing. The last thing he could remember was the sight of compelling blue eyes and - a black spider above them.

That evening a more sinister theft was discovered. One of the noble horses at the Cydonian testing station had disappeared from the pasture after dark. Gobän, the centaur, had been gravely hurt while trying to protect his charges. One precious stallion was taken, but how it had been possible, could not be explained.

In the afternoon, nobody knew anything about the theft, as Túvar was still at work.

Alun's family sat around the dining room table and listened to the kidnapping-story. What in the name of the Earthmother could anyone want with the Lady's young protégés? How shocking an incident!

A sad Túvar arrived late and told them about the stolen horse. Father Harun quickly made the connection between the kidnapping attempt and the stallion. Edfun was on the rise again!

He instructed his adopted son to guard the young guests, since he was the only Gabari in the family. They understood that Túvar was to act as their bodyguard and felt a little safer for it.

After dinner, Túvar accompanied them to the back of the house and settled for the night on the spare bed in Trevor's room. They held an emergency meeting under the watchful eye of the giant boy.

"What do we do now?" Chryséis asked and sat down next

to Trevor.

"I'm scared. They were invisible. What if they come back?"

"The Lady of Cydonia will protect us," Trevor said with confidence.

"How do we know that?" Katherine snapped.

"I trust her."

"So why did they try to kidnap us in the first place?"

"It wasn't the Alesians."

"Who was it then?"

"We'll have to find out. Harun said something about Edfunians."

"Edfun again!"

"I don't care who it was. We should just leave now."

"How? The Lady has our TPFs and Túvar is watching us like a fox," Trevor warned.

"Then what? We can't just steal the TPFs. We don't even know where they are," Katherine moaned.

"You're right!"

"And Kheton's wedding is tomorrow," Chryséis said. They couldn't leave just now! The Lady of Cydonia surely knew about the incident at the market and she would protect them as she had promised.

20 THE WEDDING

The following morning, Chryséis woke up to loud noise and music in the yard. She rubbed her eyes.

"Wake up, Katherine. It's the wedding."

"What?"

"The wedding. Get up!" Chryséis said.

It took the girls no time to get ready. It took Trevor a little longer. Túvar had left early without waking the young house guests.

Chryséis was getting impatient and wanted to see what was going on outside. As they walked through the passage, they saw Alun and Túvar standing by the fountain behind the house, dressed all in white. They were handing out red and turquoise ribbons to arriving guests.

"Shelanti athenai. Come and join us!" Alun laughed and tied a turquoise ribbon around Katherine's wrist. Today, they wanted to forget about dangerous Edfun.

The bridegroom's entourage arrived. They brought with them a citadel maiden official called Oruwen. She would perform the 'joining ceremony'.

The celebrations started off with the riotous 'bringing home' ritual. Nobody remembered where it came from, but it was great fun.

Drums sounded a repetitive rhythm, as the play was enacted in the front yard. The veiled bride was directed to the bridegroom waiting outside the gate. Only to be kidnapped by a large monkey. It was hilarious. The screeching ape was chased down and the bride rescued to much hullabaloo and laughter. The monkey was of course a friend of Kheton's in an ape costume.

The laughing couple was led toward the house, hung with garlands of flowers and sprinkled with rose-scented water. Lelani wore a flowery headdress, called the maidenhead.

She had spent months embroidering her burgundy dress. The groom sported a narrow headband and was dressed in a splendid white tunic and trousers.

A choir received them in the entrance hall with a hauntingly beautiful tune. Then the official ceremony began.

The maiden Oruwen held an impressive speech about the meaning of married life and one's role in the community. Then she tied the couple's wrists together with the red ribbons of matrimony.

They walked several times around a fire, lit in a polished metal bow, to much applause by the guests. It was Alun's job to throw herbs into the flames every time they completed one round.

After the last round they put a sweetmeat in each other's mouths to symbolize an easy life together. Then the maidenhead, made of large red and pink bataleia flowers, was taken off and handed to the bride's father. It was replaced for the day with a traditional circlet of polished crystals.

"Atri idam arpaṇam," Kheton recited.

"Here, take this offering."

After the placing of the marital crown, the couple received new suits with red stripes along the hems. The sign of matrimony. They nodded and were seated at the head of the big dining room table.

The squares in the middle were now filled with water. Flowers and candles floated on top. The joining ceremony was complete and the maiden Oruwen took her leave. The marriage needed to be recorded on the eastern wall of the citadel, for all citizens to see.

Platters of delicious food were brought in and Kheton's

mother received much praise with a proud smile. She showed good manners by pointing to the aunts, who had helped with the preparations.

The stuffed ptarmigan was deposited in the middle of the table. The guests made merry with jokes on the groom, before the band started performing wedding songs.

No Alesian celebration was complete without a sing-along and individual recitals. Almost like karaoke. When it was her turn, Chryséis belted out 'Greensleeves' to well-meaning laughter and applause. "Alas my love, you do me wrong…"

The wedding guests were fascinated by the strange words. Although their meaning was unknown, everybody soon joined in the refrain.

"Gweensleeves was allmajoye…"

Trevor didn't want to be a spoilsport and sang his favourite tune from the musical 'Hair' as best as he could. Katherine on the other hand felt too self-conscious to participate.

She slunk away through the entrance hall and towards the yard, when nobody was looking. Large eggs, stained bright red, were hanging on the walls as a symbol of prosperity. Perhaps they were ostrich eggs, they were so big… the answer would have been quite a surprise.

Somebody followed her quietly outside. In the failing light, she saw plants in terracotta containers along the garden wall. The red and white fruits the size of cherry tomatoes. The ground under the tree was swept clean of leaves and walnut buds. Later it would serve as a dance floor.

From a table, Katherine took a drink of home-made ginger beer and a piece of cake and watched red and turquoise streamers swaying in the breeze.

She took a deep breath. Ah, to take a break from everything was bliss. The memory of being transported through the air by an invisible giant crossed her mind. But she pushed the thought aside. Not now!

She took a bite of the cake and leaned against the walnut tree closing her eyes for a moment. The mild evening air was filled with the sweet scent of flowers and the rich flavours of wedding dishes.

Katherine didn't notice Túvar, hovering in the shadows. He kept a watchful eye on the children even in the midst of the wedding revelry.

Soon, lamps were lit all over the garden. Ribald music and song burst through the open windows and feet were tapping irresistibly to the beat. The musicians moved outside into the illuminated the garden followed by a happy procession of dancing guests.

Young women in red veils started twirling around and waved red handkerchiefs. A couple of youngsters grabbed Katherine by the arm, spilling her ginger beer.

Soon they were spinning and jiving around the couple and proceeded to dance around the house. Katherine's quiet moment had passed.

"Did you get some pictures?" Chryséis asked Trevor.

"Yip..." He made sure that the little camera didn't fall out of his shirt pocket, while being twirled around by two elderly matrons.

Kheton and Lelani left for the peninsula of Kalkan with the first rays of the morning sun. There was still eating, drinking and singing until the early hours of the morning.

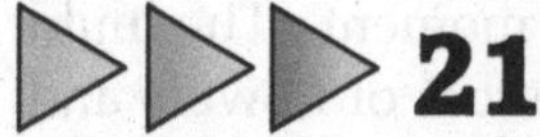 **21**   THE HOUSE OF LIFE

Chryséis, Katherine and Trevor were waiting for an audience with the Lady of Cydonia. They needed to speak to her urgently. About what had happened at the market and their travel plans. Túvar was hanging around somewhere near the stairwell. Afterwards, they had an appointment at the 'House of Life'.

The time travellers knew by now that the House of Life on the citadel grounds was tasked with the health of all life forms.

"She seems busy today," Katherine said after a while.

"No wonder, something's wrong with that country up north," Trevor said. "I hope there'll be peace as long as we're here."

"Mhmm." Katherine didn't quite listen. She studied a wall hanging that showed a tree with golden apples on the opposite wall.

"I can't wait to go to the citadel school," Chryséis suddenly said. "Imagine, a school in prehistory."

"I hope we learn the language there," Trevor said.

"Yip, about time."

"But if we can't travel anymore, it's pointless," Katherine sighed.

Soon the Lady was ready to see them. Túvar watched them enter the room. Then he posted himself next to the door.

"I apologize on behalf of all righteous Alesians for the distress caused to you at the market," the ruler of Cydonia said before they could get a word out. Of course, she already knew the reason for their visit.

"I hope, your ankle is fully healed," she said to Chryséis.

Chryséis nodded. "Yes thank you for asking. But please explain, why somebody tried to kidnap us. It was real scary."

"I will try to explain the situation as much as possible."

She told them about the war-like giants Edfun, about the 'Great Ones' and that Túvar was the heir of the royal lineage of true Gabari.

"Túvar?" Katherine whistled admiringly.

"So Túvar is a prince, really," Chryséis said.

"I suppose you could say that."

"But what do they want with us, these Edfunians?" Trevor asked.

"It is possible that the Highpriest of Shuruk learned about your presence in Cydonia under my protection. He must have thought you important enough to use in his scheming. He is a sorcerer you know."

"You mean he wanted to kidnap us and blackmail you... or kill us?"

"I'm sorry to say that it is possible. The Highpriest of Shuruk is a sly and wicked person. In spite of this, his subjects are devoted to him. There are spies in our midst and we cannot always intercept their thoughts. He is also shielding his fortress in Shuruk."

"Oh, brilliant. I'm feeling much better now." Trevor was being sarcastic. The thought of having an evil sorcerer as their adversary wasn't exactly encouraging.

Chryséis tried to be practical. "How do we protect ourselves then?"

"Many are looking out for your safety, but I implore you to avoid large congregations for the time being. Túvar will follow you around while you are in Cydonia. He has been informed of your identity as much as he needed to know."

So the giant boy knew that they had arrived from the future and were not abandoned by their parents.

"Is it safe enough for us, Lady, or should we rather come back some other time?" Chryséis asked.

"If you heed my advice, it will be safe enough."

"We'll have to think about the whole thing. And the bit about travelling."

"Of course." The Lady answered a few more questions about Edfun and the Sorcerer of Shuruk, then she asked Túvar to escort them to the 'House of Life'. It was time for their medical check-up.

Túvar seemed a little in awe of them and they caught him staring once or twice, wondering perhaps if they were for real.

The physician maiden and her assistants already waited in one of the round buildings. The 'House of Life' consisted of a whole cluster of such small round buildings. Patients sat waiting outside for their treatment.

The medics wore jade-coloured tunics with white and turquoise stripes along the hems. Down the front, the tunics were decorated with intertwining snakes.

"Shelanti athenai."

"Shelanti."

Katherine stared at the snakes. Strange decorations for medics, she thought. They were prompted with gestures to lie down on narrow beds. The medics then moved devices over the children's bodies and discussed the results with the physician maiden.

Katherine had a slight cough and a young man held a healing device above her chest area. To her great amazement, she felt the scratchy feeling in her throat subside.

Suddenly, the Lady of Cydonia appeared in the door frame. She was greeted respectfully by the medics.

"Shelanti, Honourable Lady!"

"Shelanti athenai!"

The medics interrupted their work and waited patiently, while the Lady first addressed the physician maiden, then spoke to the children in their strange language.

"I cannot stay long, but wish to ensure, that you understand the procedures correctly," she said.

"That's nice of you." Katherine couldn't think of anything else to say. They sat up and listened. This could be interesting.

"The examination device uses electromagnetic waves to detect any disruption of the natural energy flow within the body – and the mind for that matter. The correct wavelength is chosen to rectify the problem, should there be one." She picked up the second slightly larger device.

"With this device, we are able to heal almost any type of disturbance. From broken bones to tumours, the balancing of glands or infections. You have already witnessed the healing of a harpee bite, which is a relatively simple intervention."

"You can do all of that with electromagnetic waves?"

"Roughly speaking."

"How is that possible?"

"The body's self-healing ability is stimulated," the Lady explained. "Fast tracking, so to speak. Herbal medicines help with the healing. It depends on the gravity and type of the condition."

She put the instrument back on the table.

"We neither wish to poison nor cut bodies in an attempt to rid them of disease, if it can be avoided."

"Wow," Trevor said.

The Lady smiled. She took a bottle with a dark liquid and shook it slightly. The medicine had just been prepared for Katherine's cough.

"Special herbs are grown in our gardens, some are imported." She handed the bottle to one of the assistant medics.

"But how can you tell, which harmonics to use?" Chryséis demanded to know.

"My dear, these methods have been in use for a very long time. Thanks to the wisdom of the true Gabari, we still have their ancient methods available to us."

"But what about modern medicine? It's quite advanced as well... mostly," Trevor said. "What about x-rays and MRIs and brain surgery?"

"Rest assured that your scientists will soon discover similar methods to these. Perhaps even in your own lifetime." For the first time they were given a glimpse into their future.

"Right." It wasn't quite the answer he had expected.

The Lady of Cydonia conferred with the physician in a low voice and then explained further.

"See here, Trevor." The Lady pointed to a small bump on Trevor's left arm. "You broke this arm in a fall at about six years of age. We'll readjust the energy flow in your arm to help you regain its full use."

"Okay." Could they find out all these details with a device?

The physician maiden made a few adjustments to the healing tool and moved it over Trevor's arm. He felt a slight tingling that lasted for a few minutes.

"Chryséis, dear child, you had a viral infection last year and the virus still hides inside your liver."

"Really?" Chryséis was stunned. Since that flu, she had lost her interest in sports.

"The good doctor here will deactivate the virus now and reverse the damage."

"She can do that?"

"Yes. This will also help with your headaches and a special tea will strengthen your immune system. And Katherine, your cough medicine is right here in this bottle. One spoonful three times a day."

The Lady handed her the little têrakhon bottle with the dark liquid, she had shaken earlier.

"One last thing. The condition of your teeth is not ideal. Caused by incorrect diet and cleaning practices. The medics will take steps to regrow the enamel and the dentin underneath. The fillings will become superfluous. Don't be afraid, it will not hurt."

"That sounds amazing." Trevor was stunned by everything he heard.

Katherine sighed. She loved chocolate and cake just too much.

"A slight discomfort occurs and you must refrain from

eating for a few hours after each procedure," the Lady said. Nothing new there.

The physician maiden smiled encouragingly, guessing at what the Lady had just told her young patients.

"Thank you good medics," the Lady of Cydonia spoke to the health workers in Alesian and nodded appreciatively. Then she continued in English.

"I must leave now. Once the treatment is finished, I expect to see you again. I will teach you some basic Alesian."

The children nodded. "Okay, that sounds good."

"Shelanti all."

"Shelanti, Honourable Lady. Shelanti."

Soon the youngsters were on their way to the Lady's quarters again. Their teeth were itching, but other than that they felt good. Tonight, they would write everything down they had seen and heard today.

"We should take before and after pictures of our teeth, " Trevor suggested.

"Mhm. It's nice of her to spend so much time with us," Chryséis said.

"Maybe we're that important."

"Yeah sure, terribly important." Katherine rolled her eyes at Trevor.

They walked between grassy sports fields, where groups of children played curious ball games.

Singing and laughter came from one of the buildings. They would join them tomorrow. But they needed to understand more of the language in order to follow their teachers. And they had much more to learn.

In Alesia, every child enjoyed a good education. A small school and kindergarten adjoined the local library in each district. Teachers were held in high esteem by the community. Alesians believed that their offspring held the key to the future and needed to be nurtured.

Careful guidance ensured a happy new generation. According to individual ability, sports were played by boys and girls alike. A subject called 'life in the community' was taught early on. Spoken and written Alesian, mathematics, science and artistic expression were added in due course. Later on, other subjects were taught according to inclination and choice of profession. Alesians were a sophisticated and well-skilled people.

"We still have to talk about what we'll do. The Lady wants to know if we want to stay or not," Chryséis suggested.

A garden bench was nearby.

"Okay, let's sit down and talk. What do you think?" Trevor said.

They debated, while Túvar kept a watchful eye. It didn't take them long to come to a decision.

They went through the Lady's private garden back to the audience room. This time, they were allowed to enter immediately.

"Dear Lady of Cydonia," Katherine said without much ado. "We have decided to stay."

Chryséis and Trevor nodded in agreement and the Lady just smiled. Clearly, she already knew.

Now, their first language lesson could begin.

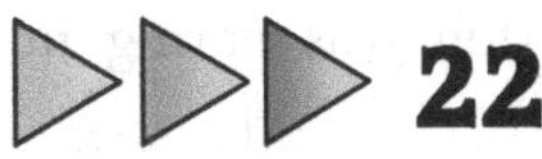 **22**   # LESSONS IN TIME

"Parâṇi manah," teacher Adami praised Katherine. "Very good memory."

Katherine beamed. Things were beginning to make sense. It was well into their first week at the citadel school and the crash course in Alesian began to pay off.

The time travellers could now say simple sentences like 'How do I get to the market, please?' and 'Thank you, the concert was wonderful'.

They were making steady progress, but Alesian was a lot easier to understand than to speak, never mind read or write. Despite that, Chryséis added new words to her glossary every day.

They liked school. Lessons were short - only about 20 minutes - and the teachers were nice too and never yelled at all. They liked especially the maiden Oruwen, who taught plant lore.

She made jokes they didn't understand, but her classes were always upbeat. Túvar was older, of course, but he always sat at the back of the room. He took this guard-thing really seriously!

Alun attended a much more advanced class, but they saw him often during break-time.

"What did you learn today?" He would ask and they had to tell him in Alesian. Then he chatted to Túvar for a while.

Many things that Alesians took for granted were still a mystery to the young time travellers. Physics for example. Not the same as good old physics at home. In Alesia, there were different dimensions to deal with.

On the plus side, they had already learned how to

prepare a bone knit-pack in an emergency situation. They had also studied the basic rules of civilised law and some mathematics and astronomy. Pemberton was boring in comparison.

They practised their mind-reading as often as possible and the Lady insisted on teaching them some subjects personally, as her busy schedule allowed. History for example. This morning, the Lady of Cydonia was going to tell them about recent earth history. Recent in prehistoric Alesian terms. They couldn't wait.

"We'd like to learn more about your world," Trevor said in halting Alesian.

"Very good, my friend," the Lady of Cydonia praised him. "Well said."

"Shukri. Thank you," he answered politely.

"Let us begin with the lesson without delay." She spoke English now. "I understand that you are familiar with virtual images in your own time. If I remember correctly you call such images 'motion pictures'." She pronounced the word slightly exaggerated.

"Yes that's right," they laughed. Movies were after all virtual images...

"You will not be too surprised then, if I show you 'motion pictures' or *mirages* as we call them. Unlike our good man Gunniva, who hid behind his chair, believing them to be the devil's work."

No wonder if he was from the 16th century. Imagine, prehistoric movies! Poor guy.

"I think, we're alright with that," said Chryséis.

"These are silent movies, allowing the teacher to speak," the Lady said. She took one of five short rolls from a shelf against the wall.

The rolls were similar to the ones in Alun's living room. The Lady of Cydonia put the roll into a wall socket and in the middle of the room a holographic image came to life. The children oohed and aahed.

"Much knowledge has been lost over time, but I'd like to share with you what we still understand."

They gaped at the moving 3-D images. This was so cool!

"The first mirage shows how much the continents have changed in the past millennia. This is a short demonstration used at schools."

She explained the animated maps, which appeared before them. Coloured areas that moved and shifted. The Lady pointed to a red continent in the Pacific Ocean, wrapping itself around the African 'Cape of Good Hope' and stretching into the Atlantic Ocean.

"This gigantic landmass over here is the continent of *Mûr*. It hosted civilised nations many aeons ago. Mûr occupied most of the Pacific Ocean, which is called the Still Ocean in our time."

That was hard to believe! There was hardly anything there.

Before Trevor could ask what had happened with all that land, she said, "sadly, there is not much left of this magnificent land. Some islands remain, the peaks of once great mountain ranges. Underwater volcanoes caused Mûr to sink rapidly to the bottom of the sea, burying its civilisation beneath the waves."

Lava shot into the air and boiling water swallowed broken rocks that had been tossed into the maelstrom. A city, built of black lava-blocks sank in all this chaos. In complete silence. Then, the hologram suddenly disappeared.

"Many rises and declines of landmasses happened in earth history. Some in living memory," the Lady explained further. "If one landmass sinks, another one rises through the sheer pressure. This often creates stark mountains."

They sat with their mouths open. Did she mean the Alps and the Himalayas? But the Lady did not stop to answer.

"Patches of coastland in Pushkara, or what you call South America, rose abruptly to heights never seen before, then fell and rose again in a matter of days. Such elevated land, like the Tepuis Highland, can still be found in your own time."

The hologram supported this with riveting visuals. Seawater gushed off such flat mountains before they sank back into the ocean again.

"Some believe that such catastrophes were punishment for the wicked ways of humankind," the Lady said.

"How can that be?" questioned Trevor.

"It may seem unlikely to you, but in our culture we believe that evil thought forms of greed and violence may unleash forces too powerful to control."

Evil thought forms? The children were horrified. They had more than enough of those in modern times.

"Amongst other things. As you know, flooding will afflict the Known World. In about 500 years from now - in your reckoning. The oceans will overflow and cover most of our great coastal cities and fertile land for many years to come."

Of course, the young scientists knew about such floods, but that cities had perished in the process was new to them. The Lady of Cydonia had travelled to the future and knew what she was talking about. Awful.

Katherine scribbled excitedly notes on her exam pad.

"The reasons for this have not been established yet, but the authorities of the day will save our civilisation, if they choose to heed the warnings."

"But haven't they done so? I mean we are here, but..." Katherine was dumbfounded.

"The future can still shift, only the past is established."

"That's scary."

"It basically means, one can influence the future from this time, but not from our future, because then it's already in the past."

"Basically."

"Hopefully, nothing crazy happens in the meantime," Trevor said and shook himself.

"One can only hope."

A song drifted over from the school buildings, but the three friends hardly paid attention to the lovely melody. They had to concentrate.

"Distant memories of a 'Golden Age' have survived as legends to this day. Entire libraries were found in underground caves. The books had often decayed with age, but many were still legible. Especially those made from thin metal foil or quartz-disks."

"Aha." Katherine suddenly understood the use of metal foils hanging in holders at Alun's house. She plucked up her courage and asked, "Lady, was this continent in the Pacific Ocean... Atlantis?"

"No child, *Mûr* existed in extreme antiquity. Parts of Atlantis still exist to this day. You will see for yourself."

The hologram changed again. An animation this time. A continent began to pile up in the Atlantic Ocean, seawater streaming off its edges. The continent grew larger and mountain ranges formed. All of that in fast motion!

The Lady called the continent *Atland*. Then it broke up into islands in the east, then the south. In the west a large piece, called Bresil, sank in one go.

Africa was clearly visible to the right. Europe appeared and disappeared a couple of times in the mirage. Only the northern parts, the Lady called Amoorland, remained above water. Ice-free land called *Mount Meru*, shifted farther north into the Arctic Circle

There was land where it shouldn't have been and vice versa. Asia was dominated by a large inland sea, the Lady called *Thetis*. Some islands, such as England and Sri Lanka were still joined to the mainland. The view zoomed into cities with paved roads and buildings made from large rocks.

The whole thing was mind-boggling, to say the least. It went totally against anything they had ever learned about earth history. The mirage gradually faded.

"Got it?" Trevor asked softly.

"Yes," Chryséis said in the same tone and switched the little camera off.

"This showed roughly the time around the birth and death of Atlantis."

"When was *that*?" Chryséis asked.

"Oh, about 40,000 years ago, in your reckoning."

The Lady of Cydonia sat down in her chair and poured mint tea into cups shaped like snails. She let them recover for a few moments.

"40 thousand? That's the bomb!" Chryséis blurted out. "Why don't *we* learn about stuff like that?"

The Lady changed mirage rolls. "You must give your scientists some credit, children. They try to explain the facts available to them. Much land has completely vanished into the innards of our planet. And along with it almost all traces of its civilisations."

"Holy moly! Isn't there any proof of this?" Trevor was skeptical.

"How do you prove something that no longer exists? The records have never been explored and too much has been forgotten."

"I suppose," Chryséis mumbled.

"How were those gigantic walls built?" Trevor asked.

The Lady of Cydonia laughed a little.

"That's a really good question. The Titans learned it from the 'Gods', how these large blocks were cut and transported. Obviously not that difficult if one considers the stature of those large people. The softening and hardening of solid rock was done with certain sound waves. Apparently. We understand that's how they were made to fit so tightly. Unfortunately, many wise men perished and the knowledge died with them. Our scientists are still experimenting."

She thought for a moment.

"What we do know is that certain sound waves play an important role in reducing the weight. I have received reports from Gabari engineers in *Ta Mery* - the country of Egypt in your day - who made breakthrough discoveries when it comes to the science of building."

Egypt? Pyramids perhaps? Could it really be done this way? With sound waves?

The Lady activated the next mirage. It was longer than the previous ones. "Now a little geography. This 'motion picture' will show you our beautiful Alesian country and the continents of Patala and Pushkara."

First, the mirage travelled along the western coastline of Alesia. It was largely uninhabited after recent earthquakes and flooding. The mirage showed this in riveting detail: a firestorm raged and the ground shook silently. Houses and a citadel collapsed. Ships anchored in the harbour sank in great waves or were pushed out to sea. The children shrank back in horror. It felt so real.

The Lady of Cydonia responded to their thoughts. "The western provinces were the jewels in Alesia's crown. The devastation caused great sadness to the people."

They couldn't quite get used to this mind reading thing yet and they stared at her bewildered.

The view changed and they moved through the rough Northern Territories.

"A mountain range forms the natural border with Edfun. The climate is cooler in those regions, yet people live mostly in daub and wattle huts. A few fortresses are also surrounded by such dwellings."

The mirage showed inland seas. A close-up zoomed in on one of the lakes. It was frozen over. Dense, dark pine forests covered much of the far north and glaciers hugged the flanks of mountains. Nomadic tents were huddled together on the snow-covered ground. Sled dogs were tied up outside the tents, small by Gabari standards. Could Indians be living in this cold place?

Hulking animals lumbered through a snowstorm. They looked like mammoths. Further south herds of grazing buffaloes appeared.

"The plains were once temperate. This particular one is still called the 'Valley of the Gods'."

The mirage swerved to the right and revealed the eastern coastline. The coast was rugged with soaring cliffs, white rivers flowing into the sea. The Lady of Cydonia called it the 'Saturnian Sea'. The southern seaboard was warmer and dotted with charming fishing villages. It had to be somewhere nearby. Nets were laid out to dry on beaches between upturned fishing boats. Then the wilderness became subtropical.

"That's the peninsula of Kalkan."

"Weren't Kheton and Lelani spending their honeymoon here?" They wanted to know.

"Yes, they are about here." The Lady pointed to a spot on the hologram.

A couple of larger harbours appeared, ships and many people. Then the view continued in the central parts of Alesia and moved across farmland. They'd already seen some of that. Most of the cities were also located here.

What a difference to the bleak and cold Edfun! Citadels stood out on hills amid buildings and towering structures, manicured parks, paved roads with vimaans. Just like here, in Cydonia.

"We have five major cities we call the *Pentapolis*. Fālia, Hawara, Eris, Bînah and Cydonia. Cydonia is the capital."

The Lady of Cydonia pointed out the cities.

"The Southern Continent, we call Pushkara, used to have even more great cities. Beyond the huge rainforests existed a great civilisation."

Houses and pyramid-like structures came into view, some with smaller citadels right on top. The inhabitants strolled along pavements between large rectangular basins edged with flowerbeds. Shops, similar to those in the Cydonia, were clustered around the pyramids. There were gigantic buildings and paved sports arenas.

Water flowed down the exterior of one of the pyramids and collected in the large basin in the middle of a square. Possibly for the purpose of cooling or irrigation. Much of South America was now covered in dense jungle!

But that wasn't all.

"The cities in Pushkara were connected through a road system thousands of miles above and below the ground."

Really? The image now changed to a breathtaking bird's eye's view of the countryside with roads, farms, exotic forests, lakes and rivers.

A type of airplane appeared for a few moments. It looked different to the vimaans they had seen so far. More like an elegant stealth fighter with panels in shades of blue on its broad wings.

The individual panels kept changing angles before the plane disappeared with lightening speed. Almost as if it was observing its surroundings. The Lady didn't explain this.

The scene changed and the mirage once again documented a tremendous flood. Then the western coastline began to sink and rise. The children's eyes nearly popped. It was completely different to hear about it and to actually see it.

The Lady now talked about relief expeditions to the 'Cradle of Serpents'. "In the once glorious city of Tollùn the medics help to contain the spread of disease. Serpents are actually wise people and the medics are called 'serpent skirts' by the natives. The symbol of the rod with two intertwined snakes on their tunics has no doubt something to do with it."

The hologram briefly showed the agricultural testing station of Tollùn manned by Alesian scientists. A man held up a small potato and pointed to terraced fields behind him.

"Our agricultural experts research new farming methods to avoid a famine."

Katherine still tried her hand at a sketch of the plane when the fourth and last mirage roll went into the socket.

The Lady of Cydonia now spoke about the peoples of the Alesian Epoch. "I know it might seem like a lot to take in. If you would like to take a break... "

"No, let's carry on!" Trevor called out, eyes all shiny. Chryséis gave him a worried look.

"Very well. What you see here are *Wildmen*. Mountain regions are still populated by *Wildmen* or *Konks*," the Lady explained the first images.

"As you see, some have black fur, dome-shaped heads and are rather tall. Others are covered in yellowish, long hair and have rather human faces. Others again have shorter reddish-brown hair. They are shy by nature and do not seek the proximity of humans, but are mostly harmless."

"Oh, mostly," Chryséis quipped.

"Some have even found their place in our communities and are adapting well a more civilised lifestyle."

They seriously wondered if the Sasquatch was no invention after all.

"Here we have an example of the flying people or *Nepeshai*. They are also very shy and like the 'Shadow People' can disappear at will."

A built-in virtual invisibility device! Trevor thought.

"So to speak. The Nepeshai prefer remote areas on the edge of the known world. This is Magnesia, a country bordering on Soghdiana. In Eurasia in your own time. Nepeshai like to be close to water. They often live along lake shores." The picture changed and the Lady pointed to dainty, little creatures.

"We also have nature spirits, who often occupy living things, such as springs, trees and rocks. Yes, even rocks are seen as alive."

On cue, the creatures flitted in and out of trees and rocks.

"These peoples are related to elves and fairies. *Ruta Ynis*, an island in the 'Saturnian Sea' between here and Atland, is shared by elves, fauns and monkey-like satyrs."

Monkey-like? "They may resemble monkeys, but are

very smart creatures," the Lady said. The image changed. "You have already made the acquaintance of the giant Gabari."

The massive shapes of giants, much larger than the Gabari they had met, appeared in front of a cave guarded by colossal statues. They carried boxes of some sort. Then it was already the next peoples' turn.

"Of the many *Seaborn* nations, only the *Ioannu* have survived. They once populated warm shallow oceans and can still be found in reservations along coastal waters."

The next hologram looked somewhat familiar.

"Here you see dwarfs or *Dwendis,* as we call them." The Lady pointed to a group of little people. Then the mirage morphed into a line up of humans, illustrating the change of size and features over time. There were European-looking humans, African-looking ones and Asians, who were called *Turanians.*

Another map of the Alesian Epoch appeared. All these races obviously shared the available land. African people in Europe seemed to prefer wooden houses in lakes built on poles. There were many in Africa, of course, and in Pushkara.

It was impossible to remember all the names of these different peoples.

"And these were the main races of people in our Known World." The mirage faded. Was this already the end of the lesson?

A maiden in a white tunic appeared in the doorway and exchanged whispered words with the Lady of Cydonia. She carried something slightly bulging under a simple cloth. The Lady nodded. "Shukri Nolea. Thank you. Hold it safe." Then she spoke to her visitors. "It is time for me to attend to matters that cannot wait. I shall summon you again soon, but you have to leave now. Shelanti, my young friends."

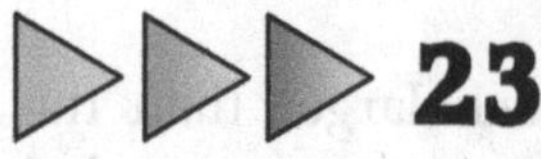

23 STOPOVER FUTURE

"Holy moly, that was some history lesson!" When they reached the bottom of the big stairs, Trevor's thoughts were still swirling around in his head. 40,000 years ago? A shifting earth crust? A recent civilisation in South America?!

"Earth history lesson," Katherine corrected him.

"Do *you* think it's true?" Chryséis asked. They were walking across the citadel square towards the big fountain. As always, Túvar was a few steps behind them.

"What, the movies she showed us?" Trevor asked absent-mindedly.

"Yes, what else?"

"I don't know. Why shouldn't it be true?"

"Who's ever heard of sunken continents?" Chryséis snorted.

"Duh! What about Atlantis?" Katherine said.

"Okay, Atlantis maybe. But that's different."

"Different, how?"

"What do we actually know about stuff like that? Diddly squat! They don't even teach you that in Pemberton!"

Túvar gave Trevor a puzzled look.

"In any case, the Lady has absolutely no reason to lie about things like that," Katherine insisted.

They passed a small hall, called the *prytaneum*. It housed the 'eternal flame of civilisation' in a raised metal basin. The front of the hall consisted of têrakhon windows. Two disk-shaped calendars were mounted to the wall behind the basin. One was golden and the other one silver. The gleaming disks were inscribed in a spiral with hieroglyphics.

The golden calendar recorded various epochs in human history, called *yugas*. The silver disk bore the details of important events since the Golden Age. They knew that much already. But the prytaneum was also important because of its 'eternal flame'. Emigrating Alesians took a lantern, lighted with the eternal flame, to the new colonies with them. The ever-burning lamps were a comforting symbol of civilisation even in the remote wilderness.

In the hall, people stood around the flame in respectful silence. Some knelt in front of the basin, praying to the Earthmother for civilisation to prevail. Hardly surprising, considering the recent problems with Edfun.

"We should have a closer look at that," Chryséis suggested.

They looked back at Túvar, pointing to the hall.

"We go there," Trevor said in bad Alesian and Túvar nodded.

As they walked towards the arched entrance, something strange happened. There was a swishing sound that seemed to be coming from everywhere. They had heard this sound before. In the vortex of the time portal. But there was no time portal! The buildings before them grew faint and disappeared into denser and denser vapour bit by bit down to their foundations.

They wanted to run away, scream - and couldn't move. The mists soon engulfed the entire courtyard. Buildings and the fountain vanished in seconds. What was happening?

The shapes of large pine trees flickered through the mist all around them. They stood rooted to the spot, staring at a faint mountain lake that appeared. The lake mirrored a blue sky where the citadel gardens had been.

The scene grew clearer. Was it a mirage again? They could feel dewy coolness rising from the water. This was no hologram!

As if all of this wasn't bad enough, something moved between the pine trees. The children huddled together on the ground. A very large bear with two cuddly brown cubs charged through the shrubbery. The bears were on their way to lunch on the abundant fish buffet in the lake. But something was wrong.

The shaggy mother bear stopped in her tracks to sniff the air. Her long snout quivered as she detected danger. The animal heaved itself up on powerful hind legs to full, frightening height and growled through menacing fangs. Her curved, black claws sliced the air. The cubs squeaked and instantly bolted back into the undergrowth. The children gasped. There was a muffled scream. The bears were only feet away.

A rather large butterfly appeared above the lake, then another one. The butterflies seemed to stand still in the air, observing the scene. The children squinted at the strange creatures. Were they butterflies at all?

Another loud growl caught their attention again. They screamed and the mother bear made ready to lunge. She took off, flying toward them.

The scene faded. The bear, the forest and the lake vanished back into misty shadows. There was no sign of the giant butterflies as vapour swirled around them. The rushing, swishing sound came back and rose and ebbed until their heads hurt. Then there was nothing but darkness and silence.

Maybe that's what death feels like, Trevor thought before he lost consciousness.

They woke up in the recovery room of the 'House of Life' to soft music and the faint scent of lavender. A fountain softly murmured in the middle of the green and lilac room. A woman medic moved a humming device over Trevor's body to stabilize his vital functions. He stirred and groaned. The girls had already been treated and lay still on soft beds.

Katherine opened her eyes just a little. Were they still alive? Chryséis leaned on her elbows and saw the Lady of Cydonia waiting patiently by the high windows. Katherine saw soft, blue lights over their beds. She couldn't see the Lady clearly, because the sunlight blinded her.

"What happened? We just wanted to see the prytaneum..." Trevor tried to sit up, but the medic pushed his shoulders gently down.

"Young friends, welcome back to Cydonia," the Lady said in a tone of relief and walked toward the beds. "You travelled into a future realm through the space-time continuum, athenai. Spontaneous dematerialisation is an uncommon side effect of time travel, but it does happen. The Earthmother be thanked for your safe return. Your good friend Túvar had the presence of mind to quickly alert the medics."

Katherine was still in shock. "The bear... where is the bear? She was so angry. She jumped at us."

"Don't fret child, there is no bear. You are safe here at the 'House of Life'," the Lady said.

The medic gave Katherine more recutis and she sank into her pillow with a sigh.

"Your electromagnetic fields have been stabilised just in time. The medics told visitors, who noticed you fainting that it was just a reaction to the hot weather."

The medic said something to her in a low voice.

"You ought to sleep now," the Lady of Cydonia translated. She left the room with the medic.

Chryséis wanted to ask about the huge butterflies, but then it didn't seem important anymore. She closed her eyes and fell asleep.

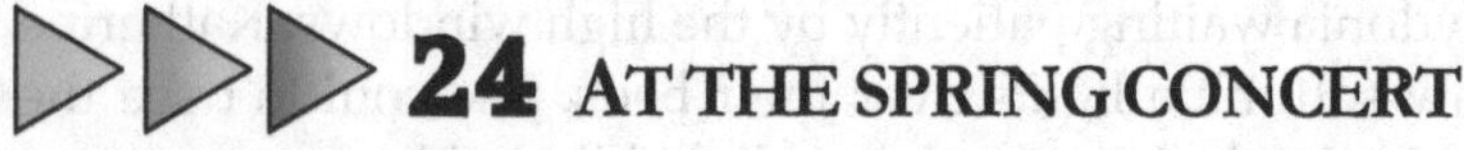

24 AT THE SPRING CONCERT

It didn't take them long to recover and the Lady of Cydonia had again assured them that there would be no more incidents of spontaneous destabilisation.

"I don't know what to think. What if it happens again?" Chryséis said and picked at a blue flower.

They sat on the maroon lawn behind the green and lilac recovery-room and had their first proper talk since the 'Thing' happened.

"Why should it happen again? She told us that they fixed the problem."

"Could have been dicey, but they got us back. We're okay," Katherine said with conviction. She felt much better about being in the past.

"Why was there no vortex?" Chryséis creased her forehead.

"I don't know. Maybe that's how it happens."

"Just imagine we had bumped into some dinosaurs."

"That would have been dangerous," Trevor said. He had not forgotten his first time travel experience in Pemberton's school garden.

"The bear was enough for me. Thank you very much," Chryséis grumbled.

"Nobody said it would be easy. Now we know what can happen. We'll be better prepared next time around," Trevor said.

"Next time around?" Chryséis laughed uneasily. "Not for a while, I hope."

"Sorry, it won't happen again, of course," he said and ran his fingers through his hair. Why did she have to nitpick?

Somebody came and put food on the table in the room.

"Come, I could eat a bear," Katherine said and stood up.

They were allowed to attend school the following day. The other children asked excited questions, but they pretended not to understand. Something like that couldn't be shared with just anyone.

Alun and Túvar already knew, of course. After the morning lessons, they had sport in one of the many parks and soon everything was like before.

The spontaneous time travel accident had crowded out something quite remarkable. Their teeth had completely regrown after a couple of treatments. Just like the Lady had promised. The fillings had just popped out. An itchy feeling had been a small price to pay.

Their health had also improved and Katherine felt a lot less anxious now. Both girls took regular walks around the neighbourhood and even raced each other on the citadel sports ground.

Trevor thought it was more fun to play 'Pigsnout', a popular team sport with a soft têrakhon ball and scoop-shaped paddles. His arm was much better when he took part in a casual match for the first time. The girls had chosen to join a lesson doing something that resembled Tai Chi, during which the maiden Oruwen demonstrated postures that the students copied.

"I like this," Chryséis whispered excitedly.

She missed doing yoga, but Katherine was struggling to stand on one foot.

"Yes, it's not bad," she said while trying to balance with her arms. The maiden changed into another posture ever so slowly. Katherine stretched and fell to the ground. Nobody laughed and one of the girls helped her up.

Meanwhile, the 'Pigsnout' game got underway. The goal consisted of a high wall with two holes in it. The holes were about ten feet apart and looked like the snout of a pig, hence the funny name.

The players had to throw the ball with paddles to each

other, aiming for the goal. The trick was to shoot into your own team's goal and not the opposite one. That wasn't so easy.

Trevor had to ask a few times, before he fully understood the rules. The playing field was roughly in a half circle. Coloured lines were drawn on the paved ground, showing the degree of difficulty.

The farther away from the wall the goal shooter hit, the more points the team was awarded. The white line was closest to the wall, then a blue line a few feet farther out and a red line was about fifty feet away from the goals. Only the most experienced players aimed at the goal from here.

Trevor tried his best. He got confused at first and shot too close to the other team's goal. He grazed his knees when he fell twice, trying to intercept the opposite players football-style.

This was not the Alesian way. The other players were patient with him. They explained again and again and he learned to aim better. In time, Trevor became quite good at 'Pigsnout' and played it often. Katherine and Chryséis preferred Tai Chi. Time passed swiftly with studies and sports. Soon they would leave the save haven of Alesia and explore more of the Known World.

They studied as much as possible of the Alesian language. Even a smattering of Gabari and other dialects of Akkadian they were likely to come across during their travels. They also learned that the payment system was based on small disk-shaped objects. The material and beauty determined the value.

The small disks had holes drilled through the middle. People carried them on strings around the neck or fastened to belts or in pouches. Although the material varied in different regions, it was often mother-of-pearl and kauri shells.

The school children had been practising for weeks and

the spring concert was held at the amphitheatre this evening. They were going with Alun and Túvar. Musical pieces with names like 'A Bee Eaters Flight' or 'Wind Carrying Clouds Across the Sky' were played on strange-looking string and wind instruments.

Rehearsals for 'A trickling brook in golden afternoon light' were still underway and the citadel grounds were full of song. The concert was a musical extravaganza. A fitting farewell from Cydonia.

Little prepared them for what happened next. Something that would throw all their plans into turmoil!

In the afternoon they killed time, walking around the citadel's herb garden. School had been cancelled because of the concert. Two gingko trees stood guard next to a wooden bench between rows of fragrant rosemary bushes. They sat down and talked until it grew dark.

Túvar sat patiently on a bench nearby and watched them. Trevor whittled away at some wooden figurine with his Swiss army knife, saying 'yes' or 'no' in strategic places.

Once in a while they caught a glimpse of a dark green tunic with a yellow sun and moon symbol. The Lady had kept her word. The grounds were swarming with citadel guards for their protection.

The air was mild and fragrant. Hidden lights illuminated the round stage in the middle. Soft têrakhon benches were already packed with people when they arrived with Túvar and Alun.

Families and older people sat close to the stage. Young people sat higher up. Young girls had tied little grass cages with glow-worms into their hair. Some wore them on bracelets around their wrists or fastened to their clothing. A common sight on festive occasions.

The music began. Two rather big harps produced magic melodies that accompanied the singing. The harps were at the back of the stage and the children's choir stood in semicircles in front. When the concert ended on a surprise note, everyone left in high spirits. Night had fallen and they had to pick their way along the sparsely-lit path back to the citadel square.

Chryséis told Túvar that the concert had been wonderful - in Alesian. The giant prince was impressed. He answered something, but neither Chryséis nor Katherine understood. They smiled anyway and Katherine tried to think what else she could say. Slowly the three of them fell behind.

Whoosh!

Alun and Trevor had just reached the courtyard when Túvar, Chryséis and Katherine suddenly disappeared in a bright beam of light. A woman screamed and angry voices approached. The two boys gawped at the empty space - no trace of the others! An alarmed murmur rose.

"Obeah!" This could only mean black magic - the thing Alesians feared the most.

"Obeah!"

"That's not possible. They wouldn't dare..." Alun said slowly.

"What was that... that thing?" Trevor was stunned.

"We must inform the Lady - at once!" Alun grew angry and gushed. "Impossible! From here, from the citadel grounds! Guests of my father's household... and Túvar."

Trevor strained to understand. "Who? What do they want from Túvar?"

They had to do something.

"Alun, contact the Lady *now!*" Trevor urged his Cydonian friend. "Do you hear me? We cannot waste time. Call for help!" He shook Alun's shoulders. Trevor didn't trust his own telepathic abilities just yet.

"You are right, friend. I must call for help," Alun stammered. At last! Alun squeezed his eyes shut and concentrated.

No doubt, he called for help telepathically. Not even a

minute later, two guards appeared with torches and one of the Lady's personal maidens in tow. She was a feisty woman with grey hair tamed in a loose bun.

"Shelanti!" The maiden Gundel almost shouted, then she composed herself. "A transporter beam on citadel grounds in broad moonlight!"

A new murmur arose. What had happened? A crime?

"Good people! I implore you." The stout maiden did her best to calm the crowd. "Please let us do our duty. You will hear more on the morrow. Go home now. Shelanti, Shelanti."

Gundel marshalled the two boys toward the 'House of Wisdom', accompanied by one of the sentry men.

Other guards searched the spot where the children had disappeared. They held spitting torches in their hands, trying to find clues. The boys were ushered into the illuminated audience room. It looked changed. Trevor had never been there after dark.

The Lady of Cydonia, who was normally so composed, seemed nervous. She began to ask them questions the minute they arrived. The answers seemed to confirm her suspicions.

She lifted her hand said, "It is as I thought. The Edfunians. There *cannot* be any doubt. The Edfunian warlords are plotting against Alesia and against our fellow Gabari of the right path. The Highpriest will try to turn Túvar against his own people. The heir to the old lineage. We failed to stop them." She slumped into her chair.

"What they want with the two girls, I cannot say. They have two unprotected innocents in their power now. The Earthmother alone knows what might happen to them." The Lady covered her eyes with her hand.

Then she had regained her composure. "We can no longer communicate with Túvar. His protection charm has been removed. The disk-necklace. The girls cannot be traced either."

Alun remembered that a Gabari man had leaned over during the concert, feigning enthusiasm for the music. He had soon left his seat. Alun reproached himself for not realising that the man had stolen Túvar's necklace.

"Alun, this is not your fault. You could not possibly have known," the Lady of Cydonia said soothingly.

"We will pray for divine intervention, Lady," the maiden Gundel said. "The Gabari leader Ranef has been notified. He will arrive shortly at the chambers."

She stared sadly at the ground, waiting for further instructions. "You are right, tell everybody to pray. I shall confer with Ranef."

Trevor couldn't believe it. The evil Edfunians were trying to overthrow Alesia! And they were right in the middle of it.

This safe utopia in prehistoric times, a haven of peace and civilisation was under threat. A sorcerer had snatched good old Túvar, because he was some kind of heir to an old lineage. And they were right in the middle of it all.

The biggest threat to their safety had turned out to be some stupid giant sorcerer. Not earthquakes or a monstrous flood. Now Katherine and Chryséis were in his power.

What if he never ever saw them again?

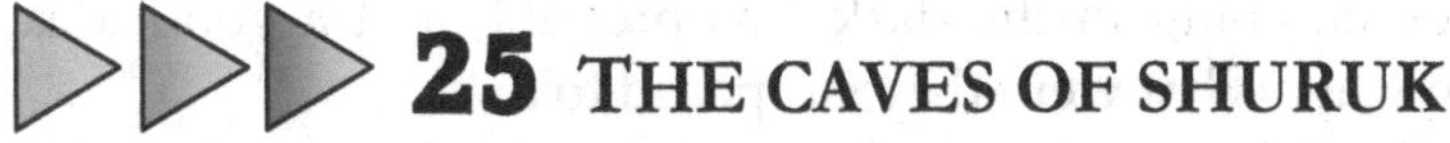

25 THE CAVES OF SHURUK

"Oh boy, not again!" Chryséis groaned. She sat dazed on the hard stone floor. The air smelled mouldy. This was definitely not the citadel of Cydonia!

"Are we disintegrating?" Katherine mumbled confused.

"I don't think so." Chryséis looked around. "Look at this place. We're in a cave! And Trevor isn't here." *What* was going on?

There were no rushing sounds. No vapour either. Just a sudden light beam and now they were inside a spacious cave. One could see that the sky was a deep blue outside - just like before. A few twinkling stars here and there and a thinning moon. They could also make out the dark tree tops of a pine forest below. That meant they were not at ground level.

Where was this place?

Growling roars rose up from the forest. Thundering stomping sounds made the cave vibrate, and then there was loud cracking of wood.

"There must be wild animals out there. Sounds scary."

The girls moved closer to the cave mouth. They caught a glimpse of rough stairs hewn into the dark rock face — and long necks above large, scaly bodies further down.

"Dinosaurs?" Katherine wondered.

"There are dinosaurs here?" Chryséis jumped back from the entrance.

Maybe they were mistaken. It was pretty dark after all, so close to new moon.

"What do we do?" Katherine stammered. "And where is Trevor?" A lengthy roar rose from the forest.

The girls froze. Climbing down into the forest was out of the question. The large beasts could be dangerous and rock climbing in the dark was probably not a good idea anyway. What were they supposed to do?

Luckily, torches were mounted against the craggy walls, casting some light on the rocky chamber. Somebody must have lit them! They stood up. Pins and needles shot uncomfortably through their legs.

"Do you think we've travelled further back in time? Stone age maybe?" Katherine briskly rubbed her left calf, then the right one.

"I hope not. Where are Trevor and the others? It doesn't make sense. One minute we're talking to Túvar and the next we are here. Alone."

"Anyway, the Lady said it won't happen again. Must be something else then."

"Well, we travelled somewhere, somehow. This is not Cydonia!"

Katherine heard faint voices coming from inside the cave. Her face lit up. They were not alone then! Chryséis also heard it as the voice grew louder.

"Oh here they are!" Katherine wanted to run to the back of the cave.

"Wait," Chryséis whispered urgently and held her back.

The voices came from behind a wall at the back of the cave chamber. The girls thought quickly.

"Let's turn invisible. It's safer," Katherine whispered back.

"Yes, good idea." They pressed the buttons on their headbands.

"It's still working Chris, give me your hand!" Their hands clasped tightly.

"Okay, so what do we do now?" Chryséis said softly. They had turned invisible not a moment too soon. A group of vicious -looking giants appeared from a concealed opening. Black capes fluttered around their hulking shapes as they strode powerfully towards the mouth of the cave.

Their hair was long and unkempt and they didn't smell very good. Katherine pulled Chryséis out of the way just in time. They pressed themselves against the wall.

One of the giants cursed angrily under his breath in a strange language. Something was wrong. The torrent of words was definitely not Alesian and the giant man seemed quite upset, wildly waving his arms around.

He suddenly stopped abruptly and looked suspiciously in the direction where Katherine and Chryséis had melted into the rock wall. His eyes were mere slits as he searched for movement. The girls held their breaths.

The other fierce men said something and seemed impatient to walk on. He hesitated for a moment then decided he must be mistaken and strutted away. The other Gabari followed. Outside, the giants began to swiftly climb up the flight of stairs.

Could these men be Edfunians? That meant they had to be somewhere in Edfun. But why? And where? The girls didn't dare move a muscle.

When they could no longer hear the hammering steps, Chryséis and Katherine moved away from the wall. At last, they could breathe again. This was no joke! They could hardly follow these violent giants out of the cave. Invisible or not.

"The sacrifice for their god has come on a platter," Chryséis said sarcastically.

"Not if I can help it."

"Of course not!"

They spun around when they heard a man's voice from the concealed opening at the back. A hissing voice. Somebody else was here! They crept along the cold, rough wall, taking care not to bump into the torches. *What was this white fluff on the opposite wall?* Katherine wondered fleetingly. The girls looked cautiously around the corner into the next cave. There was Túvar!

He sat on the ground in a recess, leaning lifelessly against the jagged rock. His face was blank. Was he dead?

But Túvar was still alive. He had been demobilised, because it was easier to control prisoners that way. And the dungeon was cleverly shielded against thought transfer. Worthless Alesians might try to rescue the boy. Not if the Highpriest could help it! The guards were vigilant - one could say, by nature - and escape was impossible.

It was here in the Caves of Shuruk that captives were punished for offences against the Edfunian law of the day. Sometimes these captives lay forgotten in the depths of the caves until cruel death released them.

That Chryséis and Katherine had landed here in the cave was mere coincidence. The Edfunian warlords had been unaware of their presence in the corner, when the teleporter beam delivered Túvar to the fortress of Shuruk.

This time they were after Túvar, the true Gabari prince. He had been stunned and dragged immediately into the inner cave. Had they seen the two girls in the corner their triumph would have been even greater.

At last, the heir to the royal line was in Edfunian power! Túvar was needed to carry out their plan. Victory would be theirs! Many others would follow him, if he were made to consent. And consent he would.

Edfun would oust the despised womenfolk from power forever and gain power over Alesia. Long had they waited for this moment. Long enough!

Katherine and Chryséis stared at the scene. The giant in front of Túvar, talking and hissing, faced the recess. He dangled a silver necklace with a moon disk pendant playfully in his right hand. They couldn't see his face, but even looking at the giant's back was scary. He seemed middle-aged, wearing a long black tunic under his dark leather armour.

This giant didn't look as brawny as the other ones, who had just left the cave in a hurry. His back was stooped, but he exuded an air of power and evil. His hair was so matted with sacrificial blood that its colour was an unnatural reddish brown. The smell was revolting, like decay. The sight made Katherine's skin crawl.

"Gross," she breathed in disgust and closed her invisible eyes.

The man turned slightly and Katherine gripped Chryséis's hand harder. A black spider was tattooed on the giant's broad forehead. Tattoos on his arms were half-hidden by the tunic sleeves.

His features seemed frozen in a hideous grin as he watched a very large black spider weaving a white web around the recess. Katherine drew in a terrified breath. The enormous spider spun relentlessly at the white curtain.

The Highpriest turned around some more and studied the cave wall. Could he see them? Did he sense their presence like the other angry giant had? But he obviously didn't, despite those x-ray eyes. Oh, why didn't Túvar just get up and run away? The web grew denser by the minute.

"So, here we are now," the Highpriest of Shuruk hissed. "How good of you to pay your clan a visit after such a long absence. We missed you. Oh yes, we did."

He played with the necklace in his hand.

"Pity about your parents. Resisting Edfun like that—" he croaked in a mean voice. "They should have known better. Could have had such a good life right here with their own kin." The moon disk pendant dangled.

There was despair in Túvar's eyes. Nothing else. If they could just understand what this hideous creature was saying to their poor friend.

"Oh young kinsman, you will *not* reject our hospitality now, will you?" The man in black seemed to enjoy his little game with the helpless Túvar. Both giants knew that he was no relative of Túvar's.

"A great throne awaits you, son. Power! To be shared of course... once you have come to your senses, that is. If not, well... our friendly guards here don't like to go without their usual rations for long," he laughed in a hacking sort of way.

Túvar just wanted to run. Away from this horrible cave and away from this awful man. But he still couldn't move a fibre in his body, couldn't think. How to get help? How?

"I will withdraw to my quarters now, dear kinsman. It is getting late. We will talk again on the morrow. The guard will take some time to finish. Please have a comfortable night." The sorcerer oozed false consideration and his grin revealed a mouthful of bad teeth.

The girls quietly retreated into an alcove. The Highpriest turned and walked smugly towards the cave entrance. They could see his face fully now.

His left eye was drooping slightly. A scar ran across the leathery skin. An injury he had received when the old Highpriest, he had faithfully served as an apprentice, tried to fend him off. The night he had decided to take over power as Highpriest of Shuruk.

The younger man had eventually succeeded in plunging his dagger into the older giant's throat. He had been ruler of Edfun ever since. His scar was still telling the story of that night.

They waited until the heavy steps echoed on the stairs outside the cave. As soon as the giant was out of earshot, they walked toward Túvar. At a safe distance from the grisly spider.

Katherine stumbled over a bundle of bones. They were wrapped into what looked like a white mohair blanket. The sight was puzzling. In fact, there were more of these parcels all over the floor. Along the walls of this long cave and also by the yawning black cave mouth. Oh dear. But they couldn't worry about it now.

"Túvar! We are here," Chryséis said in her best Alesian.

Túvar's eyes grew wide. There was nobody there. Had his time come? Were the ancestors calling him? Then he heard the voice again in a language he didn't understand.

"You can stop digging your nails into my hand now," Chryséis said quietly.

Katherine loosened her grip. "Sorry!"

They tried not to trip over stretched strands of spider's silk, fastened to the ground. "This is so gross. I hate spiders!" Chryséis groaned.

Túvar looked surprised when he heard the familiar voices. Was he hallucinating? He thought he recognised the voices of Chryséis and Kathín, but the girls were nowhere to be seen. If he could just move, he would crawl away from this spider's web and try to run for it.

"Are you more scared of this dumb spider than that smelly giant?" Chryséis asked randomly.

"Actually yes!" Katherine had goosebumps, just thinking about it.

"Then don't turn around."

"What, why not?" Katherine looked over her shoulder and nearly fainted.

"Can spiders see invisible people?" Chryséis asked in a matter-of-fact-voice.

"What? I don't know, I can't think right now!" Katherine whimpered. Why was Chryséis so calm?

Another spider, about ankle-height, crawled slowly towards them. Its round, hairy body was the size of a large dinner plate. The animal stopped and dribbled on the spot with hairy legs. No doubt contemplating its prey.

When the spider continued to crawl in their direction, a silent scream rose in Katherine's throat and - she stifled it at the last moment. The awful giants might hear her and come back. That much she could still think.

"Do something, do something," she sobbed.

"Okay, we should do something," Chryséis said bravely and pulled on Katherine's hand.

They tried to move away from the approaching arachnid. There was just a teeny weeny problem. On one side was the spider's net and on the other side the wall of the opening to the outer chamber.

They chose the opening. The spider followed their movement with eight marble-shaped eyes then preened its quivering front legs. Chryséis stumbled on some white fluff. They suddenly realised what these strange white parcels were. Oh no! The monstrous spider stared at them hungrily.

"Listen Katie. I will try to call for help telepathically." Chryséis shook her invisible friend. "Do you hear?"

"Yes..."

They were now back in the outer cave and away from the shielded area. Of course they didn't know that, but they could be fairly sure that nothing worse would happen to Túvar than being spun into a web. Chryséis closed her eyes and concentrated hard. *Relax!* She thought. *Relax!*

Katherine's eyes were fixed on the spider. Then she suddenly remembered the pepper spray she carried in her moon bag. She had managed to get it from an older student at Pemberton, just before the excursion to Carter Valley.

She had no idea, if the spray would work on a large bug, but she had to try and fumbled with trembling fingers nervously with the zip of her moon bag. Should they rather run for the cave mouth? But then she found the little spray can. Chryséis concentrated all the time.

Then the black spider moved leg by leg toward them. Slow, eerily slow. Sensitive heat sensors were detecting the warm bodies rather than seeing them. Venomous three-inch fangs were working in anticipation of a juicy dinner. Katherine could hardly breathe now, while she tried to stare the spider down.

The tarantula crawled faster now. Closer and closer. It was too much. Katherine screamed in desperation. She lunged forward and sprayed the monster right into its black marble eyes.

The arachnid retreated, taken by surprise. The prey

fought back!

But the pepper spray wasn't a sufficient deterrent. Food so close, so good! Chryséis opened her eyes and things happened very fast. A laser beam vaporised the animal in the fraction of a second.

Then the other tarantula and her artfully spun silk net were reduced to hot air. One giant citadel guard helped Túvar on his feet and dragged him from his 'prison cell'.

"Can you walk, Lord?" he asked.

But Túvar could barely stand, never mind speak.

Katherine and Chryséis deactivated their virtual invisibility capes. The citadel guards were surprised to see the foreign girls appear so suddenly, but they recovered at once.

"Come, quickly!" cried the other guard. They hurried after them to the cave entrance.

Out of the corner of her eye, Katherine saw more spiders crawling towards them. A whole lot of them! She closed her eyes.

Before they knew how, the teleporter beam had carried them back to safety. Back to Cydonia.

The last thing Chryséis remembered were thundering footsteps rushing down stone stairs outside the cave.

The gigantic Edfunian warlords had intercepted the thought communication coming from the cave. How had the boy managed...?

They were too late. The Edfunians never saw the flash of light. Never saw the Alesian guards and their charges disappear.

Too late did they realize that they were in even bigger trouble - the crawling spiders didn't stop for anything.

▷▷▷ **26** BORDER CONFLICTS

Despite the medics' best efforts, Chryséis still had flashbacks of the caves of Shuruk that she kept to herself. Túvar stayed at the 'House of Life' somewhat longer than the others. One could never be sure what the Edfunians did to their captives.

The Lady of Cydonia had visited them in the recovery room. "This seems to become your favourite place in Cydonia, athenai," she joked.

"Oh Lady, it was terrible. I've never seen such big spiders before." Katherine closed her eyes and shook herself.

Later that day Alun and Trevor came and took them back home. Trevor greeted his friends with a series of hugs. That was unusual for him, but given the circumstances, he didn't care what people thought.

The girls had to give an account of what had happened to the rest of the clan in long-winded, broken Alesian. Alun tried to help out as much as possible and the family followed every word in amazement. Shuruk was known to harbour evil warlords, but a dungeon under the fortress — and giant tarantula guards!

"No wonder, nobody ever escaped to tell their tale," Alun's father said.

Everyone was relieved that the foreign children and Túvar had escaped virtually unscathed and assured them that they would be safe from now on. But the time travellers had heard this before. Wasn't Túvar supposed to look after them as their body guard after all?

After a while, they excused themselves and walked to

the little park down the road. The Alesian Gabari had held their ceremony there only a fortnight ago.

"I nearly left without you," Trevor said as they sat under a jacaranda tree.

"Gee thanks for being so patient," Katherine pretended to be upset.

"Just kidding."

"Maybe that's what we should do - leave." Chryséis sounded serious.

"What's so wrong with staying here?" Trevor didn't understand why she was so negative all of a sudden. Chryséis wasn't the fearful type and everything had gone alright.

"I'm scared, okay?!" she blurted out. "I'm really scared that something like that could happen again. You weren't there, Trev. These giants…the spiders..."

Chryséis was looking for words to explain how she felt. "I… I just hated it!"

She wanted to let off steam somehow. But how? Screaming and running around the park until she could no more? This whole experiment was a mistake!

"I've just had enough!" she moaned.

Trevor and Katherine looked at each other.

"But Chris, you heard what the Lady of Cydonia said. They will get the Edfunians under control again. She promised."

"Edfunians…who cares about Edfunians? First the market, then the dungeon. I've had enough!"

"Chris, if the Lady said she'll protect us -" Katherine began.

"Yeah, I know she promised. So why did it happen then?" Chryséis ranted on. "That could have gone totally pear-shaped!"

"Chris!"

"What?"

"Keep your hair on, you're safe now," Trevor said and Chryséis glared at him. Apparently he had not said the right thing.

"Oh yes? And what about the state of war? We weren't

even supposed to leave the house, and here we are. Nobody stopped us. Come on let's go, before the Edfunians attack! We've got some packing to do -" She jumped to her feet.

It was a tempting thought - going back home. But this time Katherine sided with Trevor.

"We must keep it together," she interrupted Chryséis's flow of words. "We took the decision together and I don't think we should leave now. At least give it a chance."

Chryséis's eyes flashed, making Katherine feel uncomfortable. "What's wrong with you?" She yelled. "It's too dangerous. We have to go back now and we're all packing, alright?! If we hurry up, we'll make it up the hill before dark."

Chryséis felt trapped. Not even her best friends understood a thing.

"Now, that's not a good idea. We are safer here in town."

"No, we're going!"

"That makes one of us, Chris," Trevor said calmly.

"Oh yeah? Tell you what. You can both go and jump in the lake!" Chryséis was all red in the face now. "Oh, you drive me nuts!" She angrily kicked a rock. They were now all standing under the jacaranda tree.

Chryséis just turned around and stomped off. Katherine wanted to run after her, but Trevor held her back. They didn't argue often, but this trip back in time was taking its toll. A couple of weeks ago, Chryséis had wandered off in the middle of the night and Katherine had been the angry one.

"Let her chill out," Trevor said. "It's just nerves, that's all. And in any case I thought *you* were terrified of spiders, not Chris."

"I am. But somehow… oh I don't know. It doesn't bother me that much anymore."

Perhaps the treatment at the 'House of Life' had done the trick. Or perhaps she was just braver now.

They saw Chryséis's jade-green back retreat behind the clipped hedge by the street. What was she going to do? Would she just leave without them? Katherine was worried.

"That's not good, that's not good at all. We can't fight like this. We have to stick together. We..." she stuttered.

"Get a grip, Katie. She won't do anything stupid."

"Crummy," Katherine sighed and kicked a few pebbles off the path.

An orange-coloured lizard slithered idly from stone to stone. Pausing for a few seconds each time to make sure it was safe enough to continue. A blue and a red-dotted butterfly landed fluttering on a speckled marigold flower.

They sat quietly on the grass and watched the surrounding beauty - and felt like barbarians! Alesians never seemed to yell at each other. It was lucky that no one had been around to listen to their argument.

When they walked back to the house, the streets were deserted. People were heeding the citadel directive to stay indoors.

Tepi came bouncing across the courtyard to greet them. The yellow puppy was getting big. Katherine stroked her silky fur and the dog rolled onto her back for a good scratching. Katherine would miss Tepi when they were leaving for Aztlan. The little dog had won a place in her heart.

Back at the cottage, Chryséis lay on her bed, staring at the ceiling. She had taken a cool bath, while crying hot tears. She realised for the first time, that she really, really missed her family. Mom would know what to do. She always did.

But Mom wasn't there. She lived in the future. So far away. The future felt like a big weight on Chryséis's shoulders. Katherine opened the door.

"Chris, are you okay?" She asked gently.

"Yeah, I guess."

"We shouldn't fight, you know."

"I know." Chryséis sat up. "Sorry I blew my top." Her eyes were red-rimmed, but she seemed better. Katherine waved for Trevor to come in.

"Those Edfunians gave me the creeps..." She shivered

at the mere thought. "But then... who said that time travel was going to be easy, right?" She tried a smile. Trevor and Katherine exchanged a look. Chryséis had changed her mind!

"So, we go ahead as planned?" Trevor asked a little too quickly.

Katherine glared at him. Don't push our luck, her eyes said.

"We can't just walk out on this experiment... like you can with a bad movie."

Chryséis took a deep breath. "If something that bad *ever* happens again, we'll go back, right?"

"Well... I suppose..." Trevor stammered. Katherine nodded. Then Trevor nodded too, more reluctantly.

"It's agreed then?!"

"I guess."

"Don't make me regret this." That's what her mother would have said.

Chryséis went for further treatment at the 'House of Life' and by evening she was as good as new.

Chryséis had seen Túvar at the 'House of Life'. He made a point of thanking Chryséis for her help. She had bravely summoned the citadel guards and saved their lives, while he lay helpless in the dungeon. The citizens of Cydonia learned of the events at Shuruk only later. Right now, Alesia was at war with Edfun!

*

The three time travellers would probably not have felt so relaxed, had they known what was going on in the north of Alesia.

All along the border with Edfun, Alesian protection shields had gone up as soon as the giant prince and the Lady's two protégés were safely back on Cydonian soil.

Shuruk had ordered large numbers of troops south. In the past, Edfun had always lost such altercations. Nonetheless, Alesia was put on alert. As always in times of war, Alesian warlords were quickly appointed by the Lady of Cydonia.

They were already at work, locating the camps of the Edfunian contingent, concealed in the mountains, waiting to attack.

Delegations from citadels all over the country arrived in Cydonia and gathered for counsel at the 'House of Wisdom'. Ladies of citadels and temporary warlords conferred with the 'First Speaker' of warlords and Gabari leaders behind locked doors. The delegates were dressed in white tunics as a symbol of their purity of intent.

They sat around the large ring-shaped table in the Lady's chambers. A citadel maiden took a softly glowing stone from the conference table. She covered it carefully and put it on a corner table.

Longing looks followed her movements across the room. Two sturdy Gabari guards posted themselves on either side of the object. They were out of earshot and the discussion could begin. They were all in agreement. The situation posed a serious threat to the hard-won happiness of the Alesian people.

"If Edfun prevails, the entire 'Known World' will have to pay the price. An Edfunian incursion must be stopped," The Lady of Bînah implored the members of the meeting.

"Edfunian spies in Cydonia are difficult to detect. We have rounded up a number of them all over the country," Manu, the 'First Speaker' of the warlords reported.

"The Highpriest of Shuruk uses dark magic and mind control to get his way. Upstanding men have committed crimes under a spell of his evil eyes."

The brawny military veteran looked tired. This would be his last assignment as warlord. He'd much rather spend time on his farm breeding ptarmigans than chasing after wayward Edfunian spies. But this was a serious matter that called for personal sacrifice.

"Two scientists, one of them a true Gabari, have mysteriously disappeared. Secret knowledge pressed from them under duress."

"That's how Edfun was able to rebuild invisibility devices, teleporter drives and mind shields in such a short period of time. Still nothing compared to our own means," Ranef, the leader of the Cydonian Gabari said. A murmur of relief went around the table.

"Thank you, Lords Manu and Ranef," the Lady thanked her advisers with a grateful smile. "I am pleased that the Edfunian warlords gathered only so little of the 'Great One's' secret knowledge." She paused. "We thought we had time to prepare. But the Highpriest is as cunning as he is dangerous. He caught us off guard. "

"Well, almost. Let's meet the challenge with wisdom and inner strength," said Ranef.

Shortly thereafter, elaborate battle plans were intercepted. They seemed so fantastic that Cydonia suspected a decoy to throw the Alesians off track. Edfunian warlords were known for their skilled deceptions.

The warlords under the Lady's command began to give coded orders. Ray guns were brought into position, but their targets in Edfun weren't human.

"The abuse of electromagnetic devices to subjugate Alesia must be halted at once," the Lady of Cydonia had ordered. "We cannot compromise the effectiveness of our protection shields."

The delegates murmured approval. Some knocked their fists on the table. It was clear what she referred to.

"It is decided then. We will trace the offending instruments in Edfun and destroy them at the appropriate moment." More approval from the delegates. The Lady addressed the 'First Speaker' of the Alesian warlords again. "I take it that the defence forces are at the border as planned." Lord Manu nodded in confirmation.

"We wait for the other side to attack. Damage to all life forms must be avoided as long as we have a choice. The Earthmother be with us."

"Your command will be passed on at once, Lady," the

'First Speaker' answered briskly and excused himself from the table.

The conference continued into the early hours of the morning. Then, out of the blue, the Edfunian forefront started attacking the Alesian border in several places.

Ray guns punctured holes into the electromagnetic shields and the barrier began to disintegrate. Bloodshed could no longer be avoided.

Thinking that they had weakened the Alesian border enough, row upon row of massive warriors marched forward. The titanic men were thrown back as they tried to break through the invisible barrier with physical force, hacking and slicing at the shield with their broad swords and spears.

Some still remembered the glory days of their last attempt to control Alesia. The good warriors had fought bravely against cowardly Alesian soldiers and their allies, before the Edfunian army was overpowered. At least that's what they remembered.

The protection shields were quickly repaired. The Edfunians, who'd made it across the border were instantly immobilised. More followed, counting on the force of sheer numbers. On their warlords' command, the warriors persevered obstinately — only to be violently repulsed again and again. The protection shields held.

Being hampered by electromagnetic protection shields was inglorious. The evil warlords were enraged. Tempers flared. There had been no mention of improved border protection in the last reports from their Cydonian spies. Unlucky soldiers nearby bore the brunt of their anger.

More ray guns, stolen in Alesia under the cloak of invisibility, were brought to the stations. They would destroy these shields!

But what was this? Every single ray gun suddenly burst with a loud bang and fell to the ground in a thousand pieces. This was magic. Black magic for sure!

One electromagnetic instrument after the other was detected by the Alesians and painstakingly destroyed.

Faced with the now-useless technology at their feet, the warlords gave orders for the living war machines to advance.

The bodies of the saurians were like those of African elephants. Just as grey, only with long scaly necks. Tails flicking dangerously and spitting toxic slime, the war machines pushed ahead relentlessly. They were trained to stop at nothing. But not even the great beasts, so unafraid and lethal, were able to break through the re-enforced shields.

Advantage turned to disaster. One by one the huge animals were thrown back to the ground. Furious stomping and ear-splitting roars turned to frenzy.

More murderous thunder lizards pushed up from behind with long necks whipping about wildly struggling to get past the mounds of jerking bodies. Their small brains did not comprehend the cause for this obstruction.

The mighty war machines of Edfun were destroyed before the warlords' eyes. Utter chaos ensued as the saurians in the dark forests of Shuruk, took up the mighty cries of their dying brethren.

The rocky caves, on which stood the fortress of Shuruk, shook from the nervous drumming of feet and bellowing of the huge animals.

As ray guns and teleporter stations exploded above, the dungeons collapsed. Many of the spider guards were neglected by their injured keepers and escaped never to be seen again. Edfunians all over the country scrambled into hiding places close by. Their proud army had been defeated. Despair ran rampant.

But it wasn't over just yet.

The Highpriest had another trump card up his sleeve. On the eastern coastline, Edfunian warships waited, hidden in craggy fjords. During a surprise attack in the dark of night, the ships were to invade the less protected Alesian coastline. Then the warriors would make a victorious stab for Cydonia. A fateful decision.

A sea tremor off the coast in the northwestern 'Saturnian Sea' had been registered by seismic instruments in Aztlan. The seaquake couldn't be felt in Cydonia and did limited damage to the northern Alesian seashore.

That night, the tidal waves were higher than usual and seawater washed across front porches in Alesian fishing villages and towns. Crockery fell to the floor and fine cracks appeared in the walls of houses.

Two fishing boats tore loose in the little harbour of Harrah and were swept out to sea. No loss of life was reported. They were a worthy sacrifice to Nereus and his blessed daughters for sparing the lives of the village folk.

On Edfunian territory it was a different matter.

The seaquake had caused far greater devastation. North of the sparsely populated Snowfall Creek, fishermen and their families were surprised in their sleep by the violent flood. No trace of them or their earthen huts were found the following day.

Many a daring warrior aboard the warships perished in cold, swirling waters. The heavy vessels heaved and creaked and pounded against jagged rocks just as the ships were launched into the dark. Triumphant war cries turned to screams of horror and despair.

As the sea breathed in and out, heavy planks burst apart and the ships sank swiftly to join the monsters of the depth. With more than half of its mighty army gone in one day, Edfun had to admit crushing defeat.

The Highpriest in his wrecked fortress howled in anguish as his high-flying plans of supremacy were shattered before his eyes. Xipe Xolotle had forsaken him, forsaken his own people! The sorcerer disappeared that night, never to be seen in Edfun again.

Alesia would be safe. For now.

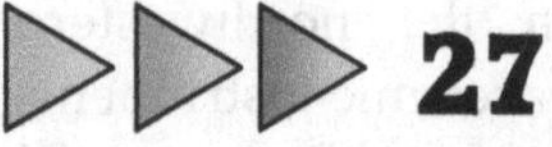 **27**   **TÚVAR'S GIFT**

The ceremony in the citadel's amphitheatre was about to begin. "Rejoice, Alesia, victory over evil has been won! A victory for freedom!"

The whole of Cydonia seemed to have congregated on citadel hill. Cydonians hadn't had so much fun since the 'Pentapolis Pigsnout Tournament' last winter. Enthusiasts from the five cities had descended on Cydonia to watch the teams from Fālia and Eris play in the finals. After a nail-biting match, Fālia had narrowly won.

People wore their best outfits today and everyone was in a festive mood. The maidens had prepared the sweetmeats especially for this day of triumph and decorated them with the emblem of Alesia.

One sauntered to and fro and greeted one another. Children with ribbons in their hair grasped fistfuls of small, tasty cakes from the tables. Hymn after song after booming hymn had been performed by the citadel choir with much enthusiasm, before the speeches started. With much vocal support from the spectators, of course.

Colourful banners flapped gaily in the breeze. The banners probably read slogans like 'Down With Evil' and 'Together We Shall Overcome' or something to that effect. At least Chryséis had said so.

The damage to Cydonia had luckily been limited. The Earthmother be thanked. Only a couple of buildings in the centre of the city had been hit before the reinforced protection shields had come up.

The hill behind the little park in Valley Cydonia, where the Gabari had held their moon ceremony, was also a bit flatter now. The top had been vaporised by a rogue laser beam.

When it was time for the formal part of the event, everyone congregated to the amphitheatre. Boisterous children were hushed. One after the other, the speakers on a wooden stage below, all of whom were honourable citizens, extolled the benefits of a civilised society.

Trevor, Katherine and Chryséis ended up standing among the Gabari dignitaries above the seats. They felt like tiny saplings among tall pine trees. The giants were gentle though and took care not to squash the foreign children by accident.

At last, the Lady of Cydonia flanked by her officials, came and spoke beautifully. The speech was short and to the point as usual.

"My fellow Alesians. Once again, we have defeated the forces of evil." Thundering applause.

"Let's remember that constant vigilance is the price of freedom. This war was over as swiftly as it began. Thanks to all your wonderful contributions another victory has been won in the name of civilisation." Her strong voice carried effortlessly across the stands. "In particular I would like to thank…"

She read out the list of dignitaries' names. Alesian border guards queued solemnly to receive praise and reward. Followed by scientists, citadel guards and warlords. Little girls dressed in pink handed the Lady gilded laurel leaves that she pinned onto proudly puffed-out chests.

"Look, over there!" Katherine had glimpsed Alun further down the aisle and waved wildly. He sat next to his parents and family members. Túvar was with them. They waved back and Alun turned around again to watch the ceremony.

The honouring of Alesian warlords was next. With much pomp and fanfare the strapping men in their tunic-uniforms were formally relieved of the temporary duty to their country.

Manu, the 'First Speaker' of the warlords beamed with pride. Each received a good piece of border land for their efforts. This was the tradition. Their achievement would be recorded on citadel walls and on the prytaneum's silver disk. For future generations to share in their glory.

The ceremony was pretty self-explanatory and they understood most of the short Alesian phrases. Teacher Adami had worked wonders with another language crash course. They were now able to have a passable conversation. Despite this Chryséis didn't understand at first when her name was called.

"Chryséis of Ethidgevee!"

She looked around fully expecting someone else to step forward. The herald called again, "Chryséis of Ethidgevee!"

There was no mistake. The Gabari moved apart and gently nudged the girl to the fore. Reluctantly she walked down the steps, looking back at her friends.

"What's going on?" She asked.

Katherine and Trevor shrugged their shoulders and shook their heads.

"Might as well find out," Trevor said.

Chryséis marched down the aisle between the seats toward the dais. Her embarrassment faded and she soon enjoyed the attention.

"Typically Chris," Trevor said.

Soon she found herself standing in front of the Lady of Cydonia, looking up at the tall, dignified woman.

"Chryséis of Ethidgevee. You are hereby honoured for your role in saving the young Lord Túvar of Cydonia. Son of the venerable Lord Hâkan and Lady Verüni of Bînah, who gave their lives for the good of all and the freedom of their people. Chryséis of Ethidgevee, you did the Alesian nation a great service. I pronounce you citizen of honour of our capital city of Cydonia." The crowd cheered.

Last year Chryséis had won in the finals of the maths-olympiad against Holly Benson. But this was so much better! The Lady of Cydonia fastened three golden laurel leaves, tied with a broad golden ribbon, to the neckline of her jade-coloured tunic. Music played somewhere. Chryséis felt like walking on air.

"Shukri, honourable Lady," she said in perfect Alesian.

Her face was flushed when she finally stepped down the stage, everybody cheered and applauded. What role had *she* played? She couldn't remember. Perhaps...ah yes, of course. The Lady must have meant that she'd called for help telepathically in the dungeons of Shuruk. Right.

Katherine and Trevor embraced Chryséis. She nearly fell into their arms for excitement. Then the phalanx of Gabari closed protectively around the foreign children.

*

Yesterday, Kheton and Lelani had returned from their honeymoon in Kalkan. They had missed all the war-action and instead told many funny stories to the assembled clan.

Of thieving monkeys stealing food from windowsills and of flying lizards, screeching incessantly before sunrise.

The time travellers had seen many of those strange little flying reptiles by now. Irritating things. Although accompanied by much gesturing, they found it difficult to follow Kheton's next story. It was about a cute baby monkey, who sat on Lelani's head trying to find lice. They laughed in all the wrong places, but nobody seemed to mind much.

The flooding had only reached the foot of the plateau on which the camp Kalkan was situated and the short-lived alarm hadn't worried the young couple too much. Or so they said. Being Alesians, they had not doubted in their minds that good would prevail in the end.

Before they all retired after supper, Kheton had requested a word with the visitors. Lelani sat next to him on one of the sofas and kept glancing proudly at her new husband. He held his wife's hand most of the time. Quite nauseating to look at - at least when you were almost a teenager.

Kheton assured them that he and Lelani would take good care of them during the coming voyage. The Lady of Cydonia had handed him the letters of passage before the victory celebrations.

'Honourable Junior Judge,' she had said. 'It is my wish that the children be safe throughout and receive every support they need. I expect regular reports.'

Their first stop-over was in D'ântilla, where Kheton's had an official mission for a couple of days. Then they would cruise a number of islands and finally arrive in Algiras, the capital of Atala.

"We will leave the day after tomorrow. You may want to ready your belongings in time, young friends. The Lady has requested to see you before our departure. We will accompany you to her quarters after the celebrations tomorrow."

"We understand and…will be pleased to do so, honourable Kheton," Chryséis said politely in halting Alesian.

Kheton and Lelani seemed pleased that the foreign children had made progress in learning about civilised ways. Everything was settled. After tomorrow was the big day. They would finally travel across the sea.

That had been only yesterday.

*

The festival was still in full swing, when Túvar tried to make a path through the dancing and singing masses. Kheton, Lelani and the three foreign children from the future followed him closely. The Lady had made time to bid her special guests farewell. Finally they reached the 'House of Wisdom' via the back garden.

That was it. They would not see her again for who-knew-how-long. The time travellers didn't want to admit it, but Cydonia had become like a second home to them.

"We will meet again, to be sure." The Lady held Katherine's hand for a moment. Her pet iguana seemed to watch them from his branch in the terrarium.

"You will return to this town after your voyage. In the name of all Alesians, I wish you a safe journey in the meanwhile. Take good care when travelling and remember the advice I gave you."

The Lady meant, of course, not to divulge their true origin to anyone and to ask for help at citadels when needed. She handed them a bulging purse made of saurian leather. The leather felt tough and durable,

"It is as tough as you, my dear friends. You might need this on your travels."

They couldn't quite understand why the little bag was important for their travels, but thanked the Lady nevertheless.

"I understand that our royal friend Túvar has a surprise for you." She spoke English now.

"A surprise? What surprise?"

But the Lady of Cydonia wouldn't tell and just winked playfully.

Túvar steered the vimaan this time. They remembered the way to the experimental farm well. The plants left and right of the road had grown a great deal.

Some of the trees lining the streets were already heavy with fruit, even though it wasn't summer yet. The warm climate and fertile soil allowed for two harvests in a year.

Again, bee-eaters warbled on the hedges and flew up as the vimaan passed. They were no longer bewildered by the saurian farm animals, even though they looked every bit as peculiar to them as before.

One herd of grazing saurians had stripes all over their backs. Almost like zebras. Others had fans of red feathers on their heads and green scales.

Since it was a holiday, little work was done at the testing station. A few workers cut good-sized heads of lettuce and cabbage in the fields. They looked up and greeted Túvar respectfully. The young prince strode around to the back of the main building to the equine enclosure and they could barely keep up.

"I hope, he doesn't want me to cuddle the harpees," Katherine said out of breath. But they only walked as far as the corral.

Gobän came galloping towards the fence. They could see the centaur's friendly bearded face properly this time. He seemed to have recovered well from injuries he had sustained during the recent theft of a precious stallion by Edfunians.

The horse minder told them sadly that the animal had not been found again. The Earthmother alone knew what had happened to him. Two other centaurs stayed with the horses and singled out four of them.

"Are you ready, Lord? Shall we proceed?" The centaur inquired. Túvar nodded. The centaurs lead the magnificent, white animals toward the fence.

"Why are we here, Túvar? Ready for what?" Trevor asked frowning.

"Athenai," the young Gabari addressed them. "We shall ride the horses today. The 'Steeds of the Gods'. I wish to show you gratitude for my rescue from the clutches of the Highpriest of Shuruk."

These Alesians really knew how to show gratitude!

One of the horses nuzzled its snout on Túvar's arm. He laughed and stroked the mare's mane. "Yes, Prïnda, just now."

He made a sweeping gesture towards the about thirty animals. "This herd is the last of its kind. They were saved from the 'Valley of Gods' when my people fled to Alesia."

They gawped at the horses. Awesome.

"Gobän and his brothers were heartbroken when our *Cintli* was taken by the Edfunians. Centaurs have been horse minders to the royal Gabari for many generations." The mare reared her head and began to dig with her hooves in the ground.

"Yes, Prïnda, we were all sad," he said to the horse. "Now, let's ride together."

Túvar lifted himself nimbly onto the back of the rather tall snowy white Prïnda. Before they knew how, they had been helped onto the backs of three of the animals. They were all equally dazzling.

In no time they were on their way to the other side of the enclosure and moved effortlessly through the rear gate and into the open field.

If these white horses had sported long, twisted horns on their foreheads, the time travellers wouldn't have been surprised. The new silver moon around Túvar's neck jumped up and down as his horse gained speed and then the horses seemed to magically fly above the ground.

That's what total freedom must feel like, Trevor thought. They went so fast, that when the children took another breath, they had almost reached the foothills.

Gobän also galloped to catch up with them.

There were only the necks and silken manes to hold onto as they floated through space. It was exhilarating. What a farewell present!

It was obvious that not many people ever received such a present from Túvar.

They would never forget this afternoon ride on their last day in Cydonia.

▷▷▷ **28** THE SEAPORT OF AZTLAN

The view of the bay was breathtaking, with a very blue sea greeting them in the distance. The vimaan made its way eastbound steadily uphill. Suddenly the road plunged towards the waterfront, giving them butterflies in their stomachs.

Their vehicle passed above pedestrians and what looked like caravans. Beasts of burden carried large baskets fastened with broad padded straps to both sides of their backs. Some of the placid animals were saurians of the striped variety.

They sometimes raised their plump heads and lowed at the vimaan whizzing past above them.

Earlier this morning, they had taken leave of their adopted Alesian family. Katherine had squeezed back a few tears. She had given a colourful, beaded Zulu bracelet among her things, as a parting gift to Alun's mother. Hopefully it wouldn't turn up in some museum 12,000 years later.

Trevor had pressed a wooden object into Alun's hand. It was a desktop computer with keyboard, screen and mouse carved in one piece. Alun wasn't sure what he was holding, but it had to be something close to Trevór's heart. Alun had thanked his foreign friend and bid him farewell with a brotherly embrace.

When they arrived in Aztlan, the sun already bathed the country in warm rays. Smaller than Cydonia, but by no means a small town, Aztlan spread out along the seashore before them.

As usual, the harbour district, the so-called *Barbican*,

with its shops, warehouses and broad wharves, teemed with activity. A seawall protected the Barbican and surrounding stretches of coastal land. Ships sailed in and out of the harbour mouth and fishing boats bobbed on the waves along the shore.

Kheton steered the vimaan towards a large white house on the hill. There were all sorts of palm trees and flowers everywhere. On a platform higher up against the hill, the acropolis of Aztlan overlooked the bay.

There was also an amphitheatre and a host of surrounding buildings. The Lady of the citadel had been informed of their presence and sent her greetings, but there were no plans for an audience.

They stared at the grand buildings and park-like gardens of the merchants' district below.

Niches in garden walls were adorned with paintings and statues of the familiar sea gods. Têrakhon vases overflowed with flowers and little offerings in front of the pictures were supposed to bring luck to voyages. For generations, the people of Aztlan had enjoyed a prosperous life, thanks to the benevolent god Nereus and his daughters.

Soon they arrived at the home of Kheton's Aunt Mellea. The vimaan went around the circular driveway with a water-spouting fountain in the middle. They slowly descended on the pavement.

White pillars supported a gabled roof over the front porch and the triangular gable displayed a carved frieze with sailing ships and billowing sails. There were sea monsters between rolling waves and Alesian letters described the mishap the pictured ship had narrowly escaped.

Chryséis read it aloud and Kheton was much impressed. "The trader, called Azaes, hereby gives thanks to the merciful god Nereus for the crew's safe return to Aztlan," she read. "... or something to that effect."

A breeze blew through the palm trees and the fountain slightly sprayed them with water. How pleasant! It was warm in Aztlan, but not quite as hot as Cydonia.

The floor of the entire front veranda was covered in mosaic tiles. Mostly yellow fish frolicking on a white background and turquoise meanders. Words in golden letters greeted the visitors underfoot at the entrance. The entrance hall was grand. Small waterfalls were let into the mosaic-covered walls on either side of the hall.

A domed têrakhon roof let light into an inner court with yet another gurgling fish-motive fountain and more floor mosaics that looked much like stone carpets.

High broad-leaved plants in large blue-glazed pots framed the court, almost hiding the rooms on the ground floor. Upholstered sofas were arranged around the fountain and further at the back stood an oval table that easily seated twenty people.

"This place is so posh! Like a palace," Katherine whispered into Chryséis's ear.

"Yeah, like a palace or a hotel. This aunt must be rich."

On cue, Kheton's aunt came bustling into the hall with two large Gabari men in tow. The plump woman did not bear much resemblance to her tall, dark-haired sister in Cydonia, but she was just as motherly.

Pretty in a corpulent sort of way, with well-coiffed reddish hair, she was every bit the wealthy trader's wife. She was a dignified matron, even at her age, deftly commanding a large household and growing brood of children.

Aunt Mellea greeted her guests with a torrent of excited words in the Aztlan accent, while clutching an astonished toddler to her ample bosom. "Shelanti all. Kheton... welcome! Welcome to you and your young bride," she gushed and embraced the newly-weds. Then the foreign children.

Lelani looked just as overwhelmed as the time

travellers. Aunt Mellea sometimes had this effect on people. Lelani grabbed Kheton's hand and smiled brightly. The time travellers got away with nodding a lot.

Mellea patted their heads and talked incessantly. She had been in Cydonia for the marriage ceremony and assured Kheton and Lelani that she had never seen a finer wedding. Apart from her own, of course.

"The cuisine was excellent, the maiden's words so fitting. Yes and how are the parents? Proud as pudding, I'm sure. And I do remember you young folk —" She looked at the children.

They mumbled something polite in confusion and addressed Mellea as 'honourable aunt', as was proper. Aunt Mellea was charmed.

"They are delightful, these young people, Kheton! Such a pity about their parents - hmm, welcome, welcome athenai!" She put the toddler down, who promptly started squalling. She ignored the outburst graciously and one of the Gabari men picked the little tot up.

"Come along now dears, food is ready."

The brief silence on the way to the table was almost deafening. They sat down at the table and the torrent of words started again.

After a hearty lunch, Katherine, Trevor and Chryséis took the chance to rest for a while and catch up on some journal writing. Trevor sat outside on the terrace in the shade of a sea grass roof and typed.

"As much as I like Cydonia and all, it's so totally awesome here by the sea," Chryséis declared. Hands folded under her head, she lay on a soft bed staring at the painted ceiling. *More* fish motives and sea monsters.

Their TPF devices were on the table. The Lady of Cydonia had handed them back a few days before the fateful spring concert. They looked different now, the sleek new casings were made of a dark têrakhon material with soft buttons. The buttons still looked much the same, but the place of their arrival in the past was now also programmed. 'Shepherd's Hill' was written in English next to the second red button.

"Feels like a luxury hotel on the Riviera," Katherine said and took off her headphones. "The food was great. I think I can't eat for at least a week."

"Mhm."

"I hope we'll never have to ever see freaky Edfunians again. All they do is kidnap people and start wars and stuff."

"Mhmmm."

"Hey Chris, are you listening?"

But Chryséis had already nodded off and snored a little. Katherine went out onto the terrace. From up here, Aztlan looked like a large park with houses. And the ocean was so big.

Two lizards landed on the grass roof and made quite a racket. Trevor shooed them away and carried on typing.

"Feels like a luxury hotel on the Riviera," Katherine repeated.

Trevor looked her in the eye. "Then at last I know how it feels to be rich. But here I can have it for free."

He saw Katherine's face. "Sorry, I didn't mean it like that," he apologised and finished the entry into the journal.

Later that day, the guests were formally welcomed by Uncle Azaes as he returned from a day's work at the Barbican. Uncle Azaes was a portly man in his forties and well-matched to his lively wife.

He was jovial and generous and never took much to heart. Like so many other Alesian clans, his family had arrived on the continent a long time ago. Azaes, the merchant, knew how to bend with the wind and roll with the punches.

Without further ado, he began to talk about business. Chryséis was used to such discussions at home. Her father was a member of the Etheridge Chamber of Commerce after all. But Trevor and Katherine barely followed.

Uncle Azaes had continued the merchant family tradition by making a fortune from trading. He owned a number of warehouses in the Aztlan harbour district. Two more on D'ântilla, one on Daitya. And Maligasima wasn't a bad choice for future business, either.

He also had an eye on the newly-navigable Nila River delta in the land of Ta Mery. Nila meant 'blue', but in the Delta, the water was not exactly that colour.

The Delta in the Kem province was well known for its impenetrable marshes and wild animals, but there was potential. The children knew that Ta Mery must be somewhere in Egypt, but that was all.

Azaes of Aztlan did not think of himself as wealthy, just blessed to serve his community. There were others, who owned fleets of shipping vessels on every ocean in the Known World.

"And they have warehouses in such distant places as Algiras on Atala, Haithabu in Lyonesse and Branam in Prydhain," Azaes marvelled.

He had recently started doing business with Tollùn on the southern continent of Pushkara. His employees were currently exploring age-old underground passages in the Tawantinsuyo. The Land of the four regions, in the magical southwest of the continent.

Chryséis remembered the mirage of Pushkara, the Lady had shown them.

"The passages could be suitable for the transport of merchandise. An advantage over traditional and more hazardous trading routes. Dangers lurk above ground," he explained over dinner.

"Worst of all, my caravans might run into herds of dangerous saurians, which are said to still roam the ancient rain forests. But a true trader can find business even in Edfun." He bellowed a hearty laugh.

"Going on like that," Aunt Mellea cut in. "You are boring our guests to tears with all these stories, old man."

Uncle Azaes laughed some more and wiped his hands on his embroidered silk tunic. They talked about local gossip for a while - now *that* Aunt Mellea had much to say about - then he returned to his favourite subject. Trade.

Chryséis listened to Uncle Azaes's stories open-mouthed. He could have been a modern businessman, just like one of her Dad's associates at the chamber of Commerce.

Some things didn't seem to change with time. Just that the stories were about attacking saurians and ancient underground passages.

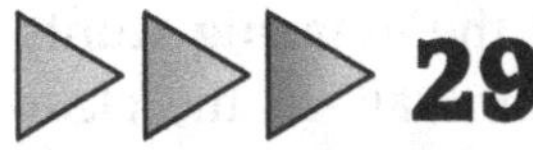 **29** **SEABORN PEOPLE**

Uncle Azaes had a younger brother called Rangan. A younger, balder version of himself. Uncle Rangan was tasked with overseeing a slender piece of coastal land south of Aztlan.

It was here, on the rocky promontory reaching out into the sea, where the 'Seaborn People' had found refuge in Alesia. There were also reservations in Helubis and Xaipán on the 'Sea of Ǧulátû', but the Seaborn population in Aztlan was the largest.

Distant cousins of the human species, the 'Seaborn People' had lived in the warm shallow oceans since the 'Golden Age'. The once mighty race was now close to extinction and needed protection. There were only about fifty such families left in the Known World. The citizens of Aztlan were proud of their fourteen *Ioannu* families.

On the promontory, the Ioannu lived in secluded settlements in small caves and in huts of twigs and seaweed over shallow dug-outs.

Visitors to the reservation used a wooden walkway that led all the way around the headland and tried to catch a glimpse of the rare creatures, while the Ioannu rested under the walkway or on the sandy beaches.

Lucky tourists could hear them sing baleful songs about the long-gone 'Golden Age'. Porpoises and seabirds shared the abundant fishing grounds and odd-looking *dugong* often fed on sea plants near the shore. The placid sea cows attracted much interest when the Ioannu were nowhere to be seen.

Close to the entrance of the reservation was the

dolphinarium. A large artificial rock pool surrounded by an amphitheatre that was often packed to the last seat.

Captivated, the spectators watched the amazing stunts of young Ioannu athletes and sea mammals in the clear water. The Ioannu had domesticated porpoises and dolphins a long time ago. Dolphins were also trained to rescue shipwrecked seafarers and often escorted ships on the oceans.

Opposite the dolphinarium, a massive 10-meter-long male *sarcosuchus* was on display in a strong enclosure. The creature was an exceptional relic of a reptile and a popular attraction. Fishermen had found the monstrous crocodile in the swamps by the 'Sea of Ğulátû' many years ago and Aztlan had been his home ever since.

When the sarcosuchus wasn't asleep, it plodded sluggishly around its spacious prison, whipping its tail lazily in all directions. Sometimes it would slide in and out the water basin, snapping great jaws at the audience or it splashed water onto shrieking spectators.

Mostly though, the sarcosuchus dozed in the warm sun with birds cleaning great sharp teeth in the enormous jaws.

In the morning, a pleasant breeze blew in from the sea and the morning mist rapidly dissolved. The guests from Cydonia enjoyed a stroll along the boardwalk. They didn't make it all the way around - that would have taken the better part of the day.

Uncle Azaes bought snacks of large fried prawns from one of the stalls on the platform, then the two brothers had to get back to work.

Uncle Rangan to his duties on the citadel hill and Uncle Azaes to his Barbican warehouse. A shipment of orichalcum copper was expected in the harbour any moment. The buyer, a gilder from Harrah, had announced his visit to the office at lunchtime. The metal was needed to coat domed roofs all over the country and sought-after

Alesian merchandise would be given in exchange for the orichalcum.

Kheton, Lelani and the three children were left in the care of a quiet Gabari man. The next show in the dolphinarium would start soon. The concept of marine shows seemed to be quite old, just that here, merpeople replaced the trainers in diving suits.

Katherine, Chryséis and Trevor were mesmerised by the human-looking merpeople. It came as a surprise that they did not have scaly-green fishtails like the mermaids in Walt Disney movies. The females sported short dark-coloured tops, embroidered with white seashells and disk-shaped beads.

"Amazing," Katherine said. "Who knew that fairytales about mermaids are based on the truth? Nobody is going to believe us for sure!"

"Well, then we need some proof, right?" Trevor began to take pictures with their tiny digital camera. On one of the photos the two Ioannu females leapt into the air and two dolphins between them jumped in succession back into the water. The mermaids praised them and rewarded the chattering dolphins with fishy snacks.

"The dolphins are a bit blurry," he said. "But otherwise, not bad."

"Well, nobody is going to believe us anyway," Chryséis noted. "They'll just think they dressed up." Trevor just shrugged. Then they oohed and aahed with everybody else at the incredible acrobatics.

The Ioannu spectators could not stand up, of course, but sat upright on front seats. There were males and females with their hair tied back into ponytails and long braids. They held cute children on - what could be called their laps. One little girl had her red hair tied into lots of tiny rat-tails.

The merpeople pensively observed the show of their young relatives, cousins Ula O Tiamat and Malindi.

Beautiful young women with long auburn hair, who instructed the energetic dolphins imperceptibly how to do their stunts.

Ula O Tiamat, the 'Jewel of the Sea', swam up to the edge of the pool right in front of the friends and nodded to them. She said something in broken Alesian with squeaking sounds in between. It didn't make understanding any easier.

"We will meet you over there, after the show," she squeaked and pointed to a spot behind a rock face not far from the pool. How thrilling! What could a mermaid possibly want to talk to them about? Ula O Tiamat threw herself back into the water and finished the show riding on a dolphin's back around the pool.

Afterwards, Kheton and Lelani agreed to wait by the reptile enclosure. They were secretly glad to have some time to themselves. This gave the Chryséis, Katherine and Trevor a chance to meet with the two Ioannu for a while.

Their Gabari guard followed at a respectful distance. It didn't matter. In fact, it was quite flattering to have a bodyguard again. The three friends sat down and waited on the rocky ledge, which seemed to serve as a launching pad into the bay.

Suddenly, two gleaming heads popped through the water's surface and the mermaids climbed onto the ledge. They looked around to make sure they were more or less alone and told the children without ado, that they knew of their unusual origin.

This came as quite a surprise! Then Malindi said something about a telepathic message the Ioannu had received from the Lady of Cydonia.

"The good Lady has asked for protection for the visitors from future times. The Ioannu will help you, athenai, to be safe by the watery realm."

That explained the meeting, of course.

Having this message out of the way, Ula and Malindi

chatted on, sounding a bit breathless at times. Seaborn People weren't used to a whole lot of talking in land-dweller fashion. They preferred to communicate telepathically in the water and on land.

"We are not fish and breathe through lungs," Malindi explained, anticipating the question. "When we dive, our lungs are compressed by the water pressure. We can stay under water without breathing for quite some time."

Ignorant landlubbers often likened them to fish. The two mermaids screeched with laughter at the thought.

The children demonstrated their growing skill in telepathic communication. Well, Chryséis did. Ula O Tiamat and Malindi were delighted and squeaked gleefully. They managed to record the remarkable voices with the discman, but later they sounded garbled.

Inquisitive Ioannu children began to play around in the water, laughing and screeching. Ula O Tiamat told them to go and play elsewhere and water splashed onto Katherine's legs as they retreated back under the water. She rolled up her trousers and hung her feet into the clear, warm water.

Malindi now spoke of the 'Golden Age', when Seaborn People had worked alongside the 'Gods' in the planet's young oceans. She told of fantastic palaces under the sea in those times, close to the shores. Transparent spheres had allowed the 'Gods' to move above and below the water to observe the marine life.

But these happy times had gone forever. The mother planet became restless, and after the last great deluge the 'Gods' had left. Only to be remembered in legends. Had the young visitors met the 'Gods' in the future?

The astonished time travellers shook their heads.

"Well, that is too bad," Malindi squeaked.

Then Ula taught them how to whistle in a special way to call dolphins to the rescue or to just greet them. Promptly, two dolphins thrust their heads through the sparkling surface and started quacking gleefully.

"Here, you try," she encouraged Katherine to copy the sound. They took turns and the dolphins danced on their tails before swimming off.

Time was passing quickly. Kheton and Lelani were probably waiting. They thanked the mermaids for their offer of protection and the whistling lesson, then Trevor took a selfie with all of them. They wouldn't look at fairytale movies with the same eyes ever again.

At the villa, a banquet had been prepared in honour of the guests from Cydonia. Uncle Rangan greeted them and was pleased that they had enjoyed their day - the Ioannu never failed to make an impression on visitors.

"Oh yes, the Ioannu are a great attraction at the reservation. We try to keep them safe and happy. They are endangered you know."

"Malindi told us about their forefathers and how they had worked with the 'Gods'," Trevor said.

"That is true. Unfortunately 'the Golden Age' is a time long past."

"Where are the 'Gods' now?"

"They left," Uncle Rangan said.

The mermaids had told them the same thing. Soon everyone was assembled around the large table. There were four robust children and more Uncles, aunts and cousins. Candles were lit in the hall and a harp player performed gentle melodies on the gallery.

Before the meal, Uncle Azaes recited a traditional verse:

"Don't save your wine up for tomorrow,
Bring out the food when guests arrive.
Place what you have into their midst,
With friendship blessed be your life."

Everyone clapped when he spilt some of his drink onto the floor in honour of the Earthmother.

The table was laden with the most incredible seafood

dishes of Alesian cuisine. Soùmi bread was dipped into delicious sauces and then the fish was scooped up. Heaps of tender fish steaks, tasty octopus and shellfish found their way into hungry stomachs.

There was lively singing and laughter, which was to be expected at an Alesian get-together. These hospitable Alesians grabbed every opportunity to celebrate. Aunt Mellea playfully bemoaned the short visit of her guests. And that they had hardly spent any time at all at her humble abode.

"I would love to show off my nephew, his bride and these lovely orphans, to the other merchant wives."

"Unfortunately, we have to embark on the *'Navis Arion'* tomorrow," Kheton apologised. "We have no choice but trade aunt's incomparable hospitality for boring official business in D'ântilla."

His aunt was flattered.

"The ship will take them straight to the capital of Kamûk," Uncle Azaes came to his nephew's aid. "My dear, you mustn't forget that Kheton will soon be the Alesian 'Honourable Junior Delegate' in Algiras. He cannot delay his voyage."

Aunt Mellea looked admiringly at her nephew.

"You are forgiven then, my sister's son. But you will have to visit and show us your offspring when you return to these shores."

Lelani flushed and everybody laughed in high spirits.

Then Uncle Azaes told engaging stories about D'ântilla. Aunt Mellea knew them all by heart. Her husband had visited many interesting places in the Known World as a young sailor.

D'ântilla was a large tropical island and above all – at a safe distance from Edfun. The recent war was discussed, but clearly nobody wanted to dwell on unpleasant matters for too long. After a while, Rangan contributed his seaman's yarn.

But could they believe him? They were not so sure. Or maybe they didn't understand properly what the stories were all about.

Were there really sea monsters in the 'Saturnian Sea'? Where was the 'Saturnian Sea' again?

Oh yes, north-east of the coast. Rangan said he had encountered elves and fauns on some island. The little buggers had tricked the captain of his ship out of half of his cargo of têrakhon panes.

Uncle Rangan had heroically seized control of the ship when the captain refused to leave a week-long feast held by their queen, and the captain had never been seen again.

Please! That couldn't be true. They had serious doubts and looked at each other skeptically. Still - it was still lucky that the 'Saturnian Sea' with its monsters was nowhere near Aztlan or D'ântilla...

What could possibly go wrong now?

In the night, they slept peacefully the under soft feather quilts and didn't even hear a stormy wind picking up along the shore. By morning the wind had died down to a gentle breeze.

But their adventures were far from over.

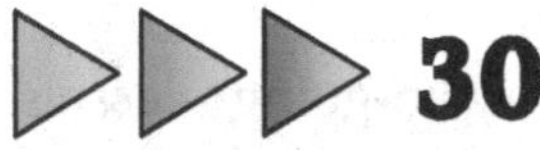 **30**   **LEAVING ALESIA**

When they arrived for boarding, the 'Navis Arion', a fast merchant ship, was still being unloaded in the Aztlan harbour and Kheton needed to sort out documents with the harbour authorities. Aztlan was a major trading hub and there was much traffic in and out of the harbour entrance.

Kheton had thanked Aunt Mellea and Uncle Azaes formally for their hospitality with a parting gift this morning. Finely worked boxes of sandalwood that fitted neatly into each other. Katherine had chosen a bouncy butterfly hairpin for Aunt Mellea.

"Shukri chachi Mellea," she had thanked the delighted matron.

"Oh, this is lovely my child. I shall wear this novel pin to the Nereus Ball." Aunt Mellea had repaid the visitors by hugging each one of them exuberantly.

Smaller sailing boats, with sails like fish fins, skippered about outside the seawall. After watching the ships in the harbour for a while, Lelani and the children went for a stroll around the *Barbican* until the ship was ready to sail. A Gabari bodyguard, who had been instructed by Uncle Azaes not to leave them out of his sight, was following them around.

The 'Navis Arion' was a middle-sized schooner, named after a famous bard in history. Arion had been on his way home from a musical contest and escaped sure drowning by riding on a dolphin to safety. A deceitful ship's crew was after the prize he'd won in the contest and had thrown him callously overboard. As a boy, Arion had healed the dolphin of its wounds. The animal remembered him and repaid Arion for his kindness. A name and a story much to Alesian liking.

Navis ships were sophisticated ocean-going vessels used for transporting cargo and passengers. Equipped with state-of-the-art radar and propulsion systems, a good many of these 'navis' were safely moored on the wharf. Violent thunderstorms, sea monsters and hidden rocks presented real dangers to marine traffic. And ever since the eternal icecaps had begun to recede, ancient sea charts had to be updated with the help of special vimaans flying at high altitudes.

The Barbican was entertaining. The children saw many shops and odd-looking people as they walked down the promenade. Some folks looked like humanoids from a science fiction series. This was so much more interesting than Cydonia!

The three friends tried not to stare at people with lots of hair. No, not just hair on their heads, it was fur covering their entire bodies. They were undoubtedly *Konks.*

The Lady of Cydonia had explained all about their tribes during one of their lessons. She had also told them that Konks were sometimes adopted into civilised families.

That explained why some of these Wildmen wore clothes. They were known to be honest and could be trusted by the merchants. Caravans seemed to go ever so smoothly, when Konks were in charge.

A particularly well-groomed Wildman couple, with a small baby sleeping in the woman's arms, caught their eye. Nobody looked at the family in a funny way, but the time travellers ogled them secretly.

They had to skip aside when a finely dressed lady with pale-green skin was swiftly carried down the wharf in an open litter. They caught a glimpse of a broad-rimmed hat and see-through lilac veil that shielded her delicate, green skin from the sun. Green skin was not unusual in the ancient rainforest country down south. The shrewd woman specialised in herbal medicines and exotic timber that were much in demand abroad.

Back home, her spacious house in the crown of a tree was directly by the water's edge. Although business with Alesia was good, she hankered for dappled shade and the humid jungle air. Seagulls squawked overhead and it smelled strongly of salt and seaweed and rotting fish.

The woman from the jungle sighed. Alas, her agents needed to be reminded, who supplied them with the best quality and at the best prices, or she would have already departed in the morning.

The time travellers didn't mean to gawk - but green skin? Trevor was stunned. "Wow! I've never seen somebody with green skin before."

"Why do you think there are no green people left in our future?"

Katherine and Trevor couldn't think of a plausible answer.

"Maybe they hunted them as trophies —"

"Sis."

"Or maybe they just died out," Trevor said.

"Yes...look over there." Chryséis pointed with her chin to a group of very tall Asian-looking traders walking along the wharf. Turanians.

They wore their black hair in topknots and their black trousers were almost covered by long brocaded shirts. The traders had just arrived and needed to stretch their legs. It had been a long voyage with stop-overs on various islands, but the journey back home to Maligasima would take only two days.

Ships could effortlessly ride the strong circular ocean current around the Atland archipelago, called 'the Wheel'. In Easterly direction, the current was faster.

The men traded in pale jade from their homeland of Maligasima and did brisk business. Jade was used for carving small *obols* for proper funeral rites. When somebody had reached the narrow passage of death, the obol was placed on the tongue. It was the proper way all over the Known World. Many wore a personal obol on a string around their necks. One never knew when it was needed.

Seawater from the harbour basin lapped over the boardwalk in a sudden gust of wind. The men from Maligasima shrieked and laughed, jumping to the other side and narrowly missed the Gabari bodyguard.

Another imposing merchant and his guards strutted right past them. Judging by their looks, they had to be from Africa. But in fact, the merchant was from Zilapán on the 'Sea of Ğulátû', beyond the 'Cradle of Serpents' on Pushkara. He had done business in Punt on the African continent, and would soon take a ship back to Pushkara.

His guards wore black and white patterned tunics as well as close-fitting leather caps, tied with straps under powerful chins.

The merchant's purple tunic was elegantly embroidered with gold thread and pearls and strings of pink pearls adorned his broad chest. His turban was made of the same material and pearl earrings in the shape of drops dangled from his fleshy earlobes directly underneath.

The guards reminded Trevor of something. Maybe a picture or a statue he had seen somewhere? There were so many intriguing sights as they walked on and he forgot about the guards.

Women in tightly pleated wine-red skirts wore finely worked silver chain-mail jewellery over their black jackets. Their stretched earlobes were pierced with a number of large silver rings and rows of silver bangles clanked merrily on their forearms.

Their dark hair was combed back into severe ponytails and black hats balanced like chimneys on top.

The women were also from Maligasima, albeit from the north of the island. They had arrived on the same ship as the jade traders, but were delegates scheduled to participate in an intercontinental conference.

The numbers of giant saurians were on the increase in parts of the Known World. They posed a danger to populated areas and urgent steps needed to be taken to curb the problem. This would be discussed at the conference.

Chryséis nudged Trevor with her elbow as she spotted girls in wide-cut dresses of a flimsy light blue material. Their loosely-bound blonde hair flowed in the breeze, adorned with precious green quetzal feathers. The magical creatures seemed to glide above the road rather than walk.

"Perhaps they are fairies," Chryséis whispered excitedly.

"Yeah, they sure look like fairies."

Had Uncle Rangan been telling the truth about meeting fairies, after all? Lelani turned right into a side road and Chryséis pulled the gaping Trevor along by the arm. Lelani seemed to know her way around the Barbican quite well.

Konk workmen in blue suits threw bales of fabric and heavy baskets onto the loading space of a boxy vimaan. Fishwives in dark work clothes were cleaning fish and crustaceans right on the wharf. They sold the fresh catch out of long trays full to the brim to haggling housewives and cooks.

Disk-shaped tender was closely inspected by the fishwives and accepted, before the fish changed hands. A gaggle of seabirds fought noisily over a pile of discarded fish heads. What a natter!

On the other side, food stalls with large grids atop drum-like barbecues offered grilled octopus. Two whole specimens, eight arms and all were placed on the grate by a short fat woman. She wore an indigo suit and a patterned kerchief hiding her hair.

The fishwife struggled with the rather long, limp octopus as lemon marinade dripped to the ground. When the octopuses were ready, she'd slice them up and serve the pieces in leaf cups. At another food stall, eager hands snapped up generous portions of crab cake.

"Crab, crab, crab, crab cakes. Fresh, hot and delicious —"

The Gabari salesman advertised his wares in repetitive jingles. He looked a bit odd with his blond hair in a high ponytail as he bellowed out the excellent qualities of his crab cakes with an admirable stamina. His wife busily packed carry nets and baskets of demanding patrons. Lelani quickly walked past the couple.

On the pebbled beach, fishermen were busy gutting a large sea animal. It would have passed for a blue whale, except it had a long neck and rudder-shaped fins. The creature's skin bore ring-shaped marks, stemming from a battle with a giant octopus.

The men neatly lugged fatty layers of blubber on top of each other with hooked poles.

Lelani didn't pay any attention to the fishermen either. She had come to this part of the market with a purpose in mind. Their Gabari bodyguard followed right behind them, making sure that nobody came between him and the Cydonian visitors entrusted in his care.

Eventually, Lelani stopped in front of a large têrakhon window. A small group of tourists already admired the dexterity of the jewellers, who carved beautiful jade objects for passersby to see. The children and their bodyguard waited outside while Lelani went into the shop.

Three market guards in bright green attire with an embroidered red feather on their chests, seemed to be searching for something. The red feather was the symbol of the citadel court.

The guards looked intently into people's faces as they walked past. Strange, they had seen market guards right by the boardwalk do the same thing.

"I wonder what they're looking for," Katherine said, but then Lelani reappeared, carrying a small pouch. She seemed less in a hurry now. When benches next to a cooking shop invited them to take a break, Lelani decided to sit down for a while.

They snacked on marinated baby octopus in bowls made of leaves while watching the crowd. Trevor wondered if the spices were some kind of curry. The cooking shop was busy at this time of the day and attracted many patrons with its Maligasima-style seafood.

A 'public house' next door sold beer. The thick, sour-smelling brew was made from roasted barley and served in cheap mugs. Lelani and the Gabari bodyguard seemed to enjoy the drink, but the children politely declined. Lelani ordered cucumber water for them, which was much better.

On the other side of the 'public house' almost hidden from view, two giants cloaked in dark coats were deep in conversation. One of them checked the road cautiously and they moved around the corner into a narrow alleyway. The shorter one walked slightly hunched over. His head was shaven and a dark cap covered the baldness. He had pulled the cap into his broad forehead as if he wanted to hide something. The other giant bent his unkempt head down between his shoulders.

"Have you got it?" The bald man hissed impatiently.

"Yes Lord." The giant looked subserviently at the 'Lord'. "It has been retrieved as you wished. Your faithful servant can be trusted."

He revealed crooked teeth and took something out of his pocket. The object was tightly wrapped in innocent-looking silk. A polished, white stone sparkled briefly as he opened the cloth. It was a precious moonstone, shaped like a large hen's egg.

A loan to the Lady of Cydonia, the *Speaking Stone* had special properties. It had come a long way from the land of Lyonesse for this purpose and was unbelievably precious.

As instructed, the giant thief had taken the 'Speaking

Stone' from the Cydonian citadel and brought it hidden to Aztlan. The cloth slipped, revealing more of the luminous object. The Gabari quickly pulled the cloth over the stone and waited with his head bowed.

"Very good. *Very* good. You shall receive your reward tonight." The 'Lord' was obviously pleased with the outcome of the venture. He took the packet and stuffed it into a satchel.

"Shukri." The thief bowed deeply, hunching his shoulders even more. The deal was done and the two giants parted in opposite directions.

*

After their meal, the tourists from Cydonia strolled over to another market down the road. Bright cloth separated makeshift booths and shaded them from the sun.

"A flea market!" Katherine cried.

Here, street traders peddled items of clothing, dress jewellery and the like. Customers were expected to bargain as it was half the fun.

Katherine bought a few useful little items. It was important to give a parting gift to their hosts and she hadn't packed much.

She also bought a woven basket, which could be neatly folded and paid with one of the smaller mother-of-pearl coins from the saurian leather purse. The disk also paid for a pair of embroidered linen shoes in bright pink, Chryséis couldn't resist. Both girls thought that fine silken veils were just the right thing to protect them against the sun on the ship.

Trevor on the other hand felt drawn to a stall with slings and knives. He purchased a sharp gutting knife and a sling. They would be quite useful, just like the Swiss Army knife he had brought with him. The gutting knife came with a sheath made from soft harpee leather. Best to be prepared.

They watched in fascination, how a large cargo vimaan

noiselessly crossing the sky, then they turned their attention back to the market. Next to them, two rather small women struggled to reach the veils at the back of the table. Katherine helped them politely and they thanked her with broad smiles. The women were *Dwendis* from Atala, visiting their local dwarf cousins.

Lelani wanted to sit down one last time by a rippling fountain and they were grateful for the brief rest. Kheton and Lelani's luggage had already been taken to the ship in the morning.

However, the children had insisted on taking their daypacks with them. Now they began to grow tired under the burden, but it was safer to keep the TPFs close by. So they had to grin and bear it.

By the fountain, musicians played lively music on four-stringed guitars, made from armadillo armours, on drums and pan-flutes. Two girls in bell-jingling knee-short red dresses, danced prettily around, clacking cymbals in moving hands.

A question popped into Chryséis's head.

"Lelani, will you miss your mother?" she asked.

"Oh yes, I do," the young bride admitted. "But I speak to her often."

By telepathy of course. Chryséis wished she could do the same.

"I cannot wait to make a home in Algiras," Lelani said. "I hear it is more exciting than Cydonia and Aztlan put together—" She seemed to listen to something.

"It's just Kheton telling me that the ship is ready for boarding soon."

On their way back to the pier, market guards strode past them quickly towards the anchored ships on the wharf.

"Maybe they've now found what they were looking for," Katherine said.

Moments later the little group lined up by the anchor

place, waiting to board their ship. Trevor leaned against a post and observed the ships. Lelani chatted with the girls about D'ântilla and mentioned an observatory they absolutely had to visit there.

The new interspace-deflector-ray-gun was said to be sensational. She had also heard about the knitted jerseys on the island of Daitya. Such a patterned jersey would make a wonderful gift for Kheton.

Suddenly, Trevor felt a sharp push to his side that took his breath away. He tripped over a rope and fell. All he saw was something dark fluttering past - then he hit the water. The bodyguard jumped after him and flipped the puffing Trevor over onto his back.

The Gabari paddled back to the pier and lifted the dripping wet boy up and into the helpful hands of two seamen from the *Navis Arion*.

Trevor spluttered and coughed. His hand was searching for the new knife in its leather sheath. It was still there. Luckily he had taken off his daypack just moments before and placed it with the others. His electromagnetic device was safe.

"Trevor, my, what happened?" Katherine giggled. "One minute you stand here, the next you jump into the water!"

"I didn't jump, okay?! I was pushed." Trevor said crossly. Chryséis made an unflattering remark and Trevor got into a huff.

"Yeah, funny, hey?" He pushed his wet hair abruptly out of his eyes and stared straight ahead. "This guy had a black cape on—" He shook his head, sending droplets flying.

Katherine and Chryséis weren't sure whether they should laugh or be concerned. Why wasn't Trevor more careful? Now he was all wet, just before they were boarding the ship.

What they didn't know was that Trevor's fall had been a distraction. An egg-shaped object, wrapped in Alesian silk, had been quickly slipped inside one of the daypacks on the wharf. In Chryséis's backpack to be precise.

The market guards had been hot on the heels of the suspects when it happened. The thieves couldn't risk being caught with a 'Speaking Stone' in their possession. They knew that the punishment would have been severe. If their plans were discovered, they could never be completed.

That's when they saw the lonely pieces of luggage sitting on the pier. They acted quickly. The 'Speaking Stone' would be retrieved from the bag later when circumstances were more favourable.

The Gabari were apprehended, but the market guards found nothing when they searched the sinister giants. The two Gabari in their black capes made quite a scene for allegedly being harassed by confused guards.

The thought pattern of the Gabari had been unmistakable. Now, they had nothing on them. The guards didn't think that the boy falling into the water had anything to do with the 'Speaking Stone' they were after. They didn't have a choice and let the men go.

The water around the *Navis Arion* suddenly swarmed with concerned merpeople.

"Is the young man hurt?" They chattered, visibly upset. "How could this have happened? Squeak".

They had to stay out of the way as other ships drifted past the *Navis Arion*. An embarrassed Trevor stood in a growing puddle and tried to explain how he had been pushed by somebody dressed in black.

"Perhaps a workman accidentally pushed the young man, while carrying a load of merchandise," one of the Ioannu men suggested.

"Such a mishap!" Malindi complained.

"Yes, but it isn't serious," Trevor insisted. "The bodyguard saved me."

Lelani interrupted the conference with the Ioannu and asked Trevor to come aboard and change his clothes for something dry from Kheton's wardrobe. She helped the boy up the gangway and handed him over to her husband.

"This klutz of a workman, squeak, why couldn't he pay attention to an important young man?"

The Ioannu said goodbye and swam off after reassuring the girls that merpeople would watch out for the foreign visitors.

By the time he returned from the cabin, Trevor had calmed down. Kheton's clothes were too big for him, but at least they were dry. Not too bad, if he rolled up the sleeves and trouser legs.

His own clothes were flapping in the wind and would be ready to wear again in no time.

Trevor couldn't shake the feeling, that the quick shove to his ribs had been deliberate. Just a feeling. Had he known how the unsuspecting time travellers were being used to hide a priceless moonstone, the 'Speaking Stone of Caradoc' would not have been smuggled out of Alesia and things would have taken a different turn.

A pale half-moon began to rise unnoticed above the harbour and looked on as the ship cast off from the pier. Captain Thëlamôn, a native of the island of D'ântilla, was an experienced seaman.

He knew that their voyage to Kamûk would be a good one today. Just a slight breeze in the air and the sea was as smooth as a têrakhon pane. Crisp sea air smelled like perfume to captain Thëlamôn. The sailing of ships was in his blood and the skipper could smell troublesome weather.

The only cargo on the *Navis Arion* was a flock of baahing sheep and a few bales of good Alesian silk fabric. They had been safely secured in their respective compartments below deck. Everything was in perfect order. Just as captain Thëlamôn liked it. He felt honoured to have such important passengers on board today. A Cydonian emissary with his young wife and three foreign orphans. Important, obviously. The letters of passage from the Lady of Cydonia left no doubt in the matter.

The ship pulled slowly out of the harbour, following the pilot boat through the broad entrance between massive seawalls. The 'Navis Arion' had passed through these walls many times before.

A handful of anglers stood at the top waving, and they waved back. Seagulls and strangely crested birds chattered wildly while darting in and out of the water around the anglers.

Before the time travellers realised it, they found themselves out in the open sea.

A prehistoric sea.

End of Book 1

Now you can look forward to the next two books in the series. The fourth book with the title 'Kingdom of the Snake' is also on its way.

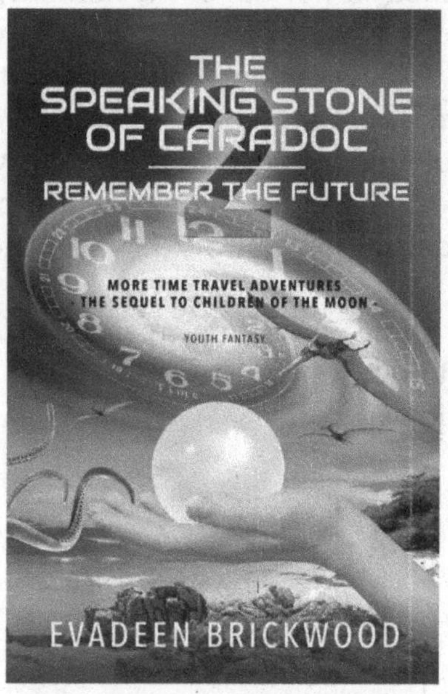

Remember the Future Book 2

Katherine, Trevor and Chryseis embark on a ship and sail to remnants of the sunken continent of Atland. When a stolen speaking stone is found in their luggage everybody suspects the three friends. Will the time travelers be punished for the theft? Suddenly everybody is after the mysterious stone from the fabled land of Lyonesse and some of the strange sea creatures are not as amusing as they seem. They escape only just a trap set by sorcerers in Prydhain and receive help from an unexpected source. Then the speaking stone has something to say...

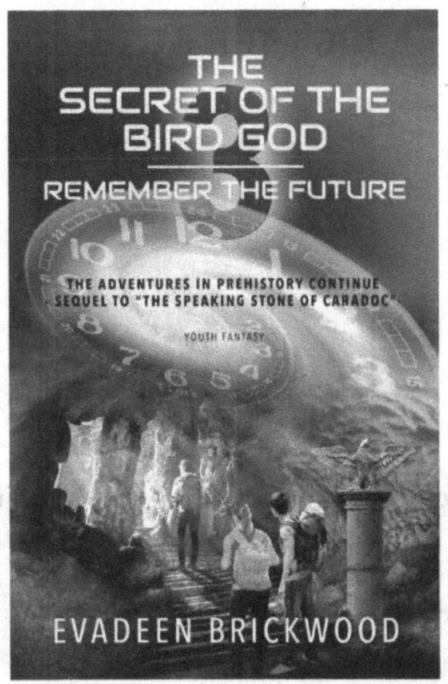

Remember the Future Book 3

Finding their way back to Alesia and their home in the future, turns out to be more difficult than the time travellers thought. War breaks out in the Mediterranean Sea and forces Katherine, Trevor and Chryséis to flee inland. Nothing here is the way they thought it would be, and who has ever heard of Egypt without pyramids? Here, they discover unbelievable books, a school of magic and that virtual-invisibility coats come in handy in prehistoric Egypt, now called Ta Mery. Somebody seems to be standing in their way and eventually, they find out the shocking truth. Can the elusive Bird God help the children get to safety in time?

ABOUT THE AUTHOR

Evadeen Brickwood grew up with two sisters in Germany and studied cultural sciences and languages. As a young woman, she travelled extensively and many of her books are inspired by her experiences abroad.

Feeling adventurous, the newly qualified translator moved to Africa in 1988 and worked for two years as a secretary and language teacher in Botswana.

The author eventually settled in South Africa, where she got married and raised two daughters. In Johannesburg, Evadeen Brickwood studied computers and management of training and worked as a corporate software trainer, professional translator and lecturer at WITS University.

In 2003, she began her writing career with youth novels in the 'Remember the Future' series, about adventures in prehistory. Book 1, 'Children of the Moon', has been published twice in South Africa and translated into German. The author now self-publishes and other books in the series are released on a regular basis.

The sequels "The Speaking Stone of Caradoc" and "The Secret of the Bird God" are now also available.

About Writing This Youth Book...

I've always enjoyed reading fascinating facts and legends from around the world, the legend of Atlantis being one of them. Sitting on stacks of material, I decided to create books for children about adventures in prehistory. Time travel seemed the logical way to arrive in ancient times and I sort of developed my own method. Whether time travel will be possible one day is anyone's guess, but it's a really cool idea.

'Children of the Moon' was first published in South Africa in 2005. Soon after the second edition in 2007, the book industry crashed and my publisher had to close down. However, I kept writing more books for the 'Remember the Future' series and will finish the fourth book soon. The sequel to book 1, 'The Speaking Stone of Caradoc' is already published and 'Children of the Moon' has just been translated into German.

Each book has an element theme, such as earth, water, air and fire and I let the time travellers learn things that could be of use in our future times.

Wherever it fit into the text, I used original expressions from ancient languages. The word 'vimaan', for example, comes from the Sanskrit word 'vimana', meaning flying vehicle; and 'shelanti', is an ancient Irish greeting with the same meaning it has in the book.

Evadeen Brickwood

This book is available from all good bookstores

The e-book can be purchased at major online stores, such as Smashwords, Kobo, Tolino, Kindle, Apple i-Store, Neobooks etc.

The author's websites:

http://www.evadeen.wixsite.com/novels
http://www.evadeen.wixsite.com/youngbooks
http://www.evadeen.wixsite.com/charlieproudfoot

Evadeen is also on social media, incl. Facebook, Twitter, Instagram, google+ and Goodreads.